Death on Beguiling Way

Also by Patricia McLinn

DEATH ON BEGUILING WAY

Secret Sleuth, Book 3

Patricia McLinn

✧   ✧   ✧   ✧

Author's Note

No yoga instructors of my acquaintance were hurt in the writing of this book …or used as models for characters. I had to seek out others' experiences to research less positive experiences than I've had. Like all the characters in my books, these are not based on real people, but are the product of my fevered imagination. I confess, some of that imagining happens during yoga class.

DAY ONE
MONDAY

CHAPTER ONE

IT WAS THE best of times, it was the worst of times.

It was the heart-soaring beginning with all things possible, it was the first step in a seven-thousand-mile walk through the desert without water.

It was the spring of hope, it was the winter of despair.

I had everything before me, I had nothing before me…

The *everything before me* was that it was nearly time to leave for my yin yoga class.

Our instructor, Liz, said we should feel at the end as if we'd had a cross between a structured nap and a massage. Who couldn't use a nap and a massage?

Especially because I'd been wrestling with *nothing before me* for hours, producing a few pathetic words insufficient to make a reader try the next paragraph, never mind a novel.

Yes, I was trying to write a novel. Specifically, a romance novel.

But, considering I just riffed off the opening of *A Tale of Two Cities,* I worried Charles Dickens had wormed his way deep into my subconscious and my ending might echo Sydney Carton's trip to the guillotine.

No matter what Hollywood thinks (have you *seen* some of the things they call romance?), cutting off the hero's head is not the route to a happy ending.

That much I knew.

Okay, okay, Carton wasn't the romantic lead of *A Tale of Two Cities*. He still ended up a hero and lost his head. I've never forgiven Dickens.

I wasn't going to do that to my readers.

If I ever had any, since I was trying to write a book for the first time.

Which would surprise the heck out of millions who considered me the author of the iconic megahit *Abandon All*.

The catch was, I didn't write *Abandon All*.

My great-aunt Kit did.

She'd masterminded my playing the public persona of *Abandon All*, investing our earnings, then ending our arrangement. She's a masterminding kind of person.

I'd happily left the *Abandon All* persona in Manhattan, re-emerging as Sheila Mackey in Haines Tavern, Kentucky, just over the Ohio River from Cincinnati.

Now I was trying to actually write.

How was it going?

Worst of times, desert marathon without water, winter of despair, nothing before me.

"What are you doing?"

I closed the laptop in front of me with extreme nonchalance.

"Nothing," I told Teague O'Donnell in an even, reasonable tone despite his sneaking up on me in the dining room of my own home.

He was a friend—acquaintance, really—from the Torrid Avenue Dog Park.

It was our dogs who were truly best buds, my Gracie and his Murphy, along with a third dog, LuLu, and her owner Clara.

But that wasn't why Teague was in my house on this early Monday evening.

He was here in his role as a carpenter.

When he'd finished building shelves for me a few months back, we'd agreed he would next reconfigure two bedroom's closets in my post-World War II colonial.

He hadn't been able to start on the project until now because he had another role—substitute teacher. Apparently, teachers developed as bad a case of spring fever as their students, so he was busy subbing right up until the school year ended.

Today was his first day on the closet job.

Based on previous experience with his methods, this day and a couple more would be devoted to measuring, planning, re-remeasuring, going over the plan, then checking his remeasurements, before, finally, writing a list of needed supplies.

"If you're doing nothing, why did you slam the computer closed?" he asked.

"I didn't slam it closed." The man clearly didn't recognize extreme nonchalance when it was right in front of him.

"You did."

"Didn't."

He leaned back against the door frame of my dining room and considered me.

Being considered by Teague O'Donnell was not the most comfortable experience. He had a way of turning his head, first one way, then the other, without shifting his gaze away, making me feel as if he were zeroing in an X-Ray machine to see below my surface. Did I mention he used to be a police detective?

And I have a few secrets I'd like to keep, starting with that *Abandon All* business.

To preserve Sheila Mackey's laid-back privacy in Haines Tavern, she—I—could not be connected to *Abandon All*. Especially if I ever hoped to write and publish without a circus.

Yeah, definitely needed to keep that secret from Teague O'Donnell, former detective.

He continued to regard me as he said, "You going to tell me next it's not your laptop?"

"Why on earth would I say it's not my laptop?"

"When I was on patrol, we'd find drugs in somebody's pants pocket and they'd say it wasn't theirs because the pants they were wearing weren't theirs. The Not-My-Pants excuse also applied to purses and underwear—men's and women's."

"Ewww. They were wearing someone else's underwear? Sure

hope—"

"They were *saying* they were wearing someone else's underwear."

"—it was clean."

"It wasn't clean. It had drugs in it."

"Different definition of clean. I wonder how dirty and clean came to be applied to drugs."

"No idea. And a different subject from slamming your laptop closed. Anyway, why aren't you using your office? Afraid I'd see what you were doing on the computer?"

I mentioned the guy had been a police detective, right? He must have been a pretty good one.

What he was not, at the moment, was a good shaver. He had scruff on his chin. Possibly a symptom of Alice Cooper's "School's Out for Summer/School's Out Forever" fever.

"Of course not." I'd thought the stairs would give me warning of his approach that I wouldn't have in the office ... and then I'd missed his approach anyway. "I thought you'd be making lots of noise upstairs."

He turned his head, adjusting the angle of his considering look.

Not an improvement, from my point of view.

"Told you I'd take a couple days to get the scope of the job since you've been changing what you want. So you knew—"

"Tweaks."

"—you could have worked in the office today. But if you don't want to tell me what you're doing on the laptop, say you don't want to tell me. Unless it's something to do with changing these closets. Again. *That* you have to tell me."

A few little design alterations, all improvements, and he hadn't even started work, so what was he complaining about?

This project started when I realized two bedroom closets sat side by side, making them deep, but too narrow for adequate hanging space.

We were going to trade depth for width by taking out the side wall dividing the closets, then building a long wall to make them back to back. In each bedroom, double doors would open to hanging space twice as wide as provided now.

"No changes—no major changes. I *did* find a better register for the vent. It's flush with the floor and matches the wood."

He groaned.

I pretended not to notice. I also changed the subject.

"Tomorrow, Clara and I are taking the dogs to the park after yoga class. Want me to take Murphy when I swing by here for Gracie? Should be early afternoon."

Two sets of dog ears perked up at the word *park*. And, again, at each of their names.

Two, because I'd told Teague to bring Murphy whenever he came to work here. No sense leaving the poor dog alone in an apartment. Besides, Murphy visiting was like giving Gracie the best toy ever.

At the moment, Gracie and Murphy were lying side by side on the rug in front of the front door, chewing on opposite ends of a rawhide, watching the humans, and looking adorable.

Gracie has an edge in the adorable stakes, being a beautiful sable and white collie with more than a passing resemblance to Lassie. And being mine, adopted from the regional collie rescue group.

Murphy, a sweet-natured lab mix, was also far above average on the cuteness scale. He just had the handicap of lying next to Gracie.

"I thought you had class this evening—the contortionist yoga you guys do."

"It's yin. Not contortionist. You should try it."

He ignored that. "Besides, Clara told me you two were taking the dogs to the park *before* class to get in the habit of going earlier for when the real heat of summer hits."

"That was on Tuesdays. We tried, but it didn't work out." It didn't work out because we arrived at yoga hot, sweaty, and smelling of dogs. After getting a lot of side looks for one class, we dumped the plan.

"Confusing."

"Not at all. Classes are Monday nights, Tuesdays lunchtime."

"Same thing two days in a row? Why not take a different class?"

"We like yin. We're discussing adding another kind, but need to figure out which one." I checked my watch. "I better go or I'll be late picking up Clara."

"I'll wait until tomorrow about having you two take Murph to the park. Your schedules will change seven times before then."

He wasn't far off. You'd think, since neither Clara nor I had a job—Clara temporarily and me permanently—scheduling would not be an issue. But it got surprisingly complicated.

"Lock up, okay?" I instructed him as I picked up my yoga bag.

"Sure. Break a leg."

He thought he was so funny.

CHAPTER TWO

WE WEREN'T LATE for class.

In fact, we were the first ones there. Just the way we liked.

It let us secure our favorite corner spots and provided a few extra minutes on our mats, letting the real world dissipate. Or, in my case, the fictional world stuck at a few words old.

But tonight, we couldn't get inside. The door was locked.

This was strange.

Our instructor, Liz, faithfully came early and opened the door for students to stretch, meditate, chat, snooze, or otherwise settle in before class.

The Beguiling Way Yoga Studio is—not surprisingly—on Beguiling Way, an alley until town leaders turned it into a no-cars pedestrian passage and loftily renamed it years ago.

It's west of the town square (which, it delights me to report, is not square but rectangular.)

The post office, library, and a hardware store occupy the first block west of one of the narrower ends of the town square. Behind them comes Tanner Street, with various historic storefronts and a café.

Next is Beguiling Way, with its no-vehicles policy. For some reason, Clara and I habitually park where aromas from the café and a nearby bakery waft around us so strongly that we almost always succumb after class.

Being at the back of a historic structure, and therefore not as regulated as the front, the studio has a large picture window and glass door. Both sport shades, allowing filtered light inside while obscuring the view of potential gawkers. A good thing, since more than a few yoga poses qualify as "Not flattering positions for photos or other viewing."

Clara peered into the window, focusing on the crack where two screens met. "This is weird."

"Liz's just running late." I set my bag, holding my rolled-up mat, towel, water, and hair clips on the sidewalk and studied a list of upcoming classes posted on the inside of the door's glass.

This yin class wasn't what you might associate with yoga if your mental images center on whippet thin bodies in perfect Warrior One, Two, Three and up, reverently pronouncing Sanskrit, completing pretzel-making maneuvers, all while demonstrating supreme spirituality, allowing no wrinkles in their high-fashion yoga attire, and displaying killer pedicures.

I haven't taken every offering at Beguiling Way Yoga Studio, so I couldn't say there weren't any such classes, but so far, so good.

Plus, yin itself is different.

Aunt Kit introduced me to it in New York. She said it reached the seat of authors' aches—sitting too many hours in a row, for too many years. It involves getting into positions with deliberation, supporting yourself with props, then remaining for minutes, with the goal of releasing connective tissue called fascia and easing seldom-stretched muscles.

"Let gravity and time do the work," Liz often said.

I'm good with that, especially with the nap and massage elements added in.

Clara twisted her neck to alter the angle of her view through the crack.

"There's somebody inside. It's not Liz," she reported. "Do you think she's sick? She acted a little strange last time."

Our instructor, Liz, was a tall, solid young woman who exuded calm. I could imagine the character of Ma Walton from the old TV series *The Waltons* being a lot like Liz in her younger days. Pleasant, but no-nonsense. Perhaps a little shy.

During last week's class, Clara had poked me while I was relaxing into a pose called Sleeping Swan that sort of feels like the splits with one knee bent.

It feels better than it sounds. At least for me. I understand other people hate the pose. Sort of the way I feel about Dragon, which should be against the Geneva Conventions.

After Clara's poke, I'd looked up at this blatant break in yoga protocol.

She whispered, "Look." Her head tip directed my focus.

Tears slid down Liz's cheeks as she listened to the soft words of the soundtrack she played at every class. The song was about a guy saying he'd always loved this girl. But, it turns out, he'd let her go. Now she'd found someone new and was happy, and here he came, back into her life, saying, "Oopsie, let's have do-overs." And he's all heartbroken the girl won't dump the good guy who's treating her well for his self-centered ass.

Not my favorite on her play list, in case you can't tell.

If it made Liz cry, maybe not her favorite, either.

But after those mid-class tears, she'd seemed to bounce back.

After class, Clara and I commented to each other about her tears, but it was otherwise forgotten in the days since.

"You think her crying last week—?"

My question ended as the door swung open abruptly.

"Hello! We have early birds! Welcome! Wonderful to have eager beavers. I'm so looking forward to this class. A rare opportunity to spread my yin wings and lead you all in a practice embracing calm and restoration. I'm Xanthe. I'll be your instructor tonight for this hour of spiritual and meditative movement."

"Is Liz okay?"

"Nothing serious from what I understand, but not attuned enough to the universe at the moment to guide you all on your journeys this evening. She needs to become realigned herself first. And your names are?"

I clenched my muscles to keep from looking at Clara.

Among Liz's positives as a yoga instructor, we'd often listed not talking *spiritual* among the top. We respect people *being* spiritual, but talking it all over the place? No, thank you.

There was also something faintly … *salesy* about Xanthe's delivery, the verbal highs and lows artificially placed for impact.

On top of that, this instructor had frazzled my rhythm.

There's a pulse-slowing, breath-deepening rhythm to yin. In the first few months, I'd found it during classes, then gradually learned to extend it after class. Recently, I'd found myself slipping into it on the way to class.

Even with today's futile writing attempt, I'd found it on the way here today.

Until Xanthe.

She was high speed, when I wanted mellow.

Xanthe had dashed behind the minimalist desk and had her fingers poised expectantly over a laptop keyboard.

The desk stood directly in front of us. On the wall to our right was a bulletin board. On the opposite end wall of this vestibule area, stacked cubes waited for students to leave accoutrements of the outside world, like phones, shoes, and wallets. To the right of the cubes and across from the front window, double glass doors opened into the studio itself.

We gave Xanthe our names, with Clara smiling back with her blazing smile.

Her smile-o-rama multiplied as Xanthe greeted the next pair of students, a harried looking young woman and one several years older who'd taken thin to extremes.

I was happy to enter the studio area through the double glass doors.

An open rectangular space stretched before us, with raw brick covered by mirrors on the long wall to our right and white-painted drywall with a barre on our left. Another mosaic of cubbies in the corner diagonally from the doors held studio-provided equipment—bolsters, blocks, straps, weights, balls, and more.

We headed straight ahead. We favored this corner formed by the barre wall and a wall to the restroom. It was no coincidence it was one of the rare areas not captured in the mirrors.

While Clara selected a bolster, block, and blanket from the cubbies,

I left my bag in my usual spot in the corner, next to her mat, and went to the restroom.

In this utilitarian space, not only was the one wall left as original brick, but someone had taken the time and effort to center the sink in front of a bricked-in archway. It was as if the brickwork had been made to frame sink and mirror. Nice touch.

I came out a moment later to find Clara, holding an armload of props and staring at two women I didn't recognize, who were in the act of pushing my bag and Clara's things from where we'd left them into the aisle between the back and front rows.

Clara, clearly, was rendered speechless by such rudeness.

Not me.

"Excuse me—" and if my tone said there was no excuse for *them*, I'd live with it. "—you've taken our spots."

They continued busily spreading their mats where our gear had been a moment ago.

"Oh, no. We couldn't have, because no one was here," said the blonde woman who was several years younger than her dark-haired companion.

"Our *belongings* were here. You know that, because you moved them."

The dark-haired woman cast an aren't-we-naughty look at the blonde. "Oh, are those yours? We thought someone left them from a previous class."

Lying to me is one thing. Not even trying to hide you are lying is another.

I took hold of my bag's straps and swung it forward, into the space where I'd left it, stepping in behind it.

The blonde woman tackled me.

Really, there's no other term for it.

It wasn't a nudge or a push or a hip check. She got her shoulder into the side of my rib cage and shoved me back. I quick-stepped to keep my balance, reaching for the support of the props' cubbies.

By the time I had caught myself, the bag swinging wildly from my gyrations, Clara was at my side, reaching out a helpful hand, and the two women were sitting side-by-side on their mats.

In our spots.

"Those are *our* spots. What do you—?"

"Did you put a deposit down? Have a lease? Hold the deed? I didn't think so. Besides, we're here now. Quit making a fuss," the blonde said, then turned to her companion. "You were telling me about your daughter's wedding plans…"

The dark-haired woman tittered, but cut it short to accept the implicit invitation. "Oh, yes. I've been working so hard on it. If other people would cooperate, I'd be much further along with our wedding."

"They can't do this," Clara said to me.

"They *have* done it."

My time in North Bend County had left me out of practice. I'd gotten soft. I hadn't reacted fast enough.

If Liz had been teaching, I might have asked her to arbitrate. Or asked her to kick them out. Certainly out of our spots, probably out of the class, maybe out of the county.

But this unknown, cheerful, *spiritual* instructor, being as much a stranger to us as we were to her, would have no idea if Clara and I were justifiably irked or whiny crybabies. Chances were, she'd default to the latter.

I said to Clara, loudly enough to be overheard, "We'll be the grown-ups and take those spots." I nodded to the two spaces next to the spot-stealers.

Mostly grown-up, anyway.

The one drawback to the corner was the security system panel on the wall of the furnace room across from the restroom, flickering bright colors that could distract someone not entirely concentrated on the practice of yin.

I hoped they'd drive the tackler crazy.

We settled in.

Sort of.

CHAPTER THREE

I MIGHT HAVE let irritation at the corner-stealers' rudeness prevent me from settling in mentally, but didn't have a chance to find out because the conversation next to us splashed loudly onto our mats.

"…can't make a single decision on the menu without me. I have a refined palate and so many followers on my Yelp reviews that restaurants all over the region know my name."

I bet they did. Probably slapped up the "Closed" sign if they saw her coming.

"What they try to pass off as suitable fare for our wedding…"

I found myself debating which of the blonde tackler's sins were worse—spot stealing or encouraging this annoying mother of the bride to babble on. The blonde didn't appear to enjoy it any more than I did, because she kept fiddling with her yoga bag in the corner where mine belonged.

As a few regulars trickled in, Clara and I received questioning glances that slid to the corner.

Berrie, a woman we knew from the dog park, stopped to voice the question, "Why aren't you two in your usual spots? And what's with Liz not being here?"

When I say we knew her, I didn't mean we were close friends.

We'd been surprised when she started attending yoga six weeks ago. From what we'd heard, her previous financial situation hadn't allowed for yoga classes. Plus, the studio didn't allow dogs and it was downright strange to see her without a pack of Boston terriers, also known as Berrie's Boston Terrors.

Donna, the all-knowing godmother of the dog park, had told us Berrie was picking up a significant number of dog training gigs. Good for her budget. Bad for dog comportment at the Torrid Avenue park.

"Liz is probably sick," was my restatement of the obvious.

"She didn't look sick when I saw her with a guy today. But what about you two?"

I pretended not to hear Berrie's repeated question. Clara said in a conspiratorially low voice, "We'll tell you later."

She needn't have bothered with discretion. The blonde tackler fidgeted with her bag while nods and uh-huhs encouraged the brunette mother-of-the-bride's soliloquy. Neither paid attention to anyone else.

"...plus, they tried to foist burlap-covered table card holders off on us. *Burlap*. Can you imagine? For our wedding? I mean, we might as well use the *standard* ones the venue offers for free."

Our wedding. Not a slip of the tongue. She clearly considered it partly—mostly?—hers. Did the bride and groom realize their duet had become a trio?

Berrie wasn't done with us.

"What do you think of this substitute, huh?"

"It's nice of her to fill in so we could still have a class when Liz is sick."

"She didn't look sick when I saw her with a guy today."

Clara rolled her eyes at Berrie's repetition.

I bent forward from the waist over one leg to stretch the hamstring and to hide my grin at Clara's reaction. Also, possibly, to encourage Berrie to move on. Even with my face practically in my knee, however, the mother of the bride's voice penetrated.

"And my poor, sweet daughter would have fallen for it, too. I told her simple does not have to be shoddy and..."

The glances from the other arrivals at the interloping pair became increasingly pointed and irritated. Except for the harried looking young woman, who apparently was too tired to look around.

I switched to stretching the other leg. The move helped the hamstring, but did nothing to drown out MOTB.

"...sweet porcelain rose on top with the bridal couple engraved on the column holding it up. Something substantial. Something the guests will take home and keep forever."

Wanna bet? Half get left at the reception. Half of the rest get thrown out at home. The final ones get tossed in a drawer to chip, shatter, and age before they, too, are thrown out.

If the equation is that the greater the temptation to say something smart-assy, the greater the honor in suppressing it, I shot up to the top of the temptation-resisting honor roll.

"And when they can't even get the table settings right, I don't know how one could ever rely on the menu being—"

The blonde popped up. "Oh. I still have my sunglasses on. Hold my spot while I put them away."

So even she needed a break from MOTB drivel.

The dark-haired mother of the bride dramatically reached an arm and leg out to rest on the blonde's mat, clearly expecting from us the same lowlife behavior she'd displayed.

I know.

Not very Zen-like thoughts.

I never said I was acing this yoga stuff.

For a few moments it was blessedly quiet. Or nearly quiet. One demonstrative breather in the front row almost blocked out the murmur of the blonde woman talking with the instructor in the vestibule.

Then she returned and the wedding planning spigot turned back on, still stuck on table card holders.

"They set a *tone*. A *brand* for our wedding. Elegance. Not burlap or feed sacks or…"

A second later, the instructor came in, closing the double doors behind her.

"Hello and good evening. Welcome to tonight's meditative journey through our practice together, in this special, spiritual community, of yin yoga. I think I met everyone already, but just in case, I'm Xanthe and I'll be leading you tonight, substituting for Liz."

A murmur of return hellos rose up like a flock of birds, then settled back into silence.

Except for the louder-than-a-murmur in the corner where Clara and I should have been by rights.

Xanthe glanced toward the corner as she walked to the center of the front row. "I hope you're all looking forward to this next hour on your mats as much as I am." She pitched the words to reach the corner.

Even with a spattering of new people, there was more room between mats than usual. We were usually close to capacity for Liz's yin yoga class. Massage and a nap, remember?

This substitute, however, seemed the type to rap the knuckles of anyone caught napping—metaphorically. She was far too cheerful and perky to actually rap anyone's knuckles.

Cheerful. Perky.

Two things to dread in any yoga instructor. Almost as bad as spiritual and skinny.

I had a bad feeling about this.

"You forgot to dim the lights," a regular said from the other end of the studio.

Liz always dimmed them, leaving on a string of Christmas lights in front of the mirrors. It was soothing, pretty, and prevented any fellow students who might not be minding their own asanas—which the instructors told us was Sanskrit for positions—from being able to see if you went ass over asana.

"We're going to leave the lights on tonight. Brighten us up. Keep us moving. While at the same time sharing a deeply spiritual experience. Right?" she said chirpily.

No one responded, too horrified to speak ... unless that was projecting my reaction.

Nor did her forceful words quiet the mother-of-the-bride.

"...put my foot down to get something *appropriate* for the table card holders, and then the next second this so-called wedding planner is trying to pass off—"

"Good evening," the instructor repeated, louder.

Most heads turned toward the MOTB, but with her back to the rest of the class she was immune to peer pressure.

I kept my eyes on Xanthe.

She reached for her yoga bag beside the speaker that instructors plugged their phones into to play music during classes.

"—what she calls rustic—*Rustic*! for my daughter and our wedding—and I call tacky—"

Clang!

The unexpected sound of metal bouncing off the hardwood floor, then against something else metal, sounded harsh in the nearly quiet room.

The two metal loops at one end of the yoga strap were there to create a cinch … or one heck of a racket when bounced off the floor and each other.

The mother of the bride jerked her head around to finally focus on the instructor.

Xanthe smiled. In the brightly lit studio, her smile looked even more salesy than I'd thought her voice was. "Sorry about dropping the strap by accident—"

I strongly suspected it hadn't been an accident. Surely fibbing went against spirituality rules.

"—but I am glad to have all of us now ready to begin our practice. To be present here, our minds and bodies together, embarking on a spiritual journey, bounded by the edges of our mat, with no thought of anything else for the complete hour."

Keeping my head aimed at the instructor, I shifted my eyes to the side enough to pick up Mother of the Bride and Blonde Tackler sitting passively on their mats. Though MOTB's mouth *was* open, presumably ready to resume at first opportunity.

"This time on your mat is to bring your awareness inside and by doing so will bring us to the infinite. To the eternal. If thoughts come into your mind, simply send them away. They are not welcomed now here."

Considering I'd previously used quiet time in this class to contemplate ins and outs of a murder, I was unlikely to be the star pupil in this category.

On the other hand, Xanthe couldn't know what was in my head.

Or that I rebelliously welcomed thinking.

"I know when Liz leads you, you do mostly floor work," Xanthe said. "But me filling in for her gives us an opportunity for something different. We want movement, don't we? Of course, we do."

"No, we don't," muttered Clara.

The woman on the other side of Clara nodded. I saw a ripple of agreement from a few more nearby.

Xanthe sailed on. "The movement activates our chakras' energy. The energy flows from the movement into our fascia. Opening, expanding, invigorating."

"Invigorating." Clara repeated the word in a bitter undertone.

"Everyone stand and we'll start with a simple sun salutation—"

"That shouldn't be so bad," I muttered back to Clara, even though sun salutation is part of the more active yoga classes this studio called flow. It had never before been included in a yin class I'd taken here or in New York.

"—repetition sequence."

Clara side-eyed me in a markedly un-Zen reproach for my optimism.

I couldn't blame her.

The sun salutation sounds benign. Like raising an arm and waving toward the sky. Maybe standing at attention to make it more official.

And that's how it starts. Standing straight and still, then reaching overhead with both arms.

From there, things go where the sun doesn't shine ... unless the sun shines from your knees or the tops of your feet. Because you bend over—a forward fold in yoga-ese—come partway up, fold again. Sometimes rinse and repeat. Sometimes on to less sunny doings.

That means you transition to plank, essentially a straight-legged pushup with your toes tucked under. I was worried about doing the pushup ... until Xanthe perkily suggested, instead of "merely" stepping back into plank, we jump into it.

Right.

My worries about jumping leapfrogged—so to speak—my worries about doing a pushup.

Two independent-minded regulars stayed the forward fold. A few others ignored the suggested modification and stepped back. The rest of us resembled jumping beans struggling to cope with triple gravity. The blonde tackler was particularly awkward as she still fidgeted with her bag. The mother of the bride said something unnuptial under her breath, proving she could speak quietly.

"Bend those elbows," Xanthe caroled joyfully.

You bend your elbows and hold there in what's called chaturanga, which sounds like a tasty Tex-Mex dish, but isn't. It's actually a way to make you miss plank.

Cobra is next. It's named after a big, old deadly snake, but at this point, you welcome it, because most of your body gets to be on the mat. Your torso and head are raised, creating a backbend—no fair pressing into your hands.

Again. *Right.*

Then you lever yourself off your mat into downward facing dog, where your body and the mat form a triangle, with your derriere the apex and the only part facing the sun.

Xanthe cheerily invited us to jump from there back into another forward fold—we weren't falling for jumping this time—then straighten to reach overhead and finally get a look back up toward the sun … if we weren't inside a building.

Oh, yes, and you're supposed to move fluidly and gracefully from position to position, making it a unified whole.

Once more. *Right.*

Most flow classes I've been in had us do three of these cycles. Xanthe said, "Let's do a fourth to be sure we're well warmed up."

We were past warmed up and into the gasping for air stage.

"Now we consciously come to our mats and our easy seats. With deliberate gracefulness," she added.

Too late.

For most of the class our descents resembled unconscious collapse. Only the too thin woman in the front row with toothpick arms and legs managed even half of the *gracefully* aspect. I identified her as the demonstrative breather from earlier.

"Recognize a ball of warmth and light residing inside you," Xanthe said. "Under your collarbone, inside your heart, at the center of your chest, even behind your third eye…"

I can't hear references to the third eye—an area of the forehead between and slightly above the eyebrows—as the opening to enlightenment without hearing Aunt Kit in my head.

"Third eye?" she'd told a shell-shocked instructor at a tony studio in Manhattan. "Sure, there's a third eye. In certain iguanas, lizards, and other lower vertebrates, which have a pineal eye—colloquially a third eye. It's a kind of receptor in the same relative position. But what grownup human aspires to something lizards need because they're badly shorted on brains."

I folded my lips to hold in a grin.

The instructor continued, unaware of Kit joining her class through my decidedly thinking thoughts.

"Wherever this ball of warmth and light lives in you, melt into it. Welcome it. Draw it wider. Spread it throughout your body. For this hour, encourage and welcome its journey throughout you until it's the focus of your entire being. Now, bring all your focus to the second toe of your right foot and breathe through it to—"

She broke off, interrupted by the sound of the street door opening.

That had never happened before during a class. With the cubes in the vestibule holding wallets, phones, keys, and other valuables, instructors locked the street door before they began class.

Xanthe must have forgotten.

She popped up as if this interruption were the one thing lacking to make her life perfect and trotted to the glass doors. As she exited, she pulled the doors partly closed behind her, but held onto the handles.

"May I help you?" she asked.

A man's voice came clearly, though he remained out of sight. Either the angle of the doors caught and broadcast his voice into the studio area or he was speaking quite loudly.

"Just wanted to let you know everything's—Hey. *What the*—? What are you doing here?"

The last part was even louder, but also faster and carrying surprise, perhaps even shock.

But why?

A woman dressed in yoga clothes in a yoga studio? Why would he be confused about what she was doing here?

"I'm teaching a class." Not so bouncy and joy-filled. "What do you want?"

"Uh, you—somebody called about, uh, water running. Just wanted to let you know it was okay. And it is. It's okay. No more water. Everything's all set."

"The call wasn't from here. There was no water running. The owner would have let me know. She's very organized. You need to go. We're in session."

"Sure, sure. As long as you know it's okay."

"Yes. Fine." She released the doorknobs, ushering him ahead of her with a gesture and moving out of sight from my angle. "Goodbye."

The sound of the street door's lock being turned came to us clearly in the listening silence. Presumably with the intruder on the outside.

Xanthe pulled the double doors closed with her back to us, drew in a slow breath, then turned with a bright smile and most of her pep back.

"Okay, now. We shake off the interruption. Come back to our breath. Breathe through that second toe. There's only here. On your mat. Nothing beyond it. There's only now. Not the past. Not even the future. Only now."

CHAPTER FOUR

CLARA AND I didn't linger after class as we sometimes did, chatting with Liz.

The toothpick-limbed woman and the younger woman with her hair tumbling down and a tank on inside out beneath a blotched-with-something orange t-shirt, waited to talk to Xanthe. The instructor currently was being battered by Berrie's barrage of words.

Or, perhaps, we didn't linger because of the lure of the café. I swear I'd picked up a sweetly delicious scent from there during class, despite the distance and multiple brick walls in between.

Clara sniffed in as we walked.

"Strawberry pie. Mmmm. Reminds me, I have a dental appointment the day after tomorrow and it's supposed to be hot that day. Could you take LuLu to the park with Gracie in the morning if I drop her off at your place? Otherwise I don't think she'll get any exercise. Poor baby."

Also, poor Clara and poor Ned, her husband. I'd seen LuLu when she hadn't had exercise. Closely resembled my Gracie.

"Of course."

As we turned toward the café, I looked back and saw the Tackler and MOTB coming up Beguiling Way toward us. I hustled Clara away from the possibility of encountering them and toward the delicious aroma.

Though, in a way, the two spot-stealers did follow us, because we griped about them and the un-yin-like yin class as we awaited our orders.

"Sure hope Liz's back tomorrow," Clara said.

"Most of my muscles agree with you."

Our griping ceased when we were served fresh strawberry pie. Hard to gripe while saying *yum.*

Clara, however, did not look as cheerful as usual.

"What's wrong?" I asked.

She streamed out a long breath. "I need to find a job."

It was a variation of my recent mental lament that I needed to find something to do—which had sparked my laughable string of words this afternoon.

"Ned's tired of you hanging around the house?" I could ask because I was sure it wasn't true, from the times I'd met Ned as well as everything Clara said about him. He was the kind of guy who watched her adoringly, said *Don't work so hard, honey,* and when she didn't listen, stood and collected the dishes himself. "Because I know LuLu loves it."

"She'd be fine with me spending all day, every day petting her with timeouts for feeding her and taking her to the dog park."

I laughed. "What dog wouldn't love that schedule?"

"And Ned's a saint. He's the one who said I should take this break after caring for his mom and he keeps saying it's not time yet and we're fine financially. But I should contribute to the household finances. Who knows when we might need an extra cushion."

"What would you like to do?"

"Stay home," she said promptly.

"Because LuLu wants it, or…?"

"Even putting aside LuLu's wants, strictly on my own account, I want to stay home. I don't mind working, but I don't want to get dressed up and be stuck someplace to do it."

"How about something online?"

"Like what? It's not like I can teach online courses—I'm not expert enough in any one thing. I know how to do a little of a lot of things."

"Let's think about your skills. You're organized and dependable and trustworthy and friendly—"

"I feel like a cross between a Girl Scout and a Labrador retriever."

I grinned, but didn't let her slow me. "You know I've talked about my relative who's an author, right? Well, she has a lot of author friends and I've talked with them and spent time with them. There's this whole network of writers the rest of the world doesn't know about and—"

"Write? Write a *book*? I can't write a book. You might know a lot of people who do it, but that doesn't mean other people—regular people—can. I mean, I know I'm organized and dependable and all the rest of what you said, but I also know I'm not writing a book. Not in this lifetime."

I squirmed. The café chair must not have been as comfortable as I'd thought.

Or maybe it was the memory of Kit and her buddies talking about how many people thought they could, said they would write a novel in their *spare time*. They would approve of Clara's practical recognition that not everyone had the skill-set or drive or desire or need to enter that peculiar writing marathon.

But how would they view my temerity in trying to write one?

And how to navigate publishing anything without being linked to the author of *Abandon All*? Because if I were linked...

Worst case scenario, comparison of my writing to Kit's in *Abandon All* could unravel the whole thing.

Best case scenario, I'd be pitched back into pretending to be someone I wasn't, pretending I'd created something I hadn't.

A pretty bad best-case scenario.

Shake it off. Focus on Clara.

"I'm not telling you to write a book, Clara. But the people who can and do write books often feel the same way about organizing and scheduling and all the practical skills you have. A number of them use virtual assistants to help."

"A virtual assistant? How does that work?"

"I can tell you about virtual author assistants, but there are other kinds, too."

"But I *love* books. Only I want to read them, not write them. I'd *love* to work with authors. What do virtual assistants do for authors?"

"It depends on the author and assistant. But you might do marketing and promotion. You might do graphics—"

She made an *emph* sound, registering as distress.

"—after you'd learned how. Or maybe coordinate and schedule with a designer the author uses. Manage calendars, possibly book travel, handle email, track data, keep other independent contractors from stepping on each other—website, cover designer, formatter—"

"I could do that. It makes my head swim, but I *could* do that. But how? I mean how would I learn to be an author assistant?" She held up a stop-sign hand. "No, I need to be a self-starter. I'll go home and Google it myself. That's what you were going to say, wasn't it?"

I chuckled. "Pretty much. I also seem to remember some established VAs offered classes. But before you sign up, send me a list of ones you're considering, and I'll see if my aunt can get her buddies to vet them. Because there are a lot of people online trying to teach what they have no idea how to do."

"Terrific. Does your aunt use a VA? Ohhh, VA sounds so cool. Like I really know what I'm talking about."

"Aunt Kit has a few people she uses."

That was accurate while simultaneously being evasive. She—or me, as the public face of *Abandon All*—had had a team at the publisher. The team dwindled, plateauing at one in-house person. At least it was the person in charge of the other in-house staff, which also had dwindled, as was the way of traditional publishing.

In addition, Kit used peoples for help with her independent publishing, but still coordinated all the writing-related, but not actually writing, tasks of her life.

"This is great, Sheila. I love this idea." Worry burst across her face. "But the VA does all this at home? Or do you need to find someone local? Because I'm not sure there are any local authors, plus going to their house would mean dressing up…"

"I wouldn't worry about dressing up." I recalled outfits Kit's fellow authors had worn to the brownstone, which meant they'd ventured out in public in them, not to mention ones Kit displayed during writing bouts. Somehow deadline eroded any sense of color coordination, not to mention fashion. "And it's mostly from home. Once in a while an author and assistant might meet in person, maybe for a big event so the assistant can help, or at a conference for the VA to learn stuff. It depends on the individual author and the agreement between the author and the VA."

"Agreement? Like a contract or—? No, I'm not going to worry about that yet. I'm going to look into this and see what's involved."

In discussing how she could find out more about being a virtual author assistant, we forgot about the oddities of the evening's yin yoga class.

DAY TWO

TUESDAY

CHAPTER FIVE

EVERYTHING WAS BACK to normal at the next day's noon-time yoga class.

Almost everything.

There was one anomaly as we approached the studio, when a North Bend County Sheriff's Department squad car rolled slowly along ahead of us on Beguiling Way. The ban on vehicles clearly didn't apply to law enforcement.

It parked across the stubby gap between the studio's building and its neighbor to the south.

"Looks like someone's parked illegally in that little alley." Clara stretched on tiptoe, trying to see over the squad car—actually, squad four-wheel drive—and almost equally bulky deputy blocking our view. This stubby alley perpendicular to Beguiling Way was barely deep enough for one vehicle to fit into it, and it didn't boast much extra space on either side.

Forget a ticket, any driver deserved a commendation for getting into the tight space without needing a new paint job. Especially the driver of a small delivery van from the flower shop on the north side of the studio, who sometimes parked there, despite the No Parking sign.

"The deputy *drove* in here to ticket the poor guy? He could have walked. The exercise might have done him good," I said from the fitness superiority of arriving for a second yoga class in sixteen hours.

The other hundred and fifty-two hours of the week were beside the point.

Once inside Beguiling Way Yoga, though, everything was definitely returned to normal.

Liz was back, greeting Clara and me by name, accompanied by her faint smile. She looked away when, in response to Clara's concerned question, she said she was feeling much better and it had been nothing serious last night.

We were the first students there and got the corner spots.

The lights were dimmed.

We stretched out on our mats, drifting in silence as more regulars came in, talking softly.

Okay, yes, there was a moment when the two corner stealers from the previous night stood at our feet and huffed angrily.

"You're in our spot," said the mother of the bride.

"It's not your spot. It's ours. As you can see." Clara's Zen calm had a decided edge.

"We want this spot. We *need* this spot," said the mother of the bride. "Go back where you were last night."

"We were there because you practically knocked Sheila to the floor while stealing *these* spots," Clara said. "We've had these spots for*ever.*"

The other woman spoke up. "We'd really appreciate it if you'd let us have these spots today."

I sensed Clara weakening. The blonde tackler had said the magic words. *Really appreciate.*

"First come, first serve," I said briskly. "We're here today and we'll take our chances other days."

Take our chances, my eye.

If necessary, we'd come even earlier, maybe take the class before this one to be in place, and we'd sharpen our elbows. I did not intend to be tackled again.

"Yeah," said tough-guy Clara from beside me.

More huffs from the mother of the bride.

"C'mon," the tackler told her. "We'll go somewhere else."

Not far, alas.

They spread their mats next to us, where we'd been last night.

The tackler sat closer to us. As the mother of the bride prattled on, whatever noise wasn't absorbed by her friend sprayed right at us.

We heard complete details of the tragedy of her daughter not being able to use the bridesmaid's shoes she'd chosen—the shoes MOTB chose, not the bride—because they didn't come in the width one bridesmaid needed or the length another needed, and these selfish females had been unwilling to undergo a day of foot-binding to satisfy MOTB's fashion dictates.

I tried hard to ignore her. Focusing on mentally releasing tension, muscles, fascia … and the MOTB headache constricting my forehead.

An interruption made me realize I'd been unconsciously extolling the unnamed bridesmaids whose too-wide, too-long feet denied a bridezilla and her mama an *absolutely darling* scooped-heel open-toed sandal.

The interruption came in the form of a question.

"Did you hear?"

I opened one eye. Now Berrie stood at our feet.

She was a spotty attender of the evening class, but a regular in this one.

She was even spottier about talking with Clara and me at yoga. Two classes in a row was a record.

I opened my second eye to confirm my guess about why she'd approached us. Yup, none of the other people here were ones I'd seen her talk to before.

"Did you hear?" she repeated.

I resisted the pull of her question. Not because I wasn't curious, but because of the asker.

It stemmed from one of my first days at the Torrid Avenue Dog Park.

Gracie, in the throes of a dog park adrenaline high, had ignored orders to come or sit. I'd snagged her collar as she flew past. Her momentum kept her shooting past me, nearly taking me off my feet. Instead, I'd spun around, barely keeping my balance. This left me behind her, roaring "Sit." Which she did, possibly from exhaustion.

That was the moment Berrie chose to instruct me I should not give commands from behind, because it was a position of weakness.

In turn, and entirely in the name of imparting useful information, I instructed Berrie she shouldn't give commands to me from behind, in front, or on the side.

I became aware the constant drone from the mother of the bride had ceased. A quick glance showed why. Her blonde buddy was standing, waiting to use the restroom, taking her yoga bag with her. What? Did she think we'd try to grab it?

"Did you hear?" Berrie asked a third time.

I still resisted.

Clara, however, did not have my willpower. "Hear what?"

"She's dead. Killed."

"What? Who?" Clara asked before I could. Willpower be damned.

"Her. You know, the yoga instructor."

"*Liz?*" Clara and I gasped together.

We'd just seen her. She was right outside in the entry area. How could—?

"No, no. The other one. The one who substituted for her last night."

Clara and I were still in unison, first with an "*Oh*" of relief Liz was not the victim, followed immediately by an "*Oh, no*," for the actual victim.

Then we diverged.

"How *awful*," Clara added.

"What happened?" I asked.

"Don't seem to know yet. I mean, it clearly wasn't a natural death. Not at her age. And she sure looked like she was in good health."

Remembering the class she put us through, making me suck in air, if not my stomach, I had to agree with Berrie, despite a general inclination not to.

"Oh, dear, an accident? Traffic around here has gotten so bad."

Clara's comment drew a reflexive "What traffic" from me, but neither she nor Berrie appeared to hear it. The only way for a former Manhattanite to consider the traffic in North Bend County bad would be to compare it to an empty road.

"Not a car accident. Or *any* accident from what I hear."

The mother of the bride listened avidly.

"What have you heard? And from whom?" I asked.

Berrie slanted me a not particularly friendly look. Some people react that way to the correct use of whom—they are people who haven't been around my great Aunt Kit, who insisted on it.

"Why? Are you going to pretend to be some big detective again?"

So, apparently the not particularly friendly look had not been sparked by my proper use of whom. Though Berrie's stance was rich, considering she'd been after us for months with questions, hoping to get the inside track on nonexistent *investigations.*

Clara came to my defense. "Pretend? Sheila figured out the whole thing. Just because you never had a clue what—*Ow.*"

Ow was an overreaction. Yes, a yoga block had gotten away from me and connected with her back, but yoga blocks are far from cement. More like Styrofoam rectangles.

"What did you hear?" I returned to what I most wanted to know.

"Well, Tina, the owner, you know, came rushing in and told Liz. She was white as a sheet. I thought she'd crumple right to the floor. Then she said she was dead. She must have been shot." Her right hand went to her chest, as if her ribs needed assistance holding her thundering heart inside. "We never used to have trouble with people being shot. Not until a different element started moving in to our county from places shootings happen on every street corner. Like New York City."

"*Was* she shot? Or—?"

"That's ridiculous." Clara staunchly overrode my words in disputing Berrie's. "You make it sound like Sheila's a gun runner."

"Well, she *is* from New York and she's practically living with a guy from Chicago."

"I am not," I said, unable to stop the instinctive return. "He's working on—"

"Teague? Why, he's an—*Ow.*"

Another yoga block escaped my hold.

I couldn't explain why I didn't want Clara to remind Berrie that Teague O'Donnell was an ex-cop. Perhaps it was the sense of listeners all around us. Or a habit of keeping secrets acquired over the years of pretending to be the author of *Abandon All*.

"I haven't even told you the weirdest part—"

Liz came into the studio area then, closing the French doors audibly enough to catch everyone's attention.

"Please take your place, Berrie," Liz said.

She shuffled quickly to her mat on the opposite side of the long room, while the rest of us watched in silence as Liz took her place in the center.

"I have some very sad news. Xanthe Anstead, who many of you know, either from her own classes or from substituting for me yesterday, has died."

The subdued reaction confirmed everyone in the room had been listening to Berrie's less than discreet tones.

"We don't have any additional information at this time. We will certainly let you know when we have arranged a suitable way to remember this important member of our community. In the meantime, we might each consider dedicating today's practice to her memory."

She adjusted a folded-up blanket and sat on it, accompanied by her usual introduction. "If you'll each take your easy seat—sukhasana— and we will open today with a few breaths together, in and out through the nose, then an om, if you choose to participate."

Omming wasn't routine with Liz.

"Breathe in." We breathed in.

"Exhale." We exhaled.

After the third *breathe in*, she adjusted to "Exhale to om."

We exhaled and ommed.

I'd swear there was a wavering crack in Liz's, which lasted longer than anyone else's.

Then we slid into the comforting routine of moving into a position as Liz described it and holding it for several minutes. My mind wandered.

Not far.

Only to what Berrie said and the little Liz added.

Plus, back in time, to last night's class.

What are you doing here?

What really caught my attention were the final three words.

You. Who did he mean? Was he talking to Xanthe? Had he expected Liz? Or hadn't he expected anyone to be here?

Doing. Was someone supposed to have been doing something? Liz? Xanthe? Was the person not performing an action the speaker expected? Or wanted?

Here. Had the speaker expected Xanthe to be elsewhere? Because when the question came down to *here* it seemed likely to be directed at Xanthe. Unless it was taken in combination with *you* and then *you* and *here* could refer to Liz, because the speaker had expected her rather than Xanthe.

Yeah, not a lot of clarity.

I hoped my muscles and fascia were doing better than my cogitations.

"**No, I'm sorry.** I don't know any more. I'm sure a notice about a memorial service will go out as soon as Tina has the information." Liz had said that at least two previous times in my hearing, responding to other students while we retrieved our belongings from the cubbies and put on our shoes.

Class had gone on as usual except for a slight ripple after the *Namaste,* when the blonde tackler tried to be the first into the restroom and was cut off by the stick woman, who took full advantage of her pointy elbows.

Clara and I now came to the edge of the desk Liz stood behind. "Liz—?"

"I'm sorry. I don't know any more. I'm sure a notice about a memorial service will go out as soon as Tina has the information."

"We were going to say we're sorry for your loss." She looked blank. "A fellow instructor. Someone who was part of your—" My gesture indicated the studio. "—professional world."

"Thank you. It is a shock. I didn't know her well, but... There is a camaraderie among the instructors. And it's sad."

"Yes. Very sad." I fought to stay focused on her while Clara tugged at my sweater.

To keep my favorite yoga-going coverup from losing shape, I skipped what else I might have said. Something brilliant, I'm sure, which would have instantly persuaded Liz to tell us everything she knew about Xanthe. Instead, patting Liz's arm, I said, "Take care of yourself."

We were out the door with the last syllable, thanks to Clara's pulling.

"Clara—"

My protest ended because I now saw what she'd spotted from her position closer to the door.

A crime scene.

CHAPTER SIX

POLICE TAPE HAD blossomed on Beguiling Way since we entered the studio.

It stretched from the deputy's vehicle, joined by other official vehicles clogging the narrow lane, across the stubby parking spot's entry.

A knot of our fellow students, along with other onlookers, had congealed in front of the barbershop directly across Beguiling Way.

The focus of official activity and civilian interest was the mini parking spot.

"Do you think…?" Clara trailed off.

But I understood her question. "Yes, I do."

This was where Xanthe had died.

I nodded toward where a deputy talked to a tall, slender woman with a long, sleek ponytail. "Tina."

The owner of Beguiling Way Yoga Studio had her arms wrapped around herself as if for warmth, though the day was warm and sunny above the tops of the shadowing buildings. She brushed fingertips across one cheek, then the other.

"Xanthe was killed here?" Clara's voice skidded up. "But… In the flower van?"

"I don't think it's the flower van. We'd be able to see its top from this angle, even with all the vehicles in between."

We exchanged a look. Then, without discussion, Clara and I opted not to join our fellow students, instead aiming for a gap between the studio building and the original vehicle on the scene, which was not spanned by police tape. We didn't push it. We stayed behind a line the tape would have formed if it had been there.

But the position let us see a silver subcompact car parked nose-in.

"Xanthe's? Was it here when we left last night?" Clara murmured.

I tried to call up the memory of leaving last night. Away from Beguiling Way, last night's sun had barely set, with plenty of remaining rays. But in here, with the buildings set alley-close, it was early gloaming most of the day. This spot was a dark shadow in my memory.

Around the deputy's shoulder, Tina caught sight of us and gave a small nod of acknowledgment.

Unfortunately, her nod caught the attention of another deputy. One we'd encountered before.

Deputy Eckles wasn't a dog lover. Need I say more?

He started toward us, then abruptly detoured. My hopes of being able to observe more plummeted when he snagged a roll of police tape, then resumed his journey toward us.

He stretched out a length of the tape, reminding me of someone about to snap a towel.

"Move along, ladies."

Ladies was a lot nicer than his expression telegraphed.

Clara, ever optimistic, tried. "But, Deputy Eckles, you should hear what we have to say—"

His face turned grimmer. "Move along. Now."

"But we—"

I hooked Clara's arm and tugged hard until she had to shuffle to keep from unbalancing. "If he doesn't want to hear," I said for her ears only, "we'll have to keep what we know to ourselves. And act accordingly. Once he stops watching us."

Her eyes widened. "Oh. *Oh*, right. Let's go."

"That's right. Move along, ladies. Move along."

Under other circumstances, I might have objected to his patronizing tone. Instead, Clara and I turned bright smiles on him, which had the pleasurable effect of making him blink in blank surprise.

✧ ✧ ✧ ✧

WE JOINED THE group in front of the barbershop.

While the others speculated in hushed voices, Clara and I watched Eckles watching us.

"We have to do something to find out who killed her." She spoke out of the side of her mouth, as if Eckles couldn't tell she was talking from the weird way her face screwed up.

"The sheriff's department might solve it," I said.

"Not likely. I mean, Eckles... Besides, look at what happened before. They're not used to dealing with *mysteries*. And you're so good at it. Plus, we're a good team. Don't you think?"

I did. Especially if she was the team's public face.

"Mmm-hmm."

"What should we do first?" she asked, fortunately forgetting the side of her mouth thing.

"Learn about the victim. But, first, since we're here..." Another deputy said something to Eckles and he turned away from staring at us. "The flower shop."

"Really? Oh. *Oh*, yes. Great. I never would have thought of that."

We left the group and casually walked north, as if headed for the outlet of Beguiling Way onto Court Street. But as soon as the angle cut off Eckles' view of us, we crossed the narrow pavement, doubled back a bit and entered the tiny flower shop next to the yoga studio.

The sound of a happily tinkling bell did not match the somber faces of a man and the teenaged assistant behind the counter. They had rectangular cardboard boxes in front of them, about six inches high, and were cutting circles into the closed tops. No one else was in the shop.

The man had a strong nose and seen-a-lot pale blue eyes under wisps of gray and blond hair combed straight back, more with the air of taking the most direct path than any effort to cover the pink scalp. The girl had blonde hair and plenty of it, along with a scaled-down version of his nose.

His nametag said Alan, hers read Mamie.

"Oh, you've heard," Clara said, reading their expressions.

They responded to her genuine warmth. The girl swallowed hard.

The man said, "We have. One of those teachers from next door, wasn't it? Horrible. Horrible."

"But it wasn't your van...?" Clara trailed off.

"Our van? Why would you think—?"

"No." Short and hard, the man, put a stop to the girl's words.

"We take classes next door," I said, "so we've seen your van parked there sometimes."

"Not often and never at night."

"Never at night?" I echoed him, digging into my memory. No instance popped up, but I couldn't swear I *hadn't* seen it there at night. "Ever?"

"Of course it's parked there for a while some evenings, Gramps. Lots of people know," the girl said. "And I tried to park there last night to load the last deliveries, because we had a really late run to the hospital in Stringer." Her words came in jerks. "A car was there. A little silver car. I'd never seen it there before. Nobody was in it. I'm sure nobody was in it."

"What time was that?"

"Eight. I left the van right outside the door with the hazard lights on and ran back and forth to load as fast as I could, because a deputy's yelled at me a couple times and said next time I'd get a ticket. But it was getting late and nobody else was around..."

"My granddaughter's worried she should have seen something or done something or called someone. I told her, but—"

"At eight she was still teaching our class, Mamie," Clara said firmly and kindly. "Nobody could have had any idea of what would happen."

The girl expelled a stream of air. The man said, "See?" to his granddaughter while giving Clara a grateful look.

"What time did you get back?" I asked.

"It took forever. There was a huge delay at the hospital and—" Her eyes popped wide. "Oh, you're thinking I came back here? I might have seen something? I didn't. I didn't come back here. We keep the van at home at night. If I'd come back last night—"

"No sense thinking of that. You didn't. You never do. And never will," her grandfather said with finality.

"Oh, Gramps."

He seemed inclined to lay down new laws for her. To distract him, I gestured toward the boxes. "What are those?"

"How we transport. We don't use fancy crates or foam systems with all sorts of inserts that cost the earth. Just cardboard boxes with holes cut into them."

"That's smart," Clara said.

Before we could get too deep into cardboard boxes, I turned back to Mamie.

"You said you'd never seen the silver car there before, but how about other cars?"

"Sure. Liz—you know, from the studio?" Clara and I nodded to show we knew Liz. "She usually teaches Monday nights. Oh, yeah, you take her class. Well, she'd parked there several times. Then one night she saw me carrying a huge load to the van around the corner. She said she was sorry and she'd never park there again. I told her not to do that, because we only have night deliveries sometimes. She gave me her phone number and said if she was ever there when I needed to park for evening deliveries, to call her.

"She was so nice about it. When I heard a yoga teacher was killed last night…"

She gulped. Her grandfather put an arm around her shoulders.

"It's not her, but it's still so horrible. So horrible," Mamie said in a small voice.

CHAPTER SEVEN

OUTSIDE, SHIFTING THE daisies I'd bought to my other hand—it had seemed wrong to leave the flower shop without buying a little something and Clara must have felt the same, because she had a bouquet of alstroemeria—I asked her, "What do you say to continuing around the block to get a clearer view of the area? I've never been past the studio."

"Sure. I'll see it with fresh eyes."

Continuing north, we passed a card and gift shop. "Smart of them to be next to each other," Clara said. "They opened about the same time. What did you think about what Alan and Mamie said?"

"It was interesting."

"Really? Why?"

"*Why* is the most interesting part—as in, why answer our questions. I even made the one about what time she got back sound like a cop, yet she answered anyway."

"You think—? What *do* you think?"

"I think Mamie wasn't telling us the whole truth and her grandfather knew it. Or at least feared it. And I think we need to see what time she got to the hospital with those flowers."

"Yeah, I wondered about that stuff about the delay at the hospital. But why on earth would she hurt Xanthe?"

"No idea if she did. Just know detectives and amateur sleuths look for inconsistencies, then follow them up."

She sighed. "I need to read more murder mysteries."

The last business on Beguiling Way before the cross street was an eye doctor's office. We turned the corner to the narrow end of the block.

"Oh, here's something I know. Zepke's." Even though we usually entered from the other direction, I recognized the display windows of Zepke's Pet Store.

Adopting Gracie from a collie rescue group had turned me into a devotee of this establishment. Not only did I spend a sizable chunk of my discretionary budget here, Gracie and I came for training. The way some women shopped for shoes, I shopped for dog toys. I figured I got the better end of the deal—no bunions, blisters, or foot cramps. Instead, I got dog hair, dog slobber, and belly laughs.

Applying what I knew of the inside layout to the buildings' outsides, I guessed Zepke's back room occupied space behind the gift shop.

"Darn. I meant to get LuLu more dental chews. She's running low." Clara had stopped by angled steps leading to a big, old-fashioned wood and glass corner door.

"We could go in…" I offered.

"No, no. Let's finish this. If she runs out—"

"You can have some of Gracie's. As long as you don't let Gracie know I gave them to you."

Directly across Tanner Street from Zepke's and also housed in a century-old building was a hardware store. Its historic front faced the square. We were looking at the business end, with a high fence enclosing supplies and equipment.

The Old Main Branch of the North Bend County library occupied a full-depth lot on the south end of the block. It was the county's original library. When Stringer, near the Interstate on the eastern edge of the county, secured a big new building and wrested away the designation of Main Library, the people of Haines Tavern didn't roll over. If this building had to be called a "branch," it was also going to be given its historic due, whether it confused newcomers or not—thus, the Old Main Branch Library.

Between these two full-depth buildings was the tiny post office, which occupied the front of its lot. A back driveway led to an area for postal trucks. This was screened by fencing, which in turn was screened by the plantings of a pocket park facing Tanner Street.

Walking south on Tanner, in addition to the backs of the square-facing institutions, we saw the fronts of buildings that sat back-to-back with those on Beguiling Way.

"You know, what they said in the flower shop made me think about the timing of Xanthe's murder, *if* she was murdered."

"But Berrie said—Oh. Yes. Berrie's our sole source for her being shot."

I nodded. "Though the way Eckles and the others were acting... Still, we shouldn't assume. So, let's look at the timing. Obviously after class. And some time before she was found, close to noon."

Clara shook her head. "It had to be at night. There's too much going on up and down Beguiling Way during the day, including morning classes at the studio. Would anybody risk killing her with all sorts of people around? If she was shot, the noise..."

"You're right. Even with a suppresser it would be risky."

"You mean a silencer?"

"Officially, it's a suppresser, not a silencer."

"You know the most interesting things."

We passed a smaller but still enticing Zepke's display window before the not-so enticing storefront for the Chamber of Commerce, followed by a financial services company named Smith-Flarenge, which seemed vaguely familiar. Then two doors apparently leading to separate sets of offices and possibly apartments on higher floors, based on listings of two lawyers, an accountant, a counselor, and several names with no occupation included.

Clara picked up the thread of our conversation. "Xanthe's body likely was there all morning without anyone noticing. I suppose with the car pulled in and how dark it stays there, nobody could see."

Slowly, I nodded. "Especially not the front seat and if her body slumped down or to the side. No one would see her unless they walked alongside the car, like a deputy writing a parking ticket and preparing to put it on the windshield."

We reached familiar territory with the bakery called simply Bake'n.

It had specialty rolls with bacon, layering on the intoxicating aroma.

A real estate agency sat between Bake'n and the café, which stretched across the southern end of the block.

Clara pulled in a deep breath, redolent with fresh-baked bread. "If I worked this close to the bakery and café, I'd weigh a thousand pounds."

A little sigh followed, informing me that referring to working reminded her of her desire for a job.

I empathized, but stuck to the topic of Xanthe's death.

"So, it's less likely she was killed this morning than last night. And, unless we find out something different, it seems more likely she was killed shortly after class than, say, in the middle of the night."

We'd parked near the café, since that's where we'd intended to end up after class. But now we virtuously continued past the entry, turning to walk north again on Beguiling Way.

"Makes sense," Clara said, "because why would she still be here? Or, I suppose, why would she leave and come back? More argument against her being killed in the morning, right? There'd have to be a reason she was here at that time."

I nodded. "Right. More likely she was killed after class. So everyone in class—"

"Is a suspect? Really?"

"Possible suspect. Also witness."

"We can see if anyone's still in front of the barbershop and chat with them."

A little odds-and-ends store was the first facing Beguiling Way. We'd stopped in a couple times and found more odds than ends.

That left the music store, which sold band instruments, supplies, and sheet music, but whose main business appeared to be giving lessons.

A pair of students stood outside it now, clearly reluctant to go inside and miss the chance to gawk at official vehicles.

Clara and I angled toward the significantly depleted knot of onlookers by the barbershop.

"Nobody from last night's class is still here," Clara muttered.

But the group did include Tina, owner of Beguiling Way Yoga.

"Tina." Clara infused sympathy, concern, and shock into two sylla-bles. She gathered the other woman into a hug.

I followed suit, though if I'd been Tina, I'd have wanted more Clara hug, less Sheila hug. The woman is a great hugger.

"How are you holding up?" Clara asked.

"I hardly know. To have this happen at the studio—well, outside the studio, but to one of ours and right here... It's horrible. Beyond horrible. I can't get my mind around it. It's like ... like sacred ground to me."

Her voice wobbled, then righted itself.

"From the moment I walked into that dark, dingy space six years ago, I just *saw* what it could be. The whole thing. All at once. A vision. There were setbacks, of course. I wanted the mechanicals where the restroom is now and I'd hope to leave the original brick walls exposed on both sides, but... It ended up being good this way because it's brighter with white on the one long wall. I do wish we'd been able to do skylights... But I love how it turned out. Love it."

"Of course you do," Clara said.

"They're inside the studio now. Searching. I told them yes when they asked because if there's any chance... But I also told them there wouldn't be anything to find there. We—none of us—keep *things* there. You know, both of you, there simply isn't space. We want all the space for classes."

True. Unless law enforcement found a secret clue tucked inside a zipped bolster, they were going to be out of luck.

"Xanthe had a key, right?"

"All the teachers do. They open up for their classes, so I don't have to be here all the time."

"And the studio has a security system..."

"Yeah. Last one out each night turns it on, first one in turns it off for the day, so using the key doesn't trip it."

That meant most, if not all, of the instructors knew the code.

"Do you have security cameras?"

She looked at me as if I hadn't spoken English. "No."

"Do any of the other businesses?"

"I have no idea. We've never had the least problem. It's perfectly safe, including at night. It's never come up."

"That's totally understandable," Clara soothed. "We're so fortunate to not have to think about those things."

I bit my tongue not to say Xanthe might have wished she had thought about it. Instead, I went with sympathy.

"This must be so hard for you, Tina, especially with knowing Xanthe so well."

"Me?" Surprise broke through her other reactions. "I mean, I'm horrified, of course, and sad. But I didn't know her well. The deputy kept asking that, too. I finally asked if he was best friends with his boss. And, really, it wasn't even as close. I hire the instructors, but I don't work with them day in and day out. They're responsible people and I can't be here for every class, for every minute. Honestly, there's so much to running the studio no one sees. It's proverbial duck feet paddling like mad under the surface while everything looks smooth and placid above, at least I hope it does." She gave a small, strangled laugh.

I took the chance to ask, "How did you come to hire Xanthe?"

"We needed a teacher for two morning classes. She had the right credentials from her training and Eloise recommended her. I think they taught together at a studio off I-275. Or maybe it was in Covington. Anyway, Eloise has recommended other people who've worked out so I jumped on the opportunity."

"Did Xanthe have another job that allowed her to do this part time?"

"No. At least I can't imagine she had another job, because she said she'd be happy to substitute. I assumed she was free to work any time because she *didn't* have another job. I didn't ask many more questions." As if the word triggered her next thought, she added, "Why are you asking all these questions?"

I raised my hands. "You know what it's like when you cross paths with someone even for a short time and then you find yourself wondering about them. About their life. What brought them to this point. Especially when something so tragic happens."

"Oh, yes, I do know. To feel as if you were brought together in the same space at the same time for a purpose, but then to have it ripped apart. It's tragic. Senseless. Such a loss. Poor Eloise is totally broken up. I had to call her before she heard about it another way. I would have gone to see her, but the deputies didn't want me to leave." She expelled a breath. "Still don't want me to leave. But also didn't want me in the studio while they search."

"I wonder... Do you think talking to us... I mean, we certainly wouldn't want to make it harder on Eloise. But somebody listening? Do you think it might make her feel a tiny bit better?"

That is what they call in the legal biz a leading question. From my contacts with Tina, it was a good bet she would think talking would do Eloise good. Whether it would be better to talk to us or a lamp post probably didn't matter much.

"Harder on her? Not at *all*. I think it would make her feel better. Absolutely. You *should* talk to her. She'll want to know her friend had an impact on students even in such a short time and you never know what open loops it might resolve for her. In addition to the yet unclosed emotional loops for you two."

I had no idea what she was talking about, but—following Clara's lead—nodded wisely.

"Here's her number. Tell her I said to call. I'm so glad you reached out. That's what the Beguiling Way studio is all about. A community. Caring. You two are demonstrating exactly what we're all about."

She hugged Clara, then me. We hugged back, with Eloise's contact information safely stashed.

With more words of caring, community, and reaching out, we headed back to where we'd parked for class, a seeming lifetime ago.

We didn't stop at the café this time. Strawberry pie didn't appeal.

CHAPTER EIGHT

DARN.

Teague's four-wheel drive was parked on the side of the driveway, politely leaving room for me to access the side of the garage near the house.

With the news of Xanthe's death, I'd forgotten he was coming back today. After months of his not being around because of substitute teaching, I needed to get reaccustomed to his presence.

Especially if I kept trying to write. Or became involved in … other things. He had not been gung-ho about the previous time Clara and I took an interest in a murder.

I stopped inside the kitchen door, trying to listen over enthusiastic and loud canine greetings. The enthusiasm came from Murphy. The loud came from Gracie.

The Lassie-type collies we know these days were bred from wily and loyal dogs who patrolled the hills and valleys of Scotland, looking for and warning of any danger to their owner's flock. Gracie upheld every decibel of the tradition. Not a nook, crag, or cranny of Scotland would have gone unwarned with Gracie around.

"Gracie, hush. It's me. This is my house. I'm not an intruder," I reminded her in vain. We'd been working on the "Quiet" command, also in vain.

Dog training advice said to first teach her to "Speak" with rewards, then alternate "Speak" and "Quiet" with rewards for getting it right. We were 0 for 17,529 so far on "Speak." Sitting in front of me with intent alertness, she absolutely refused to "Speak," despite the woofing, arfing, and other canine noises I demonstrated. I even tried catching her barking on her own and issuing the "Speak" command as fast as I could. She paid no attention. Too interested in what she was barking at.

At this rate, we'd never get to "Quiet."

But in this moment, Murphy provided the solution. Sensing Gracie was getting more attention than him, he partially curled to oh-so-subtly butt-check her out of the way. Retaliating captured enough of her interest that she stopped barking.

I strained my ears to locate the carpenter in my house. Instead of hearing Teague, though, an unfamiliar voice drifted to me.

"...murder victim was found in Haines Tavern in an area of quaint shops and businesses called Beguiling Way. The name of the victim has not been released, pending notification of family. The North Bend County Sheriff's Department is investigating. In other news..."

The report was already on the radio? I was stunned.

Local outlets here lagged a day behind on national and international news, if they reported it at all. The local news frequently seemed to forget much existed outside of these corners of Ohio, Indiana, and Kentucky. Though, they did get a fair amount of If-it-bleeds-it-leads headlines in. I supposed this was one.

"For me? You shouldn't have."

This voice was not unfamiliar. It emanated from Teague O'Donnell, whom I could see through the archway, standing over a stack of papers he'd created on my dining room table.

But his words didn't make sense.

"What?"

"The flowers." He jerked his chin toward the daisies I'd bought at the flower shop and still held.

"A little something to brighten up the place after—"

Mistake.

I saw him connect my wanting to brighten up my house with the news, linked by the proximity between the death and the yoga studio.

Before he could ask a question, I rushed to say, "Gotta change before Clara gets here. We're going to the d-o-g p-a-r-k. Happy to take

Murphy."

The last words trailed me as I chugged up the stairs.

If I was fast enough, I'd be back downstairs before Clara got here.

I WASN'T FAST enough.

I heard Clara's voice as I started down the stairs in knee-length shorts, t-shirt, and flip-flops I would swap at the dog park for old runners kept in the car.

"We're going to the dog park. See what we can find out." Clara had a knack for sounding both excited and solemn, which prevented her excitement from edging toward ghoulishness.

I regretted not warning her not to mention to Teague the murder or our discussion before I dropped her off at her house to change and collect LuLu. During that discussion, we'd agreed an initial quick and dirty gathering of information was in order. For quick and dirty, nothing beat the dog park.

"You and Murphy want to come, Teague? Or if you want to stay here and work, we can take Murphy."

As I stepped around and over the ranks of dogs at the bottom of the stairs, now swelled to three, I saw Gracie perk up at the words *dog park*. Murphy tuned in at the mention of his name. Clara's LuLu ignored the humans, happily occupied with thumping her tail on the hardwood floor while she nibbled Murphy's ruff.

"Find out about what?" Teague asked absently.

"The murder, of course. Didn't you hear? Didn't Sheila tell you?"

"No need for me to tell him," I said. "He had the radio on when I came in. It was on the news."

He raised his head, his finger sliding away from the spot where he'd been about to add a written measurement. His gaze came to me first—another of those considering examinations—then went to Clara. "The woman found murdered in town this morning? On Beguiling Way, near your yoga place?"

"Right next door," Clara said. "In fact, she was our yoga instructor. Not the regular one, but she taught our yin class last night. Then, after class today, there was police tape across the alley, with deputies and crime scene people."

"So law enforcement is working the case." In other words, according to Teague, we should stay out of it.

Clara wrinkled her nose at him. "Who knows? They wouldn't tell us anything. They—"

"They're not supposed to shoot off their mouths to civilians."

"—didn't even ask us questions or try to find out who had been at class last night. I mean, we could have been the last people to see her alive. Except for the killer, of course. But they shooed us away like pesky insects."

He dropped his head, not quickly enough. I saw the grin he tried to suppress. Because he agreed with the deputies that pesky insects described us exactly.

Pretty rude, considering we'd figured out who was behind a murder a few months ago.

Apparently, Clara did not see his expression, because she said, "We've already reconnoitered the area around the crime scene. The buildings on Beguiling Way and the ones on Tanner. You know those buildings back up to the ones on the east side of Beguiling Way, like the studio. They were among the first businesses in Haines Tavern."

"Sounds like you already know the area well."

"It's different when you're viewing it as the scene of a crime," she said solemnly.

"Okay, but the dog park's not the scene of a crime. What—"

"This time," I muttered.

"—do you think you're going to find out there?"

The dogs had started to lose interest, until he'd uttered the magic two words. Gracie and Murphy came up to a sitting position— preparation to jump around in excitement. So did LuLu, to keep nibbling Murphy's ruff.

"We picked up all sorts of information at the dog park last time."

"That involved dog park people," he pointed out.

The dogs' heads went from one speaker to the other like tennis spectators.

"This has a lot of connections to the dog park," she said airily.

"Like what?"

Before she could answer, I said, "C'mon, Clara, let's get out of here before the d-o-g-s jump out of their skins at one more mention of p-a-r-k. As for Murphy—"

"I have this sudden urge to go upstairs and break walls," Teague said, perhaps to himself.

"Really?" That was a lot faster progress than I'd expected based on his pace with the shelves. Though that might not have been my only reason for eagerness. "We're happy to take Murphy—"

"Thanks, but no need. I'm going to the dog park with you," Teague said slowly.

All three dogs jumped up and barked.

I did not share their enthusiasm.

CHAPTER NINE

CLARA ALREADY HAD LuLu out of her SUV when I got out of my car, leash in hand to get Gracie from the back.

Clara held on to LuLu's leash with both hands, which trimmed the tread-wear on her sneakers by about a third as LuLu pulled her across the parking lot in her eagerness to reach the bastion of doggy delights, the big-dog enclosure.

As Clara skidded past me—if she'd been in a "Road Runner" cartoon there would have been smoke pouring out from where her heels met the pavement—she called, "Back table? Decide who to talk to first?"

"Sure."

But we were not destined to get to our usual table immediately.

First, we had to pass the Boston terrier gantlet, especially Marcus, patriarch of Berrie's band. They were in the small-dog enclosure, but the gates to all four enclosures—two each for small and large—opened into one small area and we'd yet to slip past Marcus and the Bostons without a ruckus.

By *we* I mean *me*. Marcus loftily ignored Gracie. But until I was inside the large-dog enclosure, he caterwauled.

No idea why.

I've never done a thing to the dog. I swear. Must be mistaken identity or something.

If anything, he was in even fuller throat than usual.

The result was I could see Berrie's lips moving but not hear her. She often hung out near the gate to impart her unsolicited wisdom on all the dog owners. The fact that her strictures could not be heard over the carrying-ons of her dogs never seemed to occur to her. Its effect on me was a resolve to redouble my "Quiet" efforts with Gracie.

But this time, Berrie did not stop speaking even after Gracie and I were in the enclosure and Marcus and his fellow Bostons had trotted away, now perfectly at peace.

"What do you think of that?" she called out to Clara and me.

I might have kept going.

Clara stopped and turned. "Of what?"

"What I just said. Thought you'd be interested. But if you're not…"

Clara took a step toward the fence dividing the enclosures. "Couldn't hear you."

Berrie looked around, as if a darkly cloaked spy might be hiding behind one of the fence posts. "Come over here."

Clara obeyed, and gestured for me to join her.

That presented another layer of strange on Marcus' reaction to me. He only went nuts by the gate. He didn't make a peep when I was by the fence. Occasionally even came over to snuffle a hello.

So my reluctance was not based on another auditory assault. Not a canine one, anyway.

I looked around to see if my dog offered an excuse to walk the other way. But, no, she and LuLu were racing joyously along the far fence-line.

I assumed a smile and headed toward them.

"…and the biggest news is she was strangled."

"You said she was shot," Clara objected.

"She was strangled," Berrie repeated.

"But you said—"

"That's what I was told. But now I have better information and I'm telling you, but if you don't want to know—"

"How did you hear? Sheriff's Department hasn't announced it, have they?"

"Not yet, but they're not making a big secret of it the way they do sometimes, either. And here's another thing, the killer used something in her car."

"She had rope in her car?" That question came from an older man with a mixed breed, who'd been lurking nearby. He wore hearing aids, but with Berrie he probably didn't need them.

"It doesn't matter what, specifically, was used or—"

"Well, it must have been rope. What else can you get strangled with that someone would have in their car?"

Berrie was getting irked at the man deflating her scoop. "The important thing is she was strangled in her car."

"Well, everyone knew she was killed in her car. Even the radio said so," the man said.

"Strangled. She was *strangled*. With something from her car. You didn't know that until I told you."

"Goodness, you're testy today, Berrie."

Clara and I exchanged a look and, by the mutual agreement, excused ourselves to check on our dogs.

"Strangled by something she had in her car. A yoga instructor. Gee, what could it be?" I muttered when we wouldn't be overheard over the wrangling continuing behind us. As we crossed the scrubby grass, I looked around for Gracie.

Clara grimaced. "Yoga strap. Had to be her yoga strap."

"Mmm-hmmm." Once again, I heard the clash of metal on hardwood floor as Xanthe used the strap buckle to quiet the blonde tackler and the mother of the bride.

Clara interrupted the memory, now turned unpleasant. "Donna, what are you doing here so late?"

I turned from besottedly watching the wind ruffle Gracie's gold and burnished-bronze coat in a way that rivaled the sappiest shampoo commercial, to see the doyenne of the dog park was, indeed, in attendance at an unusual time for her.

The dog park had all sorts of sub-groups, including based on time of attendance.

Donna and her aging golden retriever, Hattie, were part of the regular mid-morning crew. After the pre-work crowd and before the lunchtimers. But here she was, with the mid-afternooners, leaning against one of the posts supporting the fence separating the big-dog and small-dog enclosures.

"Didn't get Hattie out this morning because I had a dental appointment, so excuse me if I drool as badly as a Newfie." Newfoundlands are as adorable and loving as they are large. They also need industrial strength bibs for their drool.

"Are you okay?"

"All set now. I'd lost a crown, so had to take the first appointment they'd give me."

"Darn," Clara said forcefully, "that reminds me. I have a checkup in the morning. This is not a good time with—Maybe I'll cancel."

"Don't cancel," Donna ordered. "Take care of your teeth. Listen to your elders on this. Even when you're tempted because of other *activities*." Her arch emphasis hardly needed explanation, but she added it anyway. "Heard you two were right in the middle of another murder."

"I wouldn't say that," I hedged, with one eye on the approach of Teague from the gate. Murphy had already streaked off to join Gracie and LuLu in a reunion no less joyous despite their being together minutes ago.

"But we were. Not only in the middle of it, but we solved it." Clara's head whipped to me, then beyond to see what I'd been looking at. "Why are you looking at Teague that way? Don't you like him? I know he's being a pill about our investigating, but otherwise he's nice. And smart. And attractive. And well-read. And he's nice to his dog," she concluded, having clinched the issue to her mind.

"I didn't say a word."

"You swore under your breath."

"Did I? Must have been the stone I stepped on."

"There are no stones here. Also, you said something about a beard, and it looks like he's trying to grow one. Well, *I'm* not going to make him feel bad by walking away when he's headed this way."

"I haven't said anything—"

"You don't need to," Donna said. "I'm with Clara. You don't like him?"

"I don't dislike him. I hired him, after all. Twice, in fact. It's simply a matter of not getting too friendly too fast. With him redoing the closets, he'll be around a lot anyway."

"How can it hurt to be friendly?"

I gave Clara a look meant to convey both that I didn't appreciate the question and even if I had, there was no time to answer it with the subject within a hair of hearing range.

"Good afternoon, Teague," Donna said. "Now, Clara and Sheila, tell me about this poor young woman you found murdered."

"We didn't find—" I needn't have bothered.

Teague greeted Donna, then turned a frown on me.

Hey, I wasn't the one now burbling along about Xanthe teaching our class last night, then being found murdered half a day later. *Frown at Clara, O'Donnell.*

"Terrible, terrible thing," Donna continued. "I heard about the trouble you two had with Eve and some friend of hers."

"Who?"

"Eve Kraft. She and her friend—a blonde woman named Julia Trippen—rudely took the spots you'd already claimed through yoga studio conventions."

"Oh. The mother of the—"

I didn't finish it, but Donna and Clara both chuckled.

"Yes. Eve is the mother of a bride-to-be and taking it to extremes," the older woman said. "Including at the yoga studio from what I hear."

"Your source gave all the details of their spot-stealing, huh?"

"Mmmm." In other words, she wasn't saying more on the topic of her source.

"Do you know her friend?"

"Julia? No. Though she's been in town about a year."

"Did Berrie tell you how Eve was talking on and on about the wedding, even when class started?" Clara asked.

"Berrie? Heavens no. She's entirely too pleased with herself for knowing the poor woman who was killed was strangled."

"How did you hear that, Donna?"

Teague's question sounded casual, but I thought she'd caught his attention. Understandable he'd be interested in the cause of death in a murder, considering his background.

Then he surprised me by adding, "About this mother of the bride and her friend at yoga last night?"

Was he so determined to steer us away from a murder he'd pretend more interest in a little yoga class conflict?

"Augustine Lorenson with the German shepherd told me when she was leaving the dentist's as I arrived. She'd heard it from the dental assistant, who'd heard it from her day care person..." The chain was like listening to the begats in the Bible in reverse. She clearly had no issue with sharing her sources for *this* information. "...who'd heard it from her sister, whose neighbor was in the class. I also heard Xanthe worked you all harder than you liked."

Reminded of the achiness in my legs, I shifted position. "True."

Donna chuckled. "No one shouts *Amen* louder than a convert. Just like reformed smokers."

"You mean, Xanthe wasn't always into yoga and, uh, spirituality?" Clara asked.

"Not at all into it. Wasn't the least bit what anyone would call spiritually inclined. Didn't get into yoga until a year ago or so."

I remembered sensing salesmanship in Xanthe's approach and wondered what she'd done before yoga.

Donna continued, "Ran into her at the Roger—" That was short-hand for the Jolly Roger supermarket chain, which had several outlets in the county. "—and she was happier than I'd ever seen her. Didn't know her well, but we passed a few words. Shame for her to get murdered. Shame for anybody, but after what she went through..."

"What did she go through?" It was a race to see who got the words out first, Clara or me. Clara won.

"Well, as I said, I didn't know her well. Didn't know the in-laws, either, but heard about it from a woman who used to bring her Jack Russell-dachshund mix here. Crazy." She smiled. "The dog, not the woman. Anyway, she lived next door to the Branters, Xanthe's in-laws—now ex-in-laws—and she saw a lot and heard pretty much everything. Not a family that modulated their voices.

"Xanthe and the son—Fred's his name—dated in high school. Must have done more than that, because she got pregnant and they married right after graduation. Moved in with his parents. It was rocky. And loud. They finally got their own place when the baby was a couple years old, but apparently it didn't help the family dynamics any. Money problems among other things, even though they were both working and the grandmother took care of the kid for free. Then they got divorced and things really got bad."

She looked around, as if checking how attentive her audience was. The answer was extremely attentive. Even Teague.

"Xanthe and Fred split custody and the grandmother, Joyce, said she'd keep caring for Ethan—still for free—while the parents worked. I don't suppose they could have afforded anything else, but Joyce was off-the-charts. She didn't hide she was teaching her little grandson to say things like *Mommy's a witch*, but without the "w"—and that might have been the mildest. There were also phrases about her morals and sexual habits. Disgusting. Absolutely disgusting. This neighbor heard it and was so horrified she told Fred he needed to put a stop to it for his child's welfare. Said he stared at her with his mouth open, not comprehending. So she told Xanthe.

"They went back to court. The grandmother wasn't allowed to be around the grandson without supervision and both parents had to pay for child care if they were working during their custody time. Fred was working as a stocker at the Roger, but he had financial support from his parents. Xanthe was on her own. She got a better job and worked like crazy to support herself and the kid, including saving for college. She was determined her boy would go to college. Then an uncle left her some money that let her max the college account and have a bit to spare to ease her way.

"That's when she switched to teaching yoga. Not making nearly as much money, but she didn't mind. She went for a new life." Without punctuation or a breath, she added, "Poop alert."

That might have confused other listeners.

Clara, Teague, and I all turned to see whose turn it was to pick up after their dog.

BACK IN MY kitchen, Clara and I sat at the small wall-mounted table across from the refrigerator. The dogs sprawled around our feet in satisfied exhaustion.

After Donna had left, we'd made several circuits of the enclosure, chatting with the regulars and even a few unfamiliar people. The regulars tried to grill Clara and me for information. Neither they nor the others added anything to what we knew.

"What should we look into first?" Clara's question brought Teague's head around from where he'd been filling a water bottle at the sink.

When I didn't answer fast enough for her, Clara added, "How about you, Teague? What do you think from your experience as a detective?"

This time I did speak immediately. "Let's not hold up Teague from his important work upstairs by bothering him with our speculations."

"Speculations is right. Not to mention going along your merry way poking into hornets' nests," he said.

"Don't be condescending—"

They both ignored my objection.

"You could help us investigate," Clara invited.

"I'm not interfering with the sheriff's department's investigation, but I better know what you two are up to so if you run into trouble—again—I'm up to speed."

His *again* had history behind it.

"That wasn't really our fault." Clara's staunch defense crumbled the next instant when she turned to me. "Though he does have a point. Ned about had a fit when that one reporter blabbed what happened at the dog park. And I'd been so careful about how I described it. I have no idea how she found out. She even made it sound worse than it was, like we could have been killed any second."

"You *could* have been. And your dogs," Teague said dourly.

The reminder pushed me into saying, "You can stay if you want.

But only as a silent observer."

"Good with me. I sure don't want to participate. The sheriff's department is perfectly capable of handling this. It's what they're paid and trained to do. Besides, you don't have time for this. You need to clean out your closets before I can get started."

"How many more days of measuring are you planning?" I asked with a slide toward snark.

"As many as it takes to get it ri—"

"You can't mean it, Teague." Clara turned soulful eyes on him. "Instead of checking into the murder of someone we knew, someone who was a mother, trying to give her son a better future, someone we left alive and vibrant and smiling such a short time before she was found with all that snuffed out—instead of trying to make sure justice is served for her, Sheila should clean out closets? You can't mean that."

"I can if she doesn't want sawdust and plaster dust all over her clothes." But he grumbled the words in the subdued voice of the defeated.

Nobly restraining from rubbing it in, I faced Clara, and said deliberately, "I say we start by talking with Liz."

"Oh, yes. Good. Because she would be a connection to find out more about Xanthe."

"I suppose we can find out about Xanthe from her. But I want to talk to her more because, logically, she's the most likely intended victim."

CHAPTER TEN

"LIZ?"

Clara's voice rose enough octaves I was glad I hadn't mentioned the other possibility—Liz as a murder suspect. Clara's reaction would have acted on the dogs like a dog whistle.

"You mean *Liz* was the intended target?" Clara specified.

"Possible intended target. Though it would take a pretty careless killer not to check out beforehand what kind of car his intended victim drove and to not realize Xanthe's little gray Ford was not Liz's bright green mini-SUV."

"But... *Liz?*"

"Liz," I said firmly. "Think about it, Clara. Who would be expected to be coming out of the studio, alone, last night after class? The regular instructor—Liz—not a random substitute. I'm not saying Xanthe absolutely wasn't the target. But, whatever else the sheriff's department is doing or not doing, they'll surely cover the basics on her."

I slanted a look toward Teague. As a former cop, he could easily schmooze with the locals to confirm it. He didn't meet my eyes. Not only was he going to be hands-off. He was eyes-off.

I continued, "We need to check out Liz. What do you think about how she acted at last week's class?"

"I wished she wouldn't do Sleeping Swan."

See? Some people do hate it.

"I love Sleeping Swan. Nothing else stretches—"

"There are parts of us that are not meant to be stretched and Sleeping Swan reaches all of mine."

"You know what Liz says—if you hate a pose, it means your body needs that work the most."

"Yeah? I don't see you doing Dragon."

I tried to pretend she hadn't hit a bull's-eye. "Dragon is not in my practice."

She snorted.

"Back to how Liz acted at class last week. Remember, you poked me because she was crying during that song?"

"I remember seeing her crying while I was trying to descend into the hell of Sleeping Swan and discreetly drawing your attention to it, but what song?"

I synopsized the song for her. "Oh, is that what the lyrics are about? I just like the tune. And the singer sounds sexy."

"Self-centered egotist who wants the girl to throw over the good life she has now to gamble he'll stick around this time, that's what he sounds like to me. He'd probably end up throwing her over the way he did before. Probably blather about commitment issues."

She eyed me. "Having flashbacks?"

"Nope." I wasn't going to share the restricted nature of my post-college love life—restricted by the charade of being the *Abandon All* author. "But what if Liz did? Have flashbacks, I mean. What if she turned down a former lover who wanted her back and he got angry and came after her? Someone like that might not realize it was the wrong car because he wouldn't know Liz's car now. Or, if she didn't turn him down—"

Clara's eyes widened. "But she's married."

"A husband's another suspect, with or without a former lover. How do you know she's married?"

"Ned knows him from playing volleyball together the past few winters. He's a nice guy. He and Liz met in college, but didn't start dating until a couple years after graduation when they ran into each other again. Out of the blue, at the Banks in Cincy. Totally random. Isn't that amazing?"

"What else?"

"He said Liz is teaching yoga somewhere else, too. They're trying to earn as much money as possible. Maybe to pay off student loans and stuff. She didn't want to add classes at Beguiling Way, because she didn't want to disappoint the students there when she cuts back to her regular schedule because she really likes the students." She grinned. "Which is why Ned told me about Gregson saying that.

"They bought a house a couple years ago and have been fixing it up themselves. They want to start a family. Liz worries if Gregson is traveling—Ned told me that so he could get in how he bragged about how independent I am. Just ordinary things."

If we'd been alone, I'd have asked if Ned might be persuaded to pump Gregson. Not that I expected the husband to share if she had a current boyfriend—the guy Berrie said she'd seen Liz with?—but even a tiny crack could indicate he knew something, which might give him a motive if Liz *was* the intended target.

But with Teague listening, I didn't want to give him any ammunition in case Clara's—or Ned's—answer was no.

"Oh, dear, if she has a lover, Gregson will be devastated," she said.

"We don't know if she has a lover or a former lover. Or if former, if he's tried to come back into her life. Or if she did and he did, if he would try to hurt her," I pointed out. "On the other hand, Berrie did say she saw Liz with a man. Remember? Before class. She said Liz hadn't looked sick."

"But that was Berrie, being Berrie."

"Maybe. Still… We don't *know* anything about Liz. What we do have is the fact she missed class. The fact the teacher who substituted for her was killed. And the intriguing fact she was uncharacteristically crying during a song she's heard dozens if not hundreds of times."

"I guess. She *was* acting weird. Bouncing from being sort of withdrawn, to crying, to being real friendly at the end." Clara considered her own point. "It seems terrible to consider being friendly suspicious, doesn't it?"

I wasn't the one to ask. I'd lived in Manhattan and nominally worked in publishing. Heck, yes, friendly seemed suspicious.

"Though, come to think of it," Clara added without encouragement from me, "if that's the gauge, Xanthe would be a heck of a lot more suspicious because she was really friendly."

I chuckled. "We do need to look into Xanthe and her past. But, first, how are we going to talk to Liz? We don't have class again until next week and it's not the best time anyway, with other people around. Somewhere casual, to put her at ease. Does she shop on a regular schedule?"

"I don't know, because I don't. So, I have no idea if she has a pattern or not."

"Too bad Liz doesn't bring a dog to the dog park. That would be a good time to talk to her. Casual, not rushed."

"I've never heard her mention a dog or..." Clara chewed her lip. "Wait a minute. Millie knows the family. She said *something*... Yeah, I think so. I'm almost..."

I'd lost her, but that was fine. She was hard at work.

"Yes... I'm almost positive Millie from my book club said Liz's sister signed her older daughter up for summer story time at the library, one o'clock each week day. Little kids go in the morning, but this is for kids who've started school. And Liz takes her niece for her sister. Millie was saying she wished *her* sister would do something nice like that, give her a break from having the kids all summer."

"Perfect. You and Millie are now my favorite people, Clara. I feel an overwhelming craving for story time tomorrow."

"Should we go at the beginning or the end?"

I tapped a finger on the table. "Both. If she stays for story time, we're probably better off getting her at the end, but then her niece will be with her. So if there's a chance of getting her at the beginning, that's better."

"Got it. In the meantime, we have Eloise's contact information. Let's invite her for a drink. We can get background on Xanthe and ask if Eloise has an alibi. I don't mean ask her right out, but figure out where she was. And maybe she can tell us about other people in Xanthe's life—"

"Or Liz's," I inserted.

"—to get us started on alibis along with motives. Can't hurt to try, right?"

"Right."

"Eloise?" Teague asked.

"*Silent* observer," I reminded him.

He raised both hands. Apology? Surrender? Annoyance? Hard to tell.

Clara, who'd tapped at her phone during this exchange, held one hand aloft in a silent order to be quiet. Ringing on the other end and a voice answering were audible, so Clara must have set the phone on speaker.

"Eloise? This is Clara Woodrow. From the Beguiling Way Yoga Studio? My friend, Sheila, and I had class last night with Xanthe and we were talking with Tina today about this horrible, horrible tragedy, and she suggested we call you and let you know how we feel. About Xanthe and about what happened to her. It's unbelievable. We're so very sorry for the loss of your friend and we'd like to take you out for a coffee or a drink or ice cream or whatever might appeal to you. If you'd like to?"

"I could use a drink," came immediately. "We're organizing a re-membrance gathering for Xanthe at the studio Friday and her in-laws were… Well. Thank heavens I knew her son, Ethan, from when Xanthe and I were neighbors. If it hadn't been for him, they'd shove her in a hole and walk away. Sorry. I shouldn't—Sorry. I guess it's clear I could use a drink right about now."

"Absolutely understandable. How about the Tavern?" That was local shorthand for what, more formally, was known as the Historic Haines Tavern, which occupied one of the long blocks across from the unsquared square and for which the town was named.

"Oh. That would be nice." Nicer than Eloise apparently had ex-pected. Score one for Clara.

"Twenty minutes?"

"Yes, I'll be there."

CHAPTER ELEVEN

As soon as Clara and I—without Teague—entered the Historic Haines Tavern, a brick building more than a hundred and fifty years old, we saw the bar area was full. And every person in it was talking.

Not conducive to our aims at all.

"Let's go on the deck. It should be fine in the shade."

"You get a table," Clara said. "I'll wait here for Eloise and meet you out there."

I'd settled at a well-shaded table with plenty of no-eavesdropping buffer around it—apparently everyone was inside in the bar—when Clara came out with a woman in her early thirties, of average height and build, neither showing to advantage because of the weight of emotion sagging her shoulders.

A waiter arrived as we finished introductions. Clara ordered appetizers of egg rolls made with bourbon and bacon, a crab and artichoke dip, and fried green tomatoes for the table. When we were each going to order dry white wine, we opted for a bottle of Sauvignon blanc.

"A remembrance gathering is such a great idea," Clara said to Eloise, likely continuing a conversation started inside.

"That's what Tina and I thought—a positive way for everyone to gather for memories. Tina's cancelling classes until next week and opening the studio for the remembrance. Said she'd provide anything we want or need. But you'd think it was a major imposition the way Xanthe's ex-in-laws reacted."

"Fred Branter?"

Her mouth pursed with distaste. "Yeah, and his mother."

"What about Xanthe's family? They're not from here?"

"Her parents both died when she was in high school, a horrible car wreck. And she didn't have other family except distant cousins in Alabama or Arkansas, or someplace. After the accident, she lived with the family of a friend who was a year ahead of her in school. They moved away, though, and she finished her senior year with another family that wasn't a good fit, from what I heard. Really, her family is her son, Ethan. He's asked me to help with arrangements. Even though nothing can be done until... But we figured out a lot today—the remembrance Friday, a funeral when we can. Breaks my heart to see him so..."

She swallowed. Took a sip of the ice water in front of her, and swallowed hard again.

A sudden thought hit me. "Eloise, what kind of voice does Fred Branter have?"

"Voice?"

"Speaking voice. How would you describe it?"

She looked puzzled, but game. "Kind of slow. Not very educated. Why?"

"Just curious. Someone interrupted our class last night. A man. We didn't see him—" But could any of the students near the double doors have seen him? Because her answer brought home that a description of a voice probably wouldn't eliminate possibilities unless it included something like high and squeaky or *basso profundo*. "—but we could hear him."

"Fred Branter at the yoga studio? I seriously doubt it." She made it sound like lightning would strike if he tried.

"You've known the son—Ethan—a long time?" Clara asked, probably trying to lead her to a happier topic.

"Since he was little. Six, maybe seven years old? Cute as anything running around the apartment complex—I lived next door. That's how we got to be friends. Now he's so grown up. At least Xanthe got to see him graduate high school and knew he was headed for college. She was so determined he'd have opportunities."

The waiter delivered the food and wine, pouring each of us a glass.

"To Xanthe," Clara said solemnly. "She will be missed."

We raised our glasses.

Clara gently drew Eloise into reminiscences of meeting Xanthe, of playing with the young son, of watching her neighbor change.

"Xanthe had a hard start. She clawed her way up to make things better for herself, but mostly for Ethan. I admired that. Though sometimes her methods… But she became such a wonderful soul. She traveled so far in such a short time and to have her life cut off when she could have done so much good… It's difficult for us on this plane to accept. It's so hard not to mourn her."

Clara rested her hand on the other woman's wrist. "Of course you mourn her. She was your friend."

"I should accept she's in a better place. It's important to accept."

"You can also accept your own feelings."

I scored the exchange as a win for Clara. but didn't take time for cheering, because I wanted to follow up on something.

"You said she travelled so far in such a short time. What did you mean?"

"We all have a road to travel. Some are fortunate to start on their best road early. I was. I was already involved in teaching when we became neighbors. It was tough—working, training, teaching, and taking college courses. If it hadn't been for Xanthe's encouragement—" A fleeting smile appeared. "—or downright nagging, I probably wouldn't have gotten my degree. She kept saying it would give me choices she never had, which would have kept her from making bad choices. And she was right. Having a degree helped me work in places that wouldn't have considered me otherwise. With that, private lessons, and the Beguiling Way studio, it has worked out great.

"Xanthe didn't come to yoga until a couple years ago. But then she devoted herself. It was phenomenal and uplifting to watch her progress, and then to discover her ability to share it with others. For me—" She layered her hands over her heart. "—it was fulfilling, after all the help she gave me, to help guide her to yoga. I understand both of you were in the last class she taught?"

"Yes, yes, we were." We spoke over each.

"So you know. You experienced what a transcendent teacher she was. I started as her instructor in yoga, as she had been my instructor in life. But I am confident she would have become my teacher in yoga if she'd continued on, because we can always learn from each other."

This echoed Donna's account, though with a different slant.

I might be banned from some yoga studios for saying I preferred Donna's straight-forward approach. Thankfully, the Beguiling Way studio was open-minded about those of us seeking stretching, not enlightenment from classes.

Although, thinking about it now, there was at least one element Donna missed...

I took advantage of Eloise taking another drink of wine to ask, "What did Xanthe do before she became a yoga instructor?"

"A number of jobs. When Ethan was little, she did a lot of wait-ressing."

"More recently?" I pursued.

"She was absorbed in the training, the learning of yoga. The movements, but deeper—"

"But between those two, she still worked, you said. She had to support herself and her son."

"And she clearly had a great mentor in you, Eloise." Clara slanted me a warning look. She was taking over this questioning. "You helped her find her way. Which can be so difficult when someone has been enmeshed in a life with ... Well, like that. Did you find a particular aspect most challenging in helping Xanthe change her life?"

"Money."

If you've ever heard a Temperance advocate say the word *whiskey*, that's how Eloise said *money*.

"Money?" Clara echoed. "She needed money?"

"She put too much emphasis on it. She was involved with people who thought of nothing else. It was the center of their world. And she got caught up in it. Her job, her life, her image, the guy she was involved with, it all revolved around money."

"What happened?"

"She came to her senses. No, she came to her spirituality, to her soul. Eventually, she realized how unhappy she was, despite having the *things* she'd thought she wanted. She started by coming to classes where I was teaching. She said—she thought—she was coming for physical fitness, but she found what she *really* needed. A new way of approaching the world. A new way of being herself. She started with one class, then two, then three, then she was coming every day after work."

"What kind of work?"

Eloise said, "Something in banking. But she quit the job, the man, and the life."

"Which bank?"

Eloise waved an indifferent hand. "Maybe it wasn't a bank. Something to do with money, financing, or investing or something. I don't know. I never wanted to hear about it. Then she didn't want to talk about it. Ethan knows. He insisted on inviting people from there to the remembrance. Though why he'd want them…" Her face darkened in an unserene way. "What does it matter? What does any of it matter? It's all the past."

"The past might be the answer to getting justice for Xanthe."

"Justice," she scoffed. "The universe will restore balance faster and better than we ever could. Karma."

She might be right, looking at it from the distance of the universe.

From a closer perspective, say, North Bend County, Kentucky, it was justice for Xanthe and getting a murderer off the street. Both definitely mattered to me.

"Maybe it was being in the last class she ever had a chance to teach," I said musingly, "of knowing we left her alive and then shortly after that she was killed, but justice is important for us."

"You know she was killed shortly after the class?"

"Oh." Clara's light voice drew Eloise's attention. "We assumed. Because why else would she be in that spot."

"I guess that makes sense," Eloise said, without great interest.

"It's horrifying to think of living our ordinary lives while she was being murdered. Having a piece of strawberry pie with my friend." I nodded toward Clara.

She picked it up immediately. "Me, too, having strawberry pie with my friend at the café after our class." She smiled sadly. "What about you, Eloise?"

Her eyes teared up. "Having drinks with friends after the Reds' game."

The Cincinnati Reds played home baseball games across the Ohio River and a little east of North Bend County. My brothers-induced familiarity with baseball said a night game extended at least an hour after the end of our class, depending on how long a game it was. Add on after-game drinks and Eloise had herself an alibi.

"So I know how you feel about going on with your ordinary life, having fun…" she said. "I also feel bad about drifting apart this past year-plus, ever since she bought her house."

"You haven't seen a lot of her lately?"

"Not really. You think you will. But you don't realize how much of seeing each other is spur of the moment because you're in the apartment next door."

"When was the last time you talked to her?"

"Let me think… Tina had a staff lunch at the beginning of the month, so maybe… No, wait. It was the week before last. I was coming in to set up for the lunch-time slow flow class, filling in for Natalie," she said of another regular instructor. "Nearly scared me to death because I hadn't realized anybody was there. The door was locked, like normal, so I came in and checked sign-ups on the computer first thing. Then I heard a noise in the main studio and jumped out of my skin. I was about to call the cops and get the heck out of there, when I heard this familiar sound and realized it was someone transitioning from Warrior One to Warrior Two."

Someone could recognize it by *sound?* That seemed impossible. Unless the transitioner was swearing aloud and not just in her head.

She might have seen my skepticism, because she continued, "It's a sound a lot of people's feet make moving on the mat. I peeked in and sure enough, there she was. When she finished, we talked a bit. She'd been practicing since the end of her ten o'clock class. She said she often stayed after her classes to practice herself. You can't during a class, not if you're paying attention to the students the way you should."

"Now that you know that was your last conversation," Clara picked up, "you can treasure what you talked about, how you communicated."

Eloise smiled sadly. "Nothing deep or meaningful. Just classes and teaching. A bit about her son. Nothing major."

"But those things *are* deep and meaningful—your vocations and family." After our guest nodded acceptance of this consolation, Clara said, "But underneath those elements, did you get any sense something might have been bothering her?"

She frowned. "She kept a lot to herself. And she could be hard to read if she wanted to be, so I'm not sure I could tell. But she seemed fine to me."

Which might have been helpful if Xanthe had died of a disease, but didn't advance us any.

Clara asked, "Had Xanthe become close to any of the other instructors? Liz or...?"

Eloise speared a piece of fried green tomato with her fork. "Not that I'm aware of."

"What about you? Do you know Liz or any of the others well?"

With the fried green tomato in her mouth, she shook her head, looking puzzled by the question. After swallowing, she said, "We come and go on our own schedules, mostly see each other in passing."

Crestfallen, Clara drank the rest of her wine. But I admired her trying to find out more about Liz.

I said, "Eloise, you said something about Xanthe's methods in her earlier life before she found yoga. You didn't approve?"

"I didn't know anything really. She didn't say much to start and what she did say went in one ear and out the other. It was a lot of financial stuff, investments, I think. Mostly it was sensing her no longer wanting to be in the job, of wanting something more, of turning to the life she wanted with yoga…"

She led us into a discussion of yoga that echoed Xanthe's approach from class last night—or had Xanthe echoed her?—and let me nod and *umm-hmm* while Clara batted back the conversational ball now and then. I was thinking about what Eloise had said of Xanthe.

And wondering if Xanthe hadn't only moved toward yoga and a changed life, but had run away from something.

TEAGUE WAS STILL at the house when I returned.

To my raised eyebrow, he said, "I worked late to make up for the dog park break. Was getting ready to leave. Though that Chinese takeout smells good."

Hah. He'd stuck around hoping to get an update on our talk with Eloise.

Nope. No updates for the silent observer.

"Sorry. Ordered for one. No need for you to stay late. Since you're not being paid by the hour, it's not a big deal, as long as the closets get done."

"Speaking of the closets, despite Clara's priorities, you do need to clear your stuff out. I've got more prelim stuff to double check tomorrow, then buying supplies. But I might start breaking through the day after."

"You said we wouldn't have to move the shoe shelves you built."

"We don't have to move the shelves. *You* have to move the shoes. And everything else in both closets."

I'd known that. At some level.

"C'mon, Murph, let's go." He held the door open for his dog, and looked back. "Better get it done tonight."

CLOSETS COULD WAIT. At least a while.

As I ate sesame chicken, I started on my laptop by searching Xanthe Anstead's name, saying a prayer of gratitude to the search engine gods she wasn't Mary Smith. I found only yoga references.

Next up was Eloise. More results. Mostly yoga references. Some as a student, some as a teacher, some reviews by her for clothes, shops, restaurants. None vicious.

I did the same searches for Liz and Tina. This was getting boring with all these yoga sites. At least Tina added a few women-in-business mentions in association with the studio.

I tried the flower shop. Nothing beyond good reviews. I'd have to remember that next time I needed local flowers. More local flowers, since I had those daisies in a vase on the living room mantel.

More searches produced less and less information with each step.

Okay. If there was nothing to accomplish involving the murder, I should use this time to write. In fact, that was a great idea, because if the investigation heated up, I might not have time to write for days.

I switched to the word processing program and stared at the screen.

I wrote a word. Two words. Deleted one.

By writing several words, then cutting most of them, I crept my way through a paragraph. In twenty-three minutes.

At this rate, I'd have a book written in no more than two, maybe three decades.

If I didn't become a lunatic.

Cleaning out closets suddenly became appealing.

I headed upstairs. My dog gusted an annoyed sigh and followed me with the dragging feet of duty.

CHAPTER TWELVE

THE GUEST ROOM closet wasn't bad, making it the first time a closet being small was good news.

I emptied its contents—mostly overflow from my room—onto the bed, then covered the mounds with old sheets. More old sheets protected book shelves flanking the bed, a desk and chair moved to one side, and an easy chair laboriously shifted to the other.

My closet presented more of a challenge. Since I'd sleep in the bed each night, I couldn't use it.

I'd winnowed my wardrobe significantly when I moved out of the brownstone. Not to 1940's closet standards, but way, way down.

My first pass on my Author-of-*Abandon-All* wardrobe had been easy. Those pieces were *her*, not *me*.

Mix-and-matchable classics were the next pass. I kept the most basic. Anything possibly recognizable from TV, print media photos, book jackets, public appearances went. I still mourned one jacket and silk scarf, but they had to go.

The third pass eliminated Only-for-the-Literary-Scene items.

I kept a handful of not-so-recognizable, but way beyond what I'd likely wear in Haines Tavern garments in a special hanging bag. My Maybe Someday selections.

Most days since arriving in Haines Tavern, I picked from my Going to the Dog Park collection—t-shirts, leggings, shorts. Comfort and function. Nothing that gripped dog hair. Everything washable.

My phone rang.

I was leaning toward ignoring it, until the phone recognized the number and kindly announced the caller: Great Aunt Kit.

Her beautiful home in the Outer Banks of North Carolina didn't have closet issues. It had been built far more recently than this house, plus she'd remodeled extensively before moving in.

I'd moved in my house immediately so I could adopt a dog. Dog first, renovations second.

"What are you doing?" Kit's familiar voice asked, without benefit of other greeting.

I was looking into my closet. As small as it was, it was home to a lot of stuff. I'm a good packer. And after six months I was wresting all these items from their home.

Well, I wasn't actually wresting. I was surveying the to-be-wrested.

I shared all that with Kit.

She retaliated by sharing details of a visit from one of her writing friends. They'd had a grand time walking on the beach, drinking margaritas, and watching movies to tear apart their flaws.

Gracie had come nosing along as soon as I opened the closet. She'd snuffled at the hems of all the hanging clothes, stretching up to reach the bottoms of things on the main pole, then going to ground to inspect items hanging from a temporary second pole I'd added for more space.

Shooing her away from a dry-clean-only white blouse, I caught a piece of Aunt Kit's long reply.

"… no excuse for herbicide …"

"I didn't know you felt that way about gardening, Kit." Gracie cooperatively moved away from the blouse, instead stepping on the hem of my black velvet-ish robe, then half-sitting, catching the fabric with her butt, and bringing the whole thing down off its hanger in a blink.

"Gardening? What are you talking about, Sheila?"

"Dealing with weeds. Gracie, no."

My dog ignored me. Economizing on her circling under the cir-cumstances of my telling her no, she plopped down without her usual lengthy preparation on the soft, velvet-ish bed she'd made for herself. The black velvet-ish bed, which reached out and grabbed her fur in handfuls.

"You've lost your mind," my great aunt said. "I knew it would happen in that place."

"I have not," I protested stoutly. I was a bit relieved, though. Her accusing me of having lost my mind probably meant she wasn't losing hers, despite the inexplicable subject change. Giving up on the robe and setting the phone to speaker, I removed a span of hanging shirts and slacks, took them to the bed and began folding. "I responded to what you said. About there being no excuse for herbicide."

"Herbicide? *Herb*-icide? That is not what I said. Where is your mind, girl? I said verbicide. *Verb*. In reference to that so-called dialogue in that so-called movie."

"I never heard of verbicide. Killing words?"

She snorted. "I'm not surprised you haven't heard the word. Vocabulary neglect is rampant among you young people."

Choices, choices. Deny I've neglected my vocabulary or revel in being called young?

In the meantime, I folded shirts and slacks.

"I'll tell all the others in my generation we need to tune up our vocabularies." She sniffed. There was amusement in it. "Oh, Kit, can you point me toward good information on becoming a virtual assistant for authors?"

I stashed the folded clothes in already full drawers with more determination than finesse.

As I straightened, I recognized Kit's silence was as long as it was uncharacteristic.

"You there, Kit?"

"Yes. You don't think becoming an author's assistant, even virtually, might expose you to discovery as the author of *Abandon All*?"

I gripped an armful of longer hanging items and started downstairs toward the guest closet.

"Public face of *Abandon All*, not author." It took another second to comprehend what else she'd said. "Me? The information's not for me. My friend Clara wants to get a job and when I asked what her ideal job was, she said one where she could stay at home. I immediately thought of being a VA. Told her some and mentioned author assistants—she knows I have a relation who's an author—and she's excited."

"Ah." A single syllable wasn't characteristic, either. "Why are you huffing and puffing?" That tart question was.

"Just took a bunch of clothes downstairs. Going upstairs for more." I grabbed another armful and started back down.

"Why?"

"Teague—carpenter guy who built the shelves—is starting on the closets now that school's out."

"Ah."

I never thought I'd wish Kit said more, but the solitary syllables were getting on my nerves.

"He's measuring stuff to get supplies, but might start demo soon. You know there's a sidewall between the existing closets and he has to expand the openings for the doors on both sides."

I grunted as I compressed everything in the downstairs guest closet to get this second armful in.

"Uh-huh."

Two syllables were not much improvement.

"Back to Clara," I said cheerfully, if puffily, as I went upstairs. "There are so many classes and courses and stuff offered, she needs to sort through it. I thought you and your buddies might be able to help. Would you?"

"For your friend to become a virtual author's assistant? Of course. I'll put the word out and see what we get about what's good training and what's not."

"Thanks, Kit. I appreciate that and I know Clara will, too. No need to rush. She doesn't need the job right this minute. It's not urgent."

I brought the next armful's worth of hanging clothes into the bathroom. Most were carefully disposed on three hooks on the back of the door. As long as I didn't get too wild and crazy—like opening the door all the way—they should stay put.

A couple shirts landed on the door knob. A few summer dresses went on the shower rod, farthest from the faucet. It wouldn't be disastrous if they got a little wet, but I also angled the showerhead toward the other corner while I was thinking of it.

"Not urgent because you both are busy with something else," she said.

Not a question.

Stepping back from adjusting the showerhead, I realized I was holding my breath and forced it out slowly before—brilliantly—saying, "What?"

"Sheila, I thought you knew me better. I know there's been a murder there."

"Oh, God. You're monitoring the news around here?" I perched on the edge of my bed. "You're as bad as my mother."

"Better. Because I monitor the news where she and your father and the boys are, too. If it comes to that, I keep track of the news wherever family members are and of interesting murders everywhere. *Is* this one interesting?"

"We don't know yet. It just happened—at least it was just discovered around noon today."

"One report said the victim was a yoga instructor and she was found outside a yoga studio. Is that the studio you use?"

"Yes." Forestalling her next questions, I added, "She substituted last night for a class Clara and I take. I didn't know her beyond that."

"Why did the regular teacher miss?"

Ah, Kit. I knew where I got it from.

"We don't know yet, but we have a plan to bump into her tomorrow."

"Excellent. What else?"

I told her what had happened as I lined up shoeboxes along a wall of the bedroom.

The random items left in the closet would be added to the bed in the guest room, under the protective sheet.

I sat on the edge of the bed as I finished, abruptly aware Kit had been silent for longer than usual.

"Kit? What's wrong? Or do you have an inspiration about Xanthe's murder?"

"No inspiration. Wondering if you can do this change of life thing,

becoming Sheila Mackey and forgetting the rest, the way we thought—
I thought. I might have been too cavalier about it."

I'd wondered, too. It kept getting more complicated. For one tiny
example, I used my childhood name with family members beyond my
parents and siblings and never brought up Sheila Mackey or Haines
Tavern. These relatives knew, or thought they knew, that I—the
grownup version of the childhood name—had written *Abandon All*.

My parents and siblings knew the truth. But what about their
spouses?

I worried about all this, especially with a detective in the house, but
for some reason, when Kit voiced it, I said, "Hey, I can do this. There
are people who disappear for decades and decades and they've created
a new identity, a new life. A happy, full life. Like... like that protestor
involved with a deadly bombing who turned up as a soccer mom in
Wisconsin."

"Minnesota. Sarah Jane Olson. She'd been in the Symbionese Lib-
eration Army in the '70s."

"And then there was a math teacher in suburban, uh..."

"Boston. Eliza—Liz—Spoon. She'd attacked a man with a knife
twenty-two years earlier, sent him to the hospital. Do you notice a
trend?"

"Um. They lived in suburbs?"

"They got caught."

"But they were fugitives from the law. I'm not. I'm staying well out
of the limelight."

"If you're wanted to testify at the trial in Florida you'll be back in
the limelight, and as the literary you, since you weren't known as Sheila
Mackey then. Your testimony could be vital to put away a murderer."

She was referring to my first brush with murder, during a cruise
before I dropped the *Abandon All* persona and moved to Haines
Tavern. Testifying as my *Abandon All* persona could lead to all sorts of
issues, including renewing interest in the books and thus in me—or
her, as I was beginning to think of the person I'd been then.

"I wouldn't just *not* testify. But maybe there will be a plea deal," I
ended weakly.

She snorted. "Don't count on it. You better make up your mind how you're going to handle that."

"I could tell people here I was going on a vacation. Send a few postcards. But it'll be years. It takes forever for cases to come to trial."

She skipped right over my optimistic timeline. "You better hope the trial isn't picked up by CourtTV, not to mention the regular news."

My stomach re-sank.

"Nobody from the prosecutor's office has contacted my folks to reach me yet, so it's not like it's imminent. Oh," I switched topics brightly, "but what is imminent is my poor dog exploding. Gotta run to take Gracie out. Bye, Kit."

But after disconnecting the call, I continued to sit on the bed, while Gracie continued to snooze on her black velvet-ish robe bed for several minutes before I roused her for last call.

In bed, I opened my laptop.

Clara had sent a list of possible classes—not strictly about being a VA, but also about designing ads and marketing and other skills. I forwarded it to Kit.

Then I searched news sites for updates on the murder of Xanthe Anstead.

DAY THREE

WEDNESDAY

CHAPTER THIRTEEN

CLARA HAD HER dental appointment first thing the next morning and I'd agreed to take LuLu to the dog park along with Gracie, as Clara had done for me in reverse several times.

Getting up early is not my idea of fun. I'd prepared the best I could, including showering the night before and putting out the clothes I'd wear.

That seemed a sensible precaution, not only because it would be morning when I was getting dressed, but because I'd been distracted by Kit's call and didn't know precisely what clothes were where. Not a puzzle I wanted to solve when half asleep.

Gracie paid no attention when I got out of bed, apparently expecting me to return. I will say this for her—she'd adapted readily to being a night dog.

When I didn't return to bed, despite the temptation, but continued about the process of washing and clothing myself sufficiently to make an appearance at the dog park—not exactly a high standard—her head came up and she watched me with increasing intensity.

Then a vehicle came into the driveway. She jumped up at full alert.

I swear she recognized the vehicle as Clara's—or LuLu's, which was probably how she thought of it.

I had to dissuade Gracie from joining LuLu in the back of Clara's SUV. But once we got Gracie in the back of my sedan. LuLu hopped in immediately.

"That's a lot of dog for that backseat," Clara said.

"Don't start on me like Berrie does about how I need a different vehicle for my dog," I grumbled.

Clara grinned, said, "Good morning to you, too," and departed for her appointment.

By the time we got to the dog park, I was thinking they might have a point about this car.

I didn't see much except fur in the rearview mirror and a few of their, uh, *delicate* efforts to play in the confined space had the car rocking and rolling like... Well, like what made the worthy citizen of North Bend County who pulled up next to me at a stop light burst out laughing so hard he forgot to move when the light turned green.

Glad someone was enjoying the morning.

For me, let's say nearly a hundred-and-forty combined pounds of excited dogs was not easy to corral out of the car then into the big-dog enclosure.

My morning fog started to lift as I recognized coming at this hour meant I didn't have to pass through the combined gantlet of Berrie's criticism and Marcus' noise. One bright spot.

Plus, it was impossible to not appreciate the explosion of joy when I unhooked the two dogs from their leashes and gave the release command.

They leapt and cavorted and ran straight through a sedate group of older dogs, stirring them into a trailing pack of excitement.

That left me free to meander oh-so-casually to where Donna was sitting on a roofed picnic table, talking with a group of people.

She introduced me around to the mid-morning crew, then resumed discussion with a gray-haired man about something to do with the airport.

After the gray-haired man collected a mix that might include shepherd and Australian sheep dog, with its tongue happily lolling out the side of his mouth—the dog, not the man—and left, Donna stood, stretched, called to Hattie, her graying golden retriever, and started across the open area toward the other side of the enclosure.

Ten steps away, she turned back and called, "Are you coming, Sheila?"

I hopped off the table and followed.

"You do want to talk to me, don't you?" she asked when I was close enough for her not to be overheard by others. "You don't think I'd make old Hattie take an extra walk for nothing, do you?"

"Don't think that's a worry." I tipped my head toward where Hattie had found the narrow shade of a baby tree to lie in.

Donna smiled at her dog, then frowned. "They keep planting a tree there and the dogs keep killing it. I don't know if it's the pee or chewing on it or what. I keep telling the parks people to plant it outside the fence so a tree will survive and then it can shade over the fence. They listen politely and make the same mistake."

"Why don't you run for office, Donna?"

"Are you kidding? I'd have to politely listen to all the idiot residents with their crack-brained ideas."

Did she realize that was probably what the officials she kept telling about the trees thought?

Oh, yes, she did. The glint in her eyes said so.

It also said she didn't care. She'd keep telling them until they came to their senses.

"So, what do you want, Sheila? Hattie won't last a lot longer. She and I are delicate flowers who need our air conditioning."

"Want? I didn't say…"

I let it die at her cackling chuckle.

"You and Clara are looking into that murder at the yoga studio." She didn't even make it a question.

"Is it all over town?"

"Not all over. But after how you two reacted to what happened here at the dog park and how you figured it out far before the sheriff's department did—even though you almost got yourselves killed—"

"It wasn't that bad."

"—it figured you'd start nosing around with somebody killed at your yoga studio. Not to mention your oh-so-casual questions yesterday. So, what do you want to know?"

Argue? Deny? Or get what I wanted.

"What else do you know about Xanthe Anstead, especially before she became involved with yoga?" Mom always said I was practical.

Also single-minded.

"I told you pretty much everything I know about her yesterday."

Had I gotten up early for nothing?

"But—"

That word usually meant things were taking a turn. Often for the worse. But—there it was again—this time for the better. *Had* to be for the better.

"—I have heard about that place she worked. Not the yoga studio. I mean, where she worked before. So called financial firm. Smith-Flarenge. Now *that* I have heard about. Not much good, either."

That sounded familiar, but specifics didn't surface in my morning brain.

"They talked a widow I knew from the golf course into moving all her investments to them. All of a sudden, she's having trouble making ends meet when she never had before. When her daughter looked into it, turns out Smith-Flarenge piled fees upon fees on her account. Like all those taxes and fees you get on your cell phone bill, only inflated by numerous zeroes. Absolutely shameless. Kept saying the woman chose those fancy-dancy options. No way she did. First, she's cheap. Second, she had no clue about such things. One of those idiotic women who prides themselves on knowing nothing about finances.

"And when the daughter tried to get the money out and put it back with the low-expense company, that's when the fun really started. Smith-Flarenge stalled and delayed and gave her the wrong forms to fill out, then couldn't find the right ones. Then said they'd submitted the forms, but they were lost, and she'd have to start over. All this taking months and months. They even tried to say they wouldn't deal with her because she was *unreasonable*. Had to get a lawyer involved to set them straight. And it still took forever.

"A couple from my church had been with them for a while and always said how wonderful their broker was. They were bragging about it at a family gathering, apparently—how they'd had no trouble in all these years and how Vince took care of everything for them. They trusted him completely and it was so nice he called with ideas he knew were just perfect for them. Only their niece had married some expert in mistakes individuals make investing and he asked if he could look at their statements. With it being a new marriage and all, they didn't want to say no. Well, they should've been saying no to Vince. Turns out their money hadn't grown, but Vince had made a pretty penny off them by buying and selling all the time—churn, they call it—and charging fees for every transaction.

"And then one of my second cousins inherited an account from an in-law and thought she'd leave it there and buy blue-chip stocks with it. That ended as soon as she found out their commissions and other fees—hidden, of course. Nothing's upfront or out in the open. She had the same nightmare trying to close the account and get the money out as everyone else."

Not a bank, but it fit Eloise's comments about Xanthe's previous job and bad methods.

"Xanthe did that kind of thing?"

"Mmm. I can't swear to it, but if I had to guess, I'd say she was an assistant or receptionist or something similar. That's about all I know," Donna concluded.

"Her ex?"

She shook her head, denying any further knowledge.

"Anybody else at the yoga studio, Eloise, Tina, Liz? Know anything about them?"

"Ah. That's why you're asking me without Clara. She'd doubt apparently nice people like them could do something wrong."

"Apparently?"

She cracked out a laugh. "Apparently *and* actually, as far as I know. Tina's working hard at the studio and word is she's making a go of it. As for Liz, I know her aunt's neighbor, who has nothing but good to say about any of them." She lifted one shoulder. "For whatever it's worth."

"Donna, I do believe you're a cynic."

That shoulder lifted again. "Realist. Oh. And I don't know anything about Eloise."

"Well, if you think of something else…"

"Sure." She patted my back, called her dog, and said, "All my morning folks are gone. Past time for me to leave, too."

CHAPTER FOURTEEN

I DIDN'T KNOW how I was going to explain to Clara that her dog had suddenly and inexplicably gone deaf.

Along with my dog.

I called to LuLu and Gracie, who were in the middle of the enclosure, fully intending to take them home.

They trotted away in the opposite direction, bumping each other, tails pluming high.

I should have gone after them. The most basic rule of dog training is to follow through when you give a command. I should have gone after them, put their leashes on, called them again and made them come, if necessary by reeling in the leashes.

Ninety-nine times I did.

The hundredth time always came in the morning.

Besides, I figured if they could pretend not to hear me, I could pretend not to see them.

I sat on the far covered table.

A vehicle I recognized pulled in and parked.

As Teague got out, I saw him look from the parking lot to the enclosures, obviously spotting Gracie, LuLu, and me in sole possession of the big-dog area.

Gracie and LuLu miraculously recovered their hearing, tearing toward the gate and Murphy.

Neither Gracie nor LuLu spared the human a glance, which seemed ungrateful since he'd transported Murphy and was known for bestowing liberal butt- and ear-rubbings on them.

Joining me on the table, he said, "Good morning."

I shot him a sharp look for that oxymoron, a look that snagged on the more-than-stubble.

This was past the point of excusing as accidental. This was deliberate.

"What are you doing?"

He looked around with a question in his eyes. "Watching the dogs."

"No. *This.*" I backhand-waved toward his face, slopping water out of the bottle I held. "The beard."

"Oh, that." Complacence spread out from him like the occasional puffs of sawdust or plaster dust that then rose from his shoulders when he jogged down the stairs. "Thought I'd grow one this summer."

"Why?"

"Figured it would be a fait accompli by the start of school and I wouldn't get grief from the kids when I subbed. But—" He rubbed his jaw. "Didn't know it would grow this fast. Or I would have gone ahead and started during the school year."

"No. Why a *beard.*"

"It's something I couldn't do in the department."

It seemed churlish to say it wasn't something he should do now, either.

I don't mind all beards. Especially if they're small, neatly trimmed, or on Santa Claus.

He wasn't Santa, he didn't seem to be trimming this beard, and with this rate of growth it was rapidly heading toward not-small status.

He eyed me. Apparently satisfied the previous topic had been dealt with, he said, "You're here early today."

"Thought we'd get an early start. Supposed to be hot later."

"Heard that, too. Still surprised to see you here this early." He gestured toward an empty patch of table. "And without Clara."

I mumbled something about the dentist. "What about you?"

"Thought I'd get some of Murph's energy out before we arrived at your house."

"Thanks."

We sat in silence then, as I continued my waking-up process, which had been delayed by needing to be alert to converse with Donna.

The dogs ran and ran and ran, with occasional breaks to chew on each other to their apparent mutual delight.

We talked about the dogs.

Teague asked if he could come by after the dog park to take another set of measurements he probably wouldn't need but wanted to have when he went to buy supplies. I said sure.

We talked about the dogs.

I asked if he'd substitute teach over the summer. He said he couldn't say for sure, but probably not.

We talked about the dogs.

I asked if he might be interested in giving me a bid for reinforcing a retaining wall that was supposed to hold up the back of my yard from crumbling in the creek. He said he'd look at it and let me know if he thought it was work he could do.

We talked about the dogs.

After this pleasant interlude, we loaded the dogs into our respective vehicles and caravanned to my house, where the dogs required an extended sniff around the back yard to check if anything had changed there.

In the house, they had long, cool drinks of water, requiring kitchen-floor-swabbing duty by me.

Teague went upstairs.

I opened the laptop.

My manuscript popped up on the screen.

I quickly looked around.

No one there to see it. I breathed out.

It was weird, having talked for years about writing a book I hadn't written that now I wasn't talking about a book I was writing.

But in another way, it made sense, because I wasn't writing anything like *Abandon All*.

This romance I was writing was set in the Blue Ridge Mountains.

Kit and I had spent a month there most summers while in New York and I was having a great time revisiting the area and the people in my imagination. The heroine—in romances, the lead characters are heroine and hero, not the neutral "protagonist"—was from the city. A fish out of water in this rural area. And falling for the homegrown shopkeeper with issues from his past.

That was all good.

The not-good was not being too sure about structure. I'd heard enough about the three-act structure to have a theoretical grasp of it—beginning, middle, and end, at its simplest—but was discovering pieces weren't cooperating by staying where they were supposed to.

It reminded me of baking an angel food cake as a pre-teen. I'd watched Mom a thousand times. I knew how to separate eggs. I'd even successfully beaten egg whites. But doing it in cake proportions and folding in other ingredients… I have flashbacks of trying to get it out of the cake pan. And then of how it looked on the plate, sloping from a modest height on one side down to a nearly-flat arc on the other.

Mom tried her best to mask it with strawberries and whipped cream. She and Dad praised it and ate with gusto. My brothers made faces and said I should stick with brownie mixes.

It didn't take much insight to figure that's what I was afraid of with writing—grimaces and complaints I shouldn't have tried.

I closed the manuscript file and opened email.

CHAPTER FIFTEEN

CLARA KNOCKED, THEN stepped in.

"How're your teeth?"

"All good. Just a checkup. Took so long because there was an emergency before me," she said. "What I want to know is has anything happened? Any developments? Does Teague know anything? What have you learned?"

Teague frowned at me. "You two haven't let it go, have you? I should have known your not talking about it was a bad sign."

"You thought we'd quit? We're just getting started." Then, Clara said to me, "What did you find out?"

"One fact. Eloise got it only partly right. Xanthe never worked for a bank. Donna said Xanthe worked at Smith-Flarenge."

"Huh. The money job she left behind ended up being on the other side of the block from the yoga studio."

"*That's* why it was so familiar. It's one of the buildings facing the back of the post office?"

"Yup. I was thinking at the dentist, how about Eloise? Xanthe could be a rival for her classes *and* we haven't checked her alibi."

I pointed my pen at her. "Excellent point. Though she is the one who told us about Xanthe staying late. Before that, her baseball game alibi covered her, so don't see how widening the window helps her."

"Here's a thought." Teague headed for the freezer. "She told you about Xanthe staying after class sometimes because it was the truth and Eloise has nothing to hide. Happens sometimes, even in a murder investigation. Got to leave your mind open to that possibility, too."

In silence, we watched him add ice cubes to his water bottle.

Then Clara looked at me. "We need to check her alibi."

"Absolutely."

"Should we do that first, or should we do something else next, Sheila?"

Teague said, "How about letting law enforcement do their job?"

"They needed our help last time," Clara said. "Besides—Oh, look how cute they are."

That was directed at the dogs.

With the edge taken off their energy temporarily, all three were on Gracie's kitchen bed, curled and twisted into each other in a complicated pattern reminding me of what my grandmother called a Celtic knot.

"Aren't they adorable? Thank you so much for taking LuLu—*Oh*! And talking of thanks. I can't believe I didn't say this right off. Sheila, you are a *genius*."

Clara jumped up and hugged me. Not an easy task in the small room, with Teague leaning against the stove and the already rejuvenated dogs jumping up, trying to get in on the action.

"How, exactly, did I demonstrate my genius?"

"What you said about being a virtual assistant for an author. I was already excited about what I found online last night and then the information you emailed me from your contacts. I read it twice at the dentist and I'll dig even deeper first chance I have."

"I forwarded what other people told me." I'd emailed Clara a wrap-up of what Kit and her fellow nocturnal buddies had written. There was a consensus leader, two more were solid courses, then a number designated "stay away."

"Authors?" big-eared Teague asked.

"Yes, isn't it marvelous? I'm going to try to be a VA—a virtual assistant and I hope for authors—all thanks to Sheila and her aunt, who's an author, and all her friends."

Talk about unintended consequences. Or maybe this fell under no good deed going unpunished.

The less information ex-detective Teague O'Donnell had about my life, past and present, the less his puzzle-solving brain had to work with. Yet, here, Clara's innocent exuberance and my lack of fore-thought had plopped a giant piece in his lap.

"Your aunt's an author? What's her name? What does she write?"

"Great aunt. She writes under a lot of names. Mostly romance." That should dim his interest.

"Did she write the romance novels on your bookshelves?"

Darn his observational skills. "Some."

"I'll have to try them."

"No need. It's like she told the family—you don't have to read them, just buy several copies of each."

He grinned. "I'd like to read them."

I had the feeling the grin was less at Kit's witticism and more at my discomfort. He was like some predator of secrets who sensed his weakened prey.

"Enough of this. I shouldn't have diverted us." Clara looked at Teague. "Ready to talk about the case? Or are you going to spend the day in Sheila's bedroom again."

"*Closets*," I corrected.

Teague's eyes glinted. "I can come out of Sheila's closets for a while. What do you want to talk about, Clara?"

"About Xanthe's murder, of course. I meant what I said about the sheriff's department needing our help last time. Everybody would still be wondering about the body at the dog park if it weren't for us—especially Sheila—instead of feeling perfectly comfortable taking our dogs there to have a wonderful time like always because it's all been explained and nobody's wondering if there's a murderer running around loose."

He didn't answer directly, probably because her argument had the insurmountable advantage of being true. "There are professionals and there are amateurs. Don't think every time is going to work out because your one and only effort did. What, Sheila?"

I must have made a noise. "Nothing. Really. Go ahead with your debate."

Clara said, "No debate. He's giving the automatic response that law enforcement doesn't want any help—"

"Interference."

"—from citizens who often have important information and insights—"

"Wild goose chases."

"—that could benefit law enforcement if they listened."

"Wouldn't hold up in court."

The problem with this interesting back and forth was Teague accomplished it while staring at me.

Was he building up to asking me if the death on Torrid Avenue earlier this year hadn't been my first involvement with a murder investigation?

I looked around. Mostly to avoid Teague's eyes. But when my gaze landed on the clock, I recognized a lifeline.

"It's time for the noon TV news. Let's see what they say. If the sheriff's department has the case wrapped up or a suspect in custody…"

"Do you promise to leave it alone then?"

"No," Clara said staunchly.

I felt the same way. But I worried about my secrets.

I avoided answering by leading the way into the living room to turn on the TV.

The dogs followed us, threw themselves on the living room floor with jarring thuds that would have shattered my bones—and possibly the floor—if I'd tried it. With contented sighs they rewound their Celtic knot.

"What I want to know—"

I interrupted Teague by turning on the TV.

They were teasing upcoming stories, including "The body of a beloved young yoga instructor found behind the Beguiling Way studio in Haines Tavern in North Bend County."

Clara and I exchanged a look over "beloved."

Had she been?

Not that anyone would kill over a yoga instructor making them sweat or feel like they were two hundred years old and had been out of shape for every one of them. At least I hoped no one would, or the yoga instructor population could be in big trouble.

"Behind the studio?" Teague asked. "Aren't those buildings back to back?"

"A couple are, but most are one building. Either way, she wasn't found *behind* the studio. She was found in her car in a tiny alleyway *beside* the studio. The flower shop—"

Clara waved me to silence as the anchor said, "And in Northern Kentucky, the body of a yoga instructor found dead in her car yesterday has been identified by our news team as Xanthe Anstead."

"As if they found the ID from some great investigation," Teague grumbled.

"Shh," he got in stereo.

"North Bend County Sheriff's Department investigators believe she was killed after conducting a class at the studio Monday night. Our reporter, Bianca Abernathy, spoke with sheriff's department investigators. Bianca?"

A younger woman came on the screen, nodding solemnly from in front of the sheriff's department. We all knew the building well, since it was not far from the dog park on Torrid Avenue.

"That's right, Sunny. Xanthe Anstead taught her last yoga class here Monday night, locked up the studio after her students left, and headed for her car. But she never made it home. Her body was found in her car and North Bend County authorities believe they know what happened to her."

It seemed like we all snapped to attention without moving.

They knew what happened?

The visual switched to a standard news conference shot—so much for the intimation the sheriff's department gave this station exclusive access—with a deputy standing in front of a handful of microphones. He wasn't any of the deputies I'd encountered.

The type at the bottom of the screen identified him as North Bend County Sheriff's Department spokesman Clarence Batchelder.

"I can verify that the victim, Xanthe Anstead, did not die of natural causes. Investigators' efforts have led them to the conclusion that this is another instance of violence being visited on the residents of North Bend County by criminal perpetrators passing through our county on Interstate 71/75. As you're all aware, there have been a rash of burglaries of businesses near the Interstate truck stop. We have increased patrols of the area and we are in the process of interviewing everyone who comes through the facility."

"Long gone," Teague muttered.

The deputy continued, "We'll be pursuing every possible lead to bring this murderer to justice."

"Not even he believes it." Clara's disgust with the spokesperson overrode the reporter's standard wrap-up. She took the remote from me and muted the volume. "They're saying it's a stranger to make people feel better. A stranger who passed through and is long gone. They don't even have to look for him."

"That's not—"

I talked over Teague. "A stranger on stranger murder? *That's* their theory? *That's* what they're going to *follow up*? When women, in particular, are far more likely to be killed by a significant other, a spurned lover, a—"

"You learned that from Sam?" Teague asked.

My brain scrambled for purchase on a suddenly icy slope. *Sam?*

"Or from his father, the detective?"

Oh. *That* Sam. The ex-boyfriend I'd made up with a convenient police detective father to explain my knowledge of procedure and investigative practices actually learned by joining Kit for research trips, workshops, conferences, and interviews.

"As a matter of fact I did, but so could a ten-year-old who watched a few investigative TV shows. With the sheriff's department's theory it was a random criminal off the interstate, why would they bother to look any farther? They're too busy telling everyone it's safe to go about our business because the murderer has moved on. Which will make the business community happy."

Teague pulled back, looking at me from under his eyelashes. "Anybody would think you were in law enforcement. How'd you get so cynical?"

"Skeptical. Practical. Common sense. Observation." Mentally, I added, *Education courtesy of Kit.*

Clara stepped in. "As Sheila said, are they even looking at other possibilities? Look at what we found out already. Xanthe had tense relations with her ex and his parents. She had something in her past she didn't feel good about. That could be a lead. Or look at what Sheila said about Liz possibly being the target. Is the sheriff's department considering that and who could have something against her?"

"You're starting with motive" he objected. "You don't even need motive to prosecute a case."

"We're not prosecuting. We're trying to solve a murder. And motive gives us someplace to start," I said.

Clara, with absolute sincerity, asked, "How would you go about it, Teague? Harris said you're a great detective."

He shifted to somewhere between skeptical and suspicious. "He said that when you called to check if I was who I said I was?"

After Teague told us months ago that he'd worked for a department outside of Chicago, Clara called numerous police departments, asking for Teague O'Donnell. When one said he didn't work there anymore, but would Clara like to talk to his former partner, she jumped on the chance. She'd confirmed Teague's account—as far as it went.

His former partner, Harris, had called Teague to find out why Clara was checking on him.

I had the impression Teague had been out of touch until then, but they were definitely in touch now, because I'd heard snippets of Teague's phone conversations with his former partner, both at the dog park and while Teague had been finishing the shelving projects at my house.

"Not back then," Clara said.

"When?" Teague's dark brows met in a fierce frown. I could see how he could intimidate a criminal. Not Clara, however.

"Oh, I don't remember exactly. One of our calls."

"*One* of your calls—?"

"Forget it, Teague," I advised. "She's not going to crumble at your tough guy look. She's clearly been chatting regularly with Harris, pumping him for information on you and no doubt sharing every detail of your life here."

"I wouldn't say we chat, *regularly*," Clara objected, with a hint of a twinkle.

He swung back to her. "But you *have* been pumping him about me and sharing it around?"

"Not sharing it around." She'd tacitly admitted the pumping. "We both care about you. Though Sheila doesn't like your beard."

"Don't drag me into—"

"Oh?" His frown lifted.

"Not only *your* beard," Clara assured him. "Any beards. Because of delicate skin."

"That's why some guys grow beards. To avoid shaving their sensitive skin." He was enjoying this. Did he realize she'd changed the focus on purpose?

"Not your skin. Hers. All that prickling. And I don't care what men say, it does prickle."

"Oh, look, the news is coming back on." I grabbed the remote from Clara and unmuted it.

"Recapping our top stories," said the TV anchor.

We all turned toward the screen.

"Law enforcement officials say a yoga instructor found murdered in an alleyway in Haines Tavern, Kentucky, is believed to have been the victim of a killer passing through on the Interstate."

Did none of these people know the Interstate didn't run through Haines Tavern? That their supposed killer would have had to wander for miles to reach Haines Tavern?

"Authorities request anyone who had contact with the victim the evening of her death or other information contact them at the North Bend County Sheriff's Department."

Clara and I looked at each other.

Teague groaned.

"Call the sheriff's department, Sheila. Tell them we have information, find out when they want to talk to us, then we'll go to the library to try to catch Liz," Clara said.

I tapped in the non-emergency number for the sheriff's department from the screen and explained my purpose to the voice that answered.

"Are you one of the students?"

"I am. I'm also calling on behalf of another student, Clara Woodrow. We'd like to come in together. Others have called already?"

"Yes. You're—"

"How many?"

"—all to come between three and five today. They'll take you in the order you arrive."

Unspoken—barely unspoken—was the sentiment *And get it over with, because we have to do this even though it's a waste of time.*

There'd been fifteen people in class. If, despite the short notice, all of us showed up, they'd allowed less than eight minutes each. Not in-depth interviewing.

"The wait time wasn't why I asked—"

She hung up.

Before I could express my opinion of this, Teague said, "If you're going to talk to people about this situation—"

"Murder," Clara said.

"—don't let preconceptions influence how you approach them."

I told her, "Now he's going to tell us murder isn't a crime because statutes say homicide."

He pretended he hadn't heard either of us. "You want to get at what they know, not have them parrot back what you think."

"What about the mirroring technique?"

"Another lesson from Sam and his father?" He didn't wait for my answer, which would have been delayed by trying to remember what I'd said about the mythical Sam and his equally mythical father. "That's for interrogation. And interrogation is for when you're confident you have the person. Then you *do* want them to say a specific thing—what they did and how. Interviewing, you want as much as you can get. I've seen way too many LEOs miss chances for great information by thinking they have to direct the interview, they have to drill the person with questions. Don't do that. Let them talk."

"Thank you. That's good advice." I meant it.

Clara grinned. "We'll use it whenever we ask people about their motives."

After a pause, Teague grinned back at her, looked at me, then back to her. "I'm going upstairs to wrestle with closets. You two are going to do what you're going to do. But be careful. Remember, while you're thinking this is some puzzle you're solving, where there's a murder means there's a murderer."

With the sound of his footsteps on the stairs, Clara leaned close. "So a homicide means a homicider?"

I chuffed out a laugh. Then sobered. "It does. And one the sheriff's department thinks is long gone."

CHAPTER SIXTEEN

"**JACKPOT**," **CLARA MURMURED** as we followed the walkway to the entrance steps to the Old Main Branch Library.

Liz Whyte had opened the door and started down the steps toward us.

"Liz," I called with assumed surprise and a genuine smile. I *was* pleased to see her.

"Hi, Sheila. Hi, Clara." She pushed at her eyes, as if the bright sunlight hurt them. "Are you coming for story time?" she teased, at the same time, turning away and digging in her bag. "You'll have to hurry or you'll miss the start. I just dropped off my niece."

"No, we were at the post office for Clara to pick up pre-stamped envelopes—" My co-star held aloft her prop. "—and I'm returning an overdue book." My turn to display a prop.

"You should try story time. It's fun." She pulled sunglasses out of her bag and put them on before facing us again. *Too late, Liz. Already saw the tears.* "I usually stay, but have a list of must-do errands a mile long."

I spoke quickly so Liz didn't have an opening to end this conversation before it started.

"Talking of your niece…. Kids can be such germ conduits. Was she why you missed class the night before last? We missed you."

"Thanks. Nice to be missed. I guess, indirectly, she's responsible. I picked up a bug from her. It started the night before. I hoped I'd be past it, but by Monday morning I knew there was no way. I texted Tina to see if she could find a substitute. I was sick all day."

Except Berrie said she'd seen Liz out with "a guy."

"Tina must have appreciated your giving her as much warning as you could."

She smiled mechanically. "That's what she texted back when I told her I was missing class." She angled a look, first at Clara, then at me. "How did you like class?"

"It was … different."

Liz nodded briefly at Clara's diplomatic evasion. "I've heard from a few others it was not what they expected."

"Not really what we've come to expect from a yin class," Clara agreed. "I was sort of surprised those two new students, a blonde woman and a brunette, who started with Xanthe's class, came back the next day for yours."

"They seem to intend to become regulars." From the way she looked at us, I was certain she'd heard about the conflict over the corner spots.

But that was not what I wanted to talk about. We'd settle their hash, class by class.

"Starting with the class Xanthe Anstead taught, did they know her?"

Liz shrugged. "No idea. They didn't say they did when they checked in for class yesterday. Of course that was before… before anyone knew what happened."

I assumed a frown. "Maybe I misunderstood. Is it *you* who knew Xanthe well?"

"Not really. I met her a couple times in passing when Tina got the instructors together. But her regular classes are in the morning so we don't overlap. That's the only way I've gotten to know other instructors."

"But you must know who her close friends among the instructors are? I can't imagine how hard her senseless death is for them now," I added to soften the edges of the question.

"Yes, it must be. I think… No, I don't know for sure."

Maybe she really didn't know, if she didn't even mention Eloise. Or was there another reason for her reticence?

How weird would it be to press her now? Pretty weird. But she might respond if I offered a wild guess… And it might prompt another name, so no sense using the one we already knew. "Tina?"

"I truly don't know. Sorry."

"It's such a horrible thing to happen. Right there in a place we all know," Clara started.

Liz cut her off. "It is. Nice to see you both. I need to get going so I can be back by the end of story time for my niece."

"Us, too. Get going, I mean. If I don't get this book checked in, my fines are going to rival the national debt."

We ended on a chuckle, slightly forced all-around, and went our separate ways.

Not a satisfying encounter from an investigative point of view.

And the other problem was I'd left my other overdue books at home in case we'd need them for subsequent tries. They remained on my bedside table, accruing fines.

Clara started to ask a question as we entered the library and was shushed.

Not by a librarian, since talking—or singing or dancing or playing musical instruments—no longer seems to earn that time-honored admonition in libraries, but by me.

"Later," I warned.

With us back outside, I suggested a carryout lunch on the town square. As predicted, the day was heating up in a preview of summer, but in the shade of the square's old trees it should be pleasant. "We can talk without being overheard."

Three elderly men occupied a bench facing the courthouse. We carried our takeout boxes from the café to a bench well away from theirs and with a view of anyone approaching us.

"Do you still think Liz might have been the target?" Clara asked.

"Nothing's ruled that out as a possibility."

I saw her struggle to acknowledge another possibility in her pained expression. "She couldn't have known she'd get sick."

It was a half-step. I nudged her further. "If she *was* sick. Remember what Berrie said about seeing Liz with a guy Monday."

"You're thinking… What *are* you thinking?"

I shifted on the seat. "I like Liz and I'm not saying this is likely. But if we're going to look into what happened, we have to *really* look into it, including facing possibilities we'd rather not. She was being evasive just now."

"Well, some people don't like talking about these things."

"Most would then say *I don't like talking about this.* And there was more."

I let it hang there. For Clara to truly consider this, she needed to arrive at it by her own path.

She took a bite of her sandwich. I did the same. Chewing was a good reason not to talk.

But at last, Clara said, "There was more, like why Liz was teary coming out of the library?"

I nodded. "Something's definitely bothering her."

She gusted out a breath and dropped the crusts of her sandwich into the box. "Liz is a suspect."

Carefully, I put down the remains of my sandwich. "She has to be. Her calling in sick led to Xanthe being in that spot at that time, whether that was an unfortunate chain of events or deliberate."

"She couldn't know for sure Tina would ask Xanthe to sub."

"Maybe not. But she probably knew before class who was taking her place. Remember Xanthe talking about what we usually did in class? The most likely way for her to know that was from Liz. It would have been natural for Xanthe to call Liz to find out about the class, what Liz had been doing lately."

"If she did, Xanthe ignored everything Liz said and made the class totally different."

True, but not the point.

"She couldn't have talked about how different her class was if she didn't know what we usually did. Besides, it makes sense for a sub to text or call Liz and find out. So, no matter what, Liz could count on knowing ahead of time who the sub would be. Or someone could have called Liz or texted her to check on her and mentioned who was subbing. Lots of possibilities. You heard what Liz said about Tina texting her and Tina could have said then that Xanthe was going to fill in."

"But Liz told us that—volunteered it, so—"

"Best way to disarm suspicion. Don't look so horrified, Clara. We're raising questions, not making accusations. And Liz also has to be considered as the intended victim."

"Not much better," she said bitterly. "But *why*? Why would Liz pretend to be sick or want Xanthe there or … or anything else?"

I shook my head. "No idea. We have to find out about her, like we have to find out about Xanthe and Eloise. Do you think Ned could ask Liz's husband…?"

I let it trail off because Clara was shaking her head.

"I thought you might be thinking that and I'm glad you didn't say it in front of Teague, in case he ever said anything to Ned, like when we have the cookout we've been talking about. Because I've, uh, kind of downplayed things to Ned." She chewed on her lip. "Him and Teague, huh?"

"Him and Teague, what?"

"Worrying. About us. It's kind of sweet, but it does complicate things."

"Not Teague. He's worried about the sheriff's department. His former fellows in blue—or brown or khaki—in law enforcement."

"Right." She brightened. "But I can pump Ned for what he knows already. I'm always asking him about people."

"Clara, if you don't like devoting so much time to this and missing time with Ned—"

"It's only once in a while. And he plays volleyball and cards with his pals, so…"

I wasn't sure her husband would equate her digging into murders with his pastimes. "Or if you don't think you should be looking into Xanthe's death—"

"I *want* to. I *love* it. I don't mean Xanthe's death. Or anybody else's. I hate that. And suspecting people I like, that's not fun. But I mean what we did last time. Sometimes I still can't believe I actually helped figure out a murder. It was so … so *impressive*. Probably the most impressive thing I've ever done. If we can help figure this out it'll show it wasn't … a fluke. Or even if we push the sheriff's department to look at more things, it's—" She swung her head around, as if she'd find the right word in the town square. And maybe she did. "—worth-while."

She was pleased by her found word. I didn't share her cheer.

I knew what it meant to keep secrets. To pretend you were who you weren't. I knew how it could stop relationships before they started.

Would Clara jeopardize her relationship with Ned by pretending she wasn't doing what she clearly loved? Was it my place to bring that up? … Even if I could without revealing how I knew about issues stemming from pretense.

I sighed. I'd thought coming back to the heartland would make everything simple again. Apparently, it was me, not geography that complicated things.

CHAPTER SEVENTEEN

CLARA AND I pulled into the generous parking lot for the North Bend County Sheriff's Department headquarters, which shared the complex with the county jail.

Beyond the wide, low building was a broad, green space kept well-mowed—the better to spot escapees, presumably. Trees outlining a creek bed undecided about which direction to go. On the other side sat our home away from home, the Torrid Avenue Dog Park.

It felt strange being in this part of the county without an antsy dog or dogs in the back of my car.

It also felt wrong. Like Gracie would know where I'd been—without her—when I got home.

Like I'd cheated on her.

Speaking of cheating …

Teague O'Donnell leaned on a sheriff's department vehicle, talking like old pals with Deputy Hensen. Hensen often worked with Eckles, but Hensen *was* a dog person.

They were at the end of the building, where a sign pointed toward a garage in back. I turned toward the front entrance.

He knew we were coming here. But was there any advantage in not letting him know he'd been spotted with Hensen?

Maybe.

"Look. Look." Clara craned to peek through the rear-view window as my car completed the turn. "Did you see? Teague talking with the deputy."

"Mmm-hm."

"Wonder what they're talking about."

"Last night's ballgame."

"Really? You think so?"

No. "What else could they possibly be talking about?"

"The murder," Clara said, in one of her patented say-what-everybody's-thinking moments. At least what I was thinking.

"Why? Teague's not interested. He maintains it's the sheriff's department's business and no one else's."

"He must have been called here after we left your house to talk to Liz," Clara the Innocent said. "I wonder why they want to talk to him? He wasn't there. He doesn't know any of the people."

I pulled into a spot between a giant SUV and a pickup truck.

Clara assumed the deputy sought out Teague and was asking questions. But what if our new friend initiated the conversation? While Teague spoke, looking casually toward the dog park—which kept his profile toward us—the deputy watched him intently, nodding at regular intervals.

"Should we go say hi?" Clara suggested as we exited the car into summer-swelter heat.

"No. Let's leave them to their conversation. But if we happen to hear anything…"

We didn't, because Teague's position carried his words away from us.

On top of that frustration, we practically ran into Deputy Eckles as we crossed the lobby toward a window manned by a deputy. Eckles was headed the same way.

"What are you two doing here? We don't need you interfer—"

You did last time.

Neither Clara nor I needed to speak the words because cutting himself off said he'd heard them in his head.

Clara said, "We're responding to the call for people who saw Xanthe Anstead on her last evening alive. We were in her yoga class."

He closed his eyes. Only for a moment, but it was as good as a head smack from someone else.

"We tried to tell you yesterday at the crime scene by the studio, but you wouldn't listen." Clara was so nice it almost didn't sound like rubbing it in.

He harrumphed and kept walking, opening the door beside the window.

Clara and I exchanged a satisfied look, then identified ourselves to the deputy behind the window.

"I'll buzz you in. There's a room to your right. Join the others there and wait until you're called."

His directions took us into a conference room where Clara, Teague, and I had waited—with our dogs—to be questioned about another death. I wondered if they'd ever gotten all the dog hair out.

At the moment, it held an assortment of our yoga classmates.

Monday night's spot-stealing mother of the bride—Eve Kraft, according to Donna—was seated at the table, yammering at the stick-thin woman. A rounded woman who liked to be in the precise center of the back row, sat opposite them, reading on a tablet without acknowledging them. An older man read a newspaper, but politely nodded at us before resuming.

Eve had broadened her topic from "our" wedding to complaining about Tina's decision to leave the studio closed until Monday.

"I mean, I understand respect for the dead and all, but I have so much tension in my hips from all the work I'm doing. I *need* that yin."

"Practice at home," stick-thin said without interest.

"*Alone?*"

The deputy from behind the window arrived. We hadn't even had a chance to sit.

"Deputy Eckles is ready for you now. Come this way." He held the door open, looking at Clara and me.

"I've been waiting," Eve Kraft complained. "And I don't have time for this nonsense. I have important things to do. I came here as they requested on TV, but if you're not interested in what I have to share, I will leave and get on with my *very* busy day."

I'd taken a quarter-step toward the door before I encountered Clara's extended arm, a hint she had a plan that required me to stay put.

She smiled at the deputy. "That's okay. We'll wait for Deputy Hensen. And you really should take this lady first. She is very busy." Her gesture indicated the mother of the bride.

Eve jumped up. "I am. A thousand phone calls, checking up on the so-called wedding planner, and a million other details. I must get this over with fast."

"Fine. Doesn't matter who he has to talk to first." I got the impression one civilian was like any other to this man in uniform. "C'mon."

As she swept past where we stood, Clara leaned toward her and said something I didn't catch. Eve, though, must have heard it, because she gave a sniff as she went by.

"What was that about?" I asked Clara.

"I figured, with everybody passing through, we have an opportunity to talk to people, as long as we keep delaying our interviews. Plus, a better chance of getting Hensen instead of Eckles if we wait."

"Smart, Clara." Still, my sense of justice was pricked. "But Eve didn't even thank you for giving up our spot."

Clara smirked. "This way we don't have to listen to her. Deputy Eckles won't thank me, either. I told her he has a daughter getting married soon in a very posh wedding. She would have run on about weddings anyway, but now she'll spend the whole time trying to be sure his daughter's wedding doesn't outshine her daughter's wedding."

"*Does* he have a daughter getting married?"

"He has a daughter. She must be about middle school age."

I laughed.

A voice came from over my shoulder. "I wasn't looking forward to this interrogation, but it can't be so bad if you're laughing." Berrie from the dog park must have come in as the deputy and Eve Kraft left and lurked right behind us.

She passed us and dumped an accessory resembling the offspring of a black trash bag and a tote for dozens of NBA players' shoes.

I flinched—laughing under the circumstances did feel cringeworthy.

But Clara displayed no symptoms of guilt. "We haven't been in yet.

We were celebrating avoiding the company of that woman who stole our spots. The one whose daughter is getting married."

"Oh. Her. Eve Kraft."

Clara's plan to talk to our classmates inspired me. "Berrie, do you remember during class Monday night when somebody came in the vestibule from outside and Xanthe got up to see what was happening?"

"I guess. She said who are you, he said he was there because somebody called about a problem, she said there's no problem except you being here. Get lost. Then she escorted him out."

A woman in civilian clothes opened the door to the inner sanctum and called, "Berrie Vittlow?"

Berrie raised her hand.

"Come with me." She pivoted and started out.

"Wait a minute, Berrie. You said something about seeing Liz on Monday."

She frowned at me. "What are you talking about?"

"At class Monday night. When Xanthe substituted."

She shook her head. "I don't remember. Gotta go."

The stick figure woman snorted, drawing all eyes to her.

"First the deputy invites these two, then that woman who babbles all the time about a wedding, and now you. How'd you get called before me?" she grumbled. "I was here first."

"Sh—happens. Get used to it," muttered the back-row-center woman.

I stifled a chuckle. Then had to stifle a different reaction when Berrie murmured as she picked up her belongings, "Told them the truth out front. I have an appointment with my oncologist in an hour." As she straightened, she said for everyone to hear, "I must be more important than the rest of you."

She exited the waiting area with perfect timing, with the civilian woman closing the door as punctuation.

"An oncologist? Did you know she has cancer?" I asked Clara.

"She'd tell you *had*. Still needs checkups, but she's doing great."

As more were called, the civilian woman frowned, but didn't argue when we declined our turns, letting others go ahead of us after we'd pumped them.

It did not, alas, yield a bumper crop of information.

The newspaper-reading man we'd taken to referring to as Chatty Chuck—predictably—had little to say. To questions about when he left class Monday night, the interrupting guy arriving, or anything else, he said he didn't remember.

He was called next, while the couple of two young men arrived shortly after.

The rounded woman said she'd been among the first to leave after our class, vaguely recalled an interruption, but not its cause.

A younger woman named Laura, the one who'd said she was a new mother and was pouring out woes about her baby not sleeping as we'd left the studio, was a later arrival to the waiting room. Today, the stain on her shirt was pea green. I sure hoped it was from peas.

In answer to our first questions, she absently explained, between checking her phone incessantly, she was taking classes to get rid of baby weight.

She raised our hopes by saying she took a morning class with Xanthe, then dashed them by saying she was too busy sweating and feeling miserable to note anything about the instructor except she was a relentless taskmaster.

As for the interruption to our class, we got a one-shouldered shrug that nearly engulfed her ducked head. "Some guy came in. She told him to get out. Aren't they supposed to lock the outside door before class?"

She stood and asked the others assembled if she could go in next so she could get back to her baby, because she wasn't sure about leaving the baby alone with her mother. Would she know how to handle a baby?

The two young men nodded agreeably.

Fern, a woman in her eighties, one of the class regulars, and a recent arrival in the waiting room, said, "She handled you, dear."

"But things are so different now. They're much more complicated." I could see a mounting lack of empathy for her in the faces of the older women. Then she said, "And the baby keeps having bouts of projectile vomiting."

The others unanimously agreed she could go next.

Maybe it was out of sympathy, but I suspected it had more do with not wanting to hear about projectile vomiting.

Despite telling Laura to go ahead, as soon as she left, the stick woman started muttering about karma.

"The longer we wait, the more irked she's going to get," I murmured to Clara.

She nodded and advanced on New Age Nelly.

Who said with little interest that she hadn't talked to Xanthe after class and hadn't noticed if anyone else had been there when she left the studio.

I asked about the interruption of class.

"I don't remember. No matter how loud, I didn't hear anything he said. Once I get on my mat and begin meditation and the meditative movement of yin, I shed all of daily life and a meditative shield protects me from the temporal."

We hadn't mentioned the interrupter's gender, yet she'd identified the voice as male and loud. *Some cracks in your meditative shield, girlie.*

"You take Xanthe's morning class, don't you?" Clara asked.

"Why do you think that?" she asked back.

"Because Laura, the young woman who just had the baby, said to you Monday night while we were all getting props that she hoped it wouldn't be as hard a class as the morning's because she couldn't take two in the same day." In a low-voiced aside to me, she said, "It was while you were in the restroom."

"Did she say that?" the stick woman asked without interest. "I was focused on centering myself to the moment, the space."

"She did. You must have heard her, though you did rather stare right through her." Clara fixed a wide, unblinking look on her.

"Sometimes it is necessary to withdraw from interacting on this plane to reach a higher one."

And many times on this plane, such withdrawal is rudeness.

Echoing my thoughts, Clara said, "That's not nice. To ignore her."

"Yeah? Well, she's not some sweet Madonna. What she told you about not paying attention to the teacher in the morning? Bull. You should have heard her in the morning class going off on Xylophone."

"Xanthe?"

"Yeah, right. The way she went on, you'd think Xanthe was her worst enemy. All over a dog."

"A dog?" I prodded.

"She said Xanthe was rude to leave her mutt out all the time, making noise. The barking made her baby cry and she thought she'd go mad and if the dog didn't stop it, she'd take matters into her own hands. Not so sweet, huh?"

Her descent from the spiritual heights to earth-stained gossip left her breathing heavily.

The civilian woman emerged, asked for Rowena, and the stick woman flounced out to be interviewed.

The two young men were willing to talk to us, but vague and they'd been among the first to leave the studio.

Next, we approached Fern, who usually took a spot near the double glass doors. She smiled a greeting and welcomed our questions.

"We were wondering if you remember what happened during class Monday night," Clara said.

"Well, I said hello and told her my name, because of course she wouldn't know me like Liz does. Poor Liz has been having a rough time of it. Young couples often do. Xanthe seemed very ... cheerful."

"Yes, she was. But we meant later. After we were all settled and—"

"Oh, yes, yes. I do remember. She said something about a workshop and I heard the paper rustle where the flyer is pinned to the bulletin board."

"She?" Clara repeated. "It was a man's voice."

"No, dear. It wasn't anyone I know, but I'm certain it was a woman."

Stalemate.

I raised my index finger. "Got it. Fern, you're talking about earlier, before class started when the—" I broke off from referring to her as the Tackler. "—new student, a blonde woman, went back to the vestibule to stow away her sunglasses. Clara's talking about later. After class started, when someone came in from outside, and Xanthe went to the vestibule to see what was going on. Remember?"

"Ah. *That's* what you meant. Yes, yes."

"Was it someone you know? Would you recognize him if you saw him again? Did you see him at all?"

Each question decreased in hopefulness as she shook her head.

"When the class is full, I'm quite close to the doors and I might have seen him, but with so many absent, I moved farther into the room and couldn't see the outside door. Why? Do you think—? Oh, no, he couldn't have been the killer. He sounded so *nice.*"

He also didn't walk with a limp or drool from fangs.

That was Aunt Kit's voice in my head. I sure didn't say it aloud, though I agreed with my great aunt that the generalized view of murderers was often hard to shake.

"Do you remember what he said?"

"Something about water, wasn't it?"

"That was at the end," Clara said. "How about when he first came in?"

"Mmmm. He came in talking. About everything being okay and I wondered what was okay? Which was answered in the end when he talked about the water. Someone complaining about water. But…there was something in between. Something… Did he ask her who she was? He sounded surprised." She shook her head. "I'm sorry I'm no more help. I wonder if the deputies will even want to talk to me."

"Of course—"

Clara's reassurance was cut short by the civilian woman calling Fern's name. "Deputy Hensen will see you now."

So, Hensen was sharing the questioning duties.

"This is all rather nerve-wracking, isn't it?" Fern fluttered.

"Just tell him everything you remember," I said.

We moved on as more yoga class-takers came through.

One middle-aged woman with gray roots to her auburn hair who usually took the one spot in the front row not in front of a mirror, was by far the best of the bunch. She displayed accurate recall of events and related them succinctly.

In other words, she agreed with my recollections.

She also, unprompted, listed off those who'd remained when she left—Mother of the Bride/Eve Kraft, the Blonde Tackler/Julia Trippen, the New Mother/Laura, Silent Man, and Stick Woman/Rowena—though she didn't use the same descriptors for them.

"And you two," she'd concluded, "came right behind me. Though you turned the other way. I went right on Haines Avenue, you went left."

Others added little, except for a range of memories about Xanthe's reaction to the interruption.

"*How dare you come in here during our spiritual hour.* That's what she said, and I totally agreed, because with two teenagers and a ten-year-old out of school for the summer, it's the only time I get to myself from morning to night."

"*What the blank-blank-blank are you doing in here. Get out. Get out right now you blank*—" Though he didn't leave any blanks. This was from Walter, a delivery truck driver who ran marathons and did ironman competitions, and did yin yoga to keep all his muscles from becoming one blankety-blank knot, as he told us.

The room was empty except for Clara and me when the door opened again.

"Guess we're next." Clara sounded slightly disheartened at the woeful thinness of our information crop.

But it wasn't the civilian or the deputy calling us in for our turn to be questioned. It was the Tackler/Julia, her blonde hair turning faintly green in the artificial light.

She didn't greet us.

I might have returned the ignoring. Clara wasn't that easy to foil.

"Hi. You've missed all the others." Somehow, she made it sound like a party. "We've been talking about the strange interruption of class the night poor Xanthe was murdered. You know, when the man came in and Xanthe had to stop and get him to leave."

"I have no idea what you're talking about. I don't recall any interruption," she said, with a strong subtext of *leave me alone.*

She was lying, since I'd seen her head turn toward the double doors. She *had* heard the guy come in.

Lacking the authority or equipment to shake the truth out of her, we left her alone and in minutes, the civilian woman asked for Julia Trippen.

But the civilian woman didn't move from the doorway.

"You, too, Ms. Mackey. Deputy Hensen is ready for you. And," she added as my head began to swivel, "there's nobody else left to send in before you."

CHAPTER EIGHTEEN

DEPUTY HENSEN WAS professional and thorough as he took me through the events of the class and after.

He didn't say a word about Teague O'Donnell.

Neither did I, despite swells of temptation to ask what the heck they'd been talking about.

Only one question caught me unprepared.

"Were you the last one to leave the studio?"

I went blank for a second. Had someone said I was last? Or, more accurately, we were, because Clara and I left together. We were sometimes last out when Liz taught, especially if we got chatting. And because, for some reason, I seemed to be among the slowest mat-rollers on the planet.

But that night...?

No, wait. The auburn-haired woman had said we were behind her and there were others yet to leave.

Besides, I *knew* we hadn't been last.

Yet the question left me momentarily blank.

Okay. Recreate it.

Class ends. We're all down on our mats, stretched out for shavasana, less relaxed, more exhausted than usual. Xanthe started ordering us to bring movement back into our bodies way before I was ready.

We all sit up, do the closing, she thanks us for sharing our practice with her. I mentally add, *our sweat, too.* Then...

The Tackler, now also known as Julia Trippen, hopped up—I remember resenting her enthusiasm—and fussed with her bag.

Rolled up my mat. Clara and I waited for the crush to end, then put our bolsters, blocks, and blankets away. We went up front to the vestibule to get our shoes and other paraphernalia.

A few had already left. More milled around, putting shoes on. Someone—Laura, the new mother, I thought—stood by the desk, asking Xanthe something. Yes, definitely Laura. There'd been a phrase about baby weight.

Eve and Julia came up behind us, blocked from leaving because of the traffic jam in the vestibule.

The door opened for another departure, and a gust of scent had entered.

"Fresh strawberry pie at the café," Clara murmured. "Do you want...?"

"I want."

We snaked through those left, reached the door behind—yes, the auburn-haired woman. We waved a thank you to the substitute instructor over the head of the New Mother named Laura, who was talking angrily. A continuation of the morning dog-baby conflict, if Rowena was right.

Clara and I were out the door, heading south on Beguiling Way.

We passed the music shop and reached the odds and ends store-front, its window festooned with strings of lampshades above the more sober bases at the bottom of the window, when a sound behind us made me turn.

Eve and Julia—though I'd then thought of them as MOTB and the Tackler—were emerging from the studio and heading our direction. Instinctively, I picked up the pace and Clara matched it without question. So we were in the café before they would have reached the end of Beguiling Way.

"No," I told Hensen firmly, "I wasn't the last to leave the studio. Clara and I left together and there were several people still there. In addition to Xanthe. I assume you weren't counting her, because she'd naturally be the last one, needing to lock up."

"You can open your eyes."

I did.

"Why did you take so long to answer?" he asked.

"I was recreating what happened from the end of class until Clara and I arrived at the café for strawberry pie."

"What did happen?"

I told him. Identifying Berrie, Laura the new mother, Fern, and Chatty Chuck, still being there when Clara and I left, possibly still there when I saw Eve and Julia behind us. I left out editorial and sidebar comments, as well as descriptive nicknames, so it became a fairly straight-forward account.

He facilitated identifications with photos taken today because each matched what they'd worn in the waiting room.

"...and then we got strawberry pie at the café. Clara got double whipped cream. I didn't. Saved from suspicion by the aroma of baked goods." I grinned at him.

His solemnity didn't waver.

"You could have gone back."

✧　✧　✧　✧

"OKAY, SO HE used the same line on both of us," I said to Clara. "It doesn't mean he suspects us. They're going through the motions before they finalize writing it off as the work of a random killer from the Interstate."

We were at my dining room table with ice waters, sharing the table with an outpost of Teague's tools—and a bag of his Cheetos—on a protective cloth. The main colony of tools was upstairs in the guest bedroom that backed up to mine.

We'd shared what Deputy Hensen asked us and what we'd said— Clara had followed me into the interview room, while I waited in the lobby.

"Yeah. And we *didn't* go back," she said cheerfully. "The server at the café should remember. Especially since I got double whipped cream."

"Exactly. Besides, we should be grateful to Hensen for bringing it up. Because who *did* leave last is a fascinating question."

"We can compare memories. But—No, wait. Let's each write who we remember still being there when we left so we don't sway each other's memories."

"Perfect."

I got scratch pads and pens from a kitchen drawer and brought them back to the table. We wrote in silence for three, maybe four minutes, although Clara wasn't totally silent when she crossed out one of her entries.

"Ready?" she asked.

"Ready. First say who you scratched out."

"Berrie."

"She was still there. Sitting on the bench, putting her shoes on."

She shifted in her chair uneasily. "Was she? I don't—"

"Clara. Getting these names down isn't an accusation. They're simply facts. Not even damning facts. Someone could have come along as Xanthe was leaving—"

"Like a maniac from the Interstate."

"—or been lying in wait when she left after all the students had."

"Anyone who left earlier could have doubled back and been waiting for her, like Deputy Hensen said we could have. And since she wasn't found until the next day, it could have been any time after class."

"Why would she be there in her car there, say, hours and hours after class? The most *likely* time for her death was when she came out of the studio and got in her car. Even if she stayed an hour late like Eloise said she did sometimes, that narrows it a lot."

"She could have left and then come back, like Deputy Hensen said about us."

"The killer would have to know she was coming back or followed her. Unless they just happened upon her."

"Mmm. And it doesn't seem like a break-in at the studio or any of the businesses around would be a reason. I can't imagine they leave cash or valuables worth stealing."

"Exactly. Plus, I bet the preliminary time of death fits roughly with her being killed not too long after class or the sheriff's department's Interstate theory would have included that information. Also, even with them fixed on the idea of an Interstate killer, surely they've checked if anyone spotted Xanthe after class. Not to mention Deputy Hensen asking us who left last. Why do that if evidence pointed to her being killed hours and hours later?"

"That's good." She nodded emphatically. "Let's go over the rest of our lists of who was still there when we left."

They matched up. Berrie. Eve Kraft and Julia Trippen. Chatty Chuck. Laura, the new mother. Rowena, the stick woman.

Clara hadn't seen Eve and Julia come out after us and seemed disappointed when I described their leaving while several others were still inside.

We also agreed seven had left before us.

"That doesn't eliminate them," I reminded her, "because any could have doubled back."

"Or anybody else could have shown up," she said.

"Although… I'm about to argue with myself. Maybe people couldn't have doubled back. Because, surely, the sheriff's department has checked for security cameras—after all, that could clinch their Interstate killer theory—and the cameras would also spot anybody who doubled back."

She tapped her finger on the rim of the water glass. "Problem is, how would *we* find out what they saw on any security tape. Not to mention I don't know if many places have security cameras in Haines Tavern."

"A lot more than you'd think."

Clara and I both jumped at the introduction of this new voice— Teague's.

He stood at the bottom of the staircase, flanked by our dogs.

"Some guard dog you are," I commented to Gracie, who was at his side, getting her ears ruffled.

"Some detective you are," he countered. "You didn't notice my truck?"

"Thought you'd still be up there measuring."

"I have been."

Clara brought us back on topic. "You think the Beguiling Way shops might have security coverage showing the killer?"

"No."

"But you said—"

"A lot of shops might have cameras to cover the front, especially their doors, but wouldn't aim out to where most people walk. Plus, the height of the buildings and the narrowness of the passageway wouldn't let much light get in there once the sun started going down. In a place like Beguiling Way, the artificial light is meant for ambience, not security. And then some shops' cameras record over after twelve hours or so to skimp on storage. Best you might hope for is a camera or two catching movement, but no hope of making identifications—"

"But they can enhance video—" Clara started.

"—no matter how good the enhancement, because the original's so bad."

The way he talked about all this raised a question. "Is this hypothetical? Or do you know for a fact the sheriff's department has checked security cameras and hasn't found anything useful?"

"Worst of all, no security camera shows the spot where Xanthe's car was."

A tacit acknowledgment his knowledge wasn't hypothetical.

His former partner up in the Chicago area had a friend in the North Bend County Sheriff's Department. Was he relaying information to Teague? Or had Teague received information via the direct route of Deputy Hensen?

And what else had they talked about?

CLARA WENT HOME to her husband.

We'd agreed on the first part of the next day's agenda. A morning trip to the dog park, as early as I could bear. Then to the hospital to ask about flower deliveries.

The rest of the day included hopes to try for more information on Xanthe, Liz, and anyone connected to them.

After scrambled eggs and sliced tomatoes for supper, I spent the evening researching.

First, I took another run at Xanthe's background. I came across a few legal listings from her divorce from Fred Branter. Remembering what Eloise said, I found mentions of their son, Ethan, in connection with moderate success in school sports.

Then I tackled Smith-Flarenge. The positive reviews were far outnumbered by complaints.

The complaints from all around the country sounded familiar after talking with Donna. All sorts of promises, few kept, and roadblock after roadblock to get money out.

Getting deeper into complaint sites, I found a few about the Haines Tavern office, with two mentioning a specific agent—Vincent Shornfell. One described his assistant, Xanthe, as peaches and cream before the complainer signed up and unhelpful after, deteriorating to sullen at the end.

Assuming it was the Xanthe we knew—a pretty safe assumption, because how many Xanthes could there be who'd worked for Smith-Flarenge in Haines Tavern, Kentucky?—could Vincent Shornfell be the man Eloise mentioned. The one associated with Xanthe's money-loving ways. An office romance could fit.

If so, had their relationship followed the same pattern? Peaches and cream, deteriorating to sullen at the end. Could that be a motive for murder?

More searching. No current address or phone number was listed for Vincent Shornfell in the usual spots online.

Unlisted to avoid unsatisfied customers? Or could he have left the area?

It might have been the power of suggestion, but I had vanilla ice cream topped by sliced peaches before going to bed. And had no complaints.

DAY FOUR
THURSDAY

CHAPTER NINETEEN

"DID YOU SEE?" Clara asked as I got into her SUV the next day to head to the hospital.

"Yes."

Tina had sent an email request for help this evening setting up the studio for a remembrance gathering for Xanthe tomorrow.

"Do you think—?"

"Yes."

"We've already talked to those people."

"Maybe something new will come up. And helping with the set-up means at least we'll be sure we accomplish something."

I filled her in on what I'd found about Smith-Flarenge the evening before, including Vincent Shornfell and my speculations he might have been the "money guy" Xanthe had been involved with.

"He could be the guy who came into the studio," Clara said excitedly. "That would all fit. His surprise when he saw her. Her chilly reception. That's great, Sheila. Great."

"Except we don't know he is the guy who came in and even if we did, it doesn't get us any farther."

"But he's a great suspect."

"Why? Why would seeing her after—what, almost a year?—suddenly throw him into such a rage he killed her?"

"Maybe he waited for her after class, to talk, you know, then when she wouldn't come back to him, he went into a rage."

"Maybe."

"But you don't think so."

I felt bad for dampening her enthusiasm, but said, "I don't. If they'd just broken up, I could see it more, but there's no indication he tried to get back into her life."

"That's something we could ask Eloise."

"Yes. But right now, we should ask our questions of your connection here at the hospital."

"MY FRIEND SENT flowers to a neighbor of hers who's in the hospital and the neighbor said they didn't bring the flowers into her room until she was about asleep. Does that happen a lot?" Clara asked the woman she knew at the hospital over coffee and snacks in the cafeteria.

"Not often. Though there was one day last week when deliveries ran later than usual. The girl who brings them—a sweet girl, really— was an hour later than usual, maybe a little bit more."

"I wonder if it was the same night," Clara mused. "Monday?"

"Yes. That was it." The older woman looked at me. "If you give me your neighbor's name and room number, I can check. They shouldn't deliver to a room late enough to disturb the patient. They're supposed to wait until the next day."

Barely recovered from hearing I had a neighbor in the hospital, according to Clara's improvisation, I hurriedly said that wasn't necessary. "My neighbor is being released soon."

"In fact," Clara said, "we're here to pick her up, so we better get going."

With cheerful farewells, we headed out. Clara hooked my arm when I started toward the outside door. "Picking up your neighbor, remember," she said under her breath. "C'mon, we'll go out another way."

We went up the elevator a couple floors, down a hall, then down another elevator and out a side door.

Despite the necessity of a much longer walk to reach the car, I was admiring. "Clara, you missed your calling as a spy."

"Aw, thanks. But what did you think of Mamie delivering the flowers an hour late? That's got to mean something, doesn't it?"

"There's definitely a missing hour in her timeline. If she spent it at the flower shop for some reason, it might have put her on Beguiling Way around the time Xanthe could have been killed." I grimaced at the *might* and *could*.

"But why on earth would she kill Xanthe?"

"Xanthe saw something Mamie—or a confederate of Mamie's—didn't want her to see?"

"Her grandfather…?"

"Or," I continued, "if Mamie was there an hour later than she said, she might have seen something vital without actually being involved. Either way, I think Mamie fudged the times."

"I think you're right. I think she was keeping something from Alan. If we figure out what we might use it to get her to come clean about the times. But first, let's have lunch. Then I have errands before we go to the studio to help get ready for the remembrance."

"Okay. And after lunch, while you're doing errands, I'm calling Donna to see if she can get me a name and phone number for her friend's nephew-in-law, the Smith-Flarenge critic."

DONNA CAME THROUGH. Of course.

Teague's truck was still in the drive, apparently with his canine entourage upstairs from the sounds emanating from that direction and the fact I received no four-legged greeting.

I wandered into the back yard—in case of sharp ears—to make my call.

"Hi, Professor Adronski? My name is Sheila Mackey. I'm from Haines Tavern, Kentucky. I understand through mutual friends you had conflicts with the local Smith-Flarenge office and came out on the winning side."

I braced to be asked how I'd gotten his number. I'd braced for the wrong question.

"Are you a customer of theirs?"

"No. I—"

"Former customer?"

"No."

"Journalist?"

"No."

"Writing a book?"

"A book?" How the heck did he know—? Oh. "About finances? Investing? Not in this lifetime."

"That's good. Because I am. And I don't want this coming out before the book does."

"No. I'm not writing a book or anything else about that. I don't know if you're aware a former employee—Xanthe Anstead—was recently murdered?"

"I heard from relatives in town. Someone off the Interstate, wasn't it? Wrong place, wrong time."

"Possibly. But it always behooves us to look into the background of the victim and the victim's associates." If he concluded I was with law enforcement, that was on him. He'd been quick to ask me other questions. "Did you encounter her?"

"Only in passing. She was the usual Smith-Flarenge doorkeeper. Sweetness and light if you're signing over money to them. Fire-breathing dragon if you're trying to get it back. She had quite the mouth on her."

I tried to imagine the woman who'd taught our yin yoga class as a fire-breathing dragon with a potty mouth. She'd certainly changed.

Or, had she simply assumed the sweetness and light image for yoga? Had the fire-breathing dragon with the potty mouth still existed in other areas of her life?

"Was she closely associated with anyone at Smith-Flarenge?"

He chuckled. "You mean sleeping with? That would be Vincent Shornfell. Although in a business sense she was also associated with the other advisors. As I said, she was the doorkeeper. Very important for them. Make the incoming slide as smooth as possible. Once the mark is in their clutches, bar any potential exit."

He *really* didn't like this company.

"But you're certain she had a personal relationship with Vincent Shornfell?"

"Absolutely. Caught them as close to doing the deed in the break-room as I ever want to one day when I slipped free of my keeper, pretending I needed the restroom. But she was gone before Shornfell got caught."

"Caught doing what?"

"Boy, you don't know much about this, do you?"

"I don't." It made him feel more assured I wasn't going to steal his book and it was the truth.

"He had used information of former customers' relatives—the beneficiaries to those former accounts—to create bogus accounts to get bonuses. A couple customers complained and they were told they had no standing because they were no longer account holders. The family members whose information was used were told they had no standing, since they "claimed" to not be account holders.

"Smith-Flarenge's automatic response is to stall, delay, and obfus-cate, but this time it was nuts. Unlike most of the instances involving Smith-Flarenge, he wasn't actually ripping off the customers—or non-customers in this case—but *was* ripping off the company.

"Still, it took nearly six months for the company to stop denying everything long enough to realize they were being ripped off. Then they released him."

"Released him? They didn't fire—?"

"No, no, no. That would be acknowledging some wrong occurred within Smith-Flarenge. They never admit wrongdoing of any kind.

"They hire these so-called advisors with little to no background, put them through training that leaves them with little to no back-ground, except on how to work the S-F fees and commissions structure to the company's benefit, and set them loose. The fortunate customers quickly realize they know a heck of a lot more than most of these so-called advisors and get the heck out. The middle-of-the-road customers know enough to avoid the most egregious offers, prevent the churning, and come out intact, if behind the market. The ones I feel bad for are the customers who need advice because they don't have the background, the resources, the knowledge to invest for themselves. S-F battens off the most vulnerable."

Kit would thoroughly approve of his use of batten. She often applied the word's meaning of prospering at the expense of someone else to publishers.

"I know they took advantage of your relatives—your wife's relatives."

"Among a lot of other people. I spent months interviewing people who've been ripped off by S-F. I wasn't a very nice guy to be around then. But I was particularly angry about those relatives. They're both former military. They worked hard. Raised a good family. Took care of themselves and their own, plus helped other people. And what this so-called company did was not only deprive them of income by whittling their nest egg, it also made them into people who see themselves as saps. That sucks."

"It does."

His anger gave way to a wry half-chuckle. "I was worried about using them in the book—you know, exposing their vulnerability. We're using other names for them but a lot of people know who they are. But they had an entirely different take on it. They've given me access to every bit of information they have. They figure it's their way of taking charge. They can't wait for the book to be published."

"That's—"

"Hey. Are you saying Smith-Flarenge could be involved in a murder?"

"No, no. I have no reason to think—"

"Damn. That would have made a great chapter."

CHAPTER TWENTY

"**WHAT ARE YOU** doing?" the familiar voice asked through the phone.

Sitting on a deck chair with my laptop, I'd typed notes on what Professor Andronski told me, then meandered between writing a list of possible suspects with their motives and alibis and trying to write another sentence or two on my novel… if that wasn't too grandiose for what I had.

I shied away from telling Kit about either.

Not because she wouldn't share my interest—in murder and writing—but because she did. I wasn't sure either would pan out and I felt protective of them.

Maybe it was the Teague effect, since I was not telling him about them.

As if that thought sparked my verbal centers, I blurted out, "Enjoying the peace and quiet of being in the back yard while Teague's working inside. He's the carpenter—the guy doing the closets? Well, he's starting work and—"

"Oh, I remember who Teague O'Donnell is," she said with far too much emphasis.

"—he's all over the house and—"

"*He* is?"

"His stuff is," I amended without addressing her innuendo and continuing to redirect the conversation. "All over. The dining room. The kitchen. The hallway. He made me clean out my closets, while his stuff spreads through the house. On top of which he says he's growing a beard, so I have to see this scruffy mess whenever I look at him. I swear, it's like living with the guy without the benefits."

For half a beat I thought I'd redirected this conversation right over a cliff. If I'd been talking to my mother, I'd be at the bottom of that cliff already. But not with Kit.

"What benefits? Can't think of a single benefit of living with a man. Oh. You mean sex? Good heavens, Sheila, you don't need to put up with a man in your house to have an active sex life."

Yes. There it is. My great-aunt had—and almost surely *has*—a more active sex life than me.

It might be a character flaw, but I'd found it difficult to form a relationship with anyone when I wasn't letting them in on the charade.

While I was thinking those thoughts, I'd also been updating Kit on what Clara and I had learned and speculated since we'd last talked.

"Kit, can you ask Beatrice some questions for me?"

Beatrice was Kit's beyond-sharp money manager ... as much as Kit let anyone manage her.

"Ask her yourself."

"I don't know if—"

But Kit was already connecting the three-way call. She told Beatrice I had questions—referring to me by my legal name—the one checks came to—which was neither Sheila nor the *Abandon All* name.

I blurted out Professor Andronski's name. "He's a financial writer. Is he any good?"

"Hmm. Not too bad. Wrote a couple books about how people make mistakes investing. Had a lot of fancy terms for it, but he got the behavior right."

That was reassuring. Beatrice didn't praise easily.

"What do you know about Smith-Flarenge, Beatrice?"

"Piece of—"

There went the praise.

"Have you ever used them or—"

"I have *not*. What do you take me for?" She shifted from incensed to lecturing. "And don't let me catch you—"

"I'm not, I'm not. Just... some people I know have connections..."

She humphed at my weak finish.

"Thanks, Beatrice," Kit said, taking control again. After the good-byes left Kit and me alone on the call, she said, "He's published by the non-fiction imprint of the *Abandon All* publisher. If you called your editor, you could have his phone number immediately."

I groaned. "And remind her of my existence?"

"There is that," she agreed. "He's also represented by the same agency who represents my foreign rights. It's not the slam dunk the editor would be, but let me see if I can get past the defenders and drive the lane."

"I love it when you talk basketball, Kit. But as it happens, I've already talked to him. Got his number through a contact at the dog park."

She chuffed out a laugh. "Different world."

"It is. I wanted another point of view on him beyond my own."

The sound she made this time was not laughter. "Trust your gut, kid. You have good instincts."

"Who was it who taught me to get two sources?"

I'D TAKEN A leftover roast from the freezer when a salvo of barking thundered down on me from above.

Gracie.

A collie bark is not something to fool with. It's neither an ear-piercing yap nor a deep-throated ruff. It both pierces the ear at close range and travels long distances. Remember, it was designed to be heard in the hills of Scotland. Pack that bark into a suburban house, and you've got something you can't ignore.

I sprinted for the stairs.

This wasn't her joyous bark for greeting her dog buddies or people she liked. Not her excited bark for new experiences. Not her protesting bark for going to the vet. Not her warning bark for dangers like UPS deliverymen and mail carriers. Not her DEFCON One for horrors like chipmunks and squirrels.

This bark blended excitement, protest, warning, and DEFCON

Two.

I stepped into the guest room to find Teague and Murphy standing still, watching in fascination as Gracie barked strident warnings at an extended metal tape measure that it better not pull any funny business.

"Gracie. Quiet." She couldn't hear me over her own barking. Or chose not to hear me.

I had to clap my hands to break her concentration.

"Quiet." She stopped. Side-eyeing the tape measure before trotting over to me with tail wagging in triumph. Murphy shook all over as if he'd gotten wet, then joined the greeting committee, by coming to my side. I patted each, then turned to Teague. "What are you doing?"

"Measuring."

"I mean with my dog. Why didn't you retract it?"

"Hard to measure with it retracted. Besides, wanted to see how long she'd bark at it."

"Forever. She gets in a zone."

"Yeah? I think my ears are still ringing."

"That's how she'd scare off predators going after sheep she's guarding."

"I'd sure leave her sheep alone."

"Don't tell her that. You'll encourage her."

"She barks *more* with encouragement? Hard to believe. Did you know about her reaction to tape measures?"

"No. Maybe it's only yours."

He retracted the tape measure with a faint metallic whine followed by a thwack as it landed. Gracie jerked.

"Quiet," I ordered preemptively.

She gave a muffled, *Whumpf,* having barked it into submission.

"You have sawdust in your..." I waved toward the lower part of his face.

"Beard?"

"Yeah. Sawdust."

He brushed at it. "Why don't you like beards?"

I wasn't telling him the truth. Even though he already knew one element from Clara. I did have sensitive skin. The few times I'd kissed men with beards it had hurt. And then there was the sawdust-and-more catching qualities.

"Short hair and a bushy beard? Like all those ballplayers? Looks strange. Bushy beards sticking out of football helmets. Or someone who looks like a Civil War general until he takes off his baseball cap and shows a hipster flattop with close sides … and then this bush at the bottom of his face, like a hairy goiter—"

"Boy, you *don't* like beards," he said mildly.

"—and it makes no sense. Short hair for the ease of upkeep for guys out sweating all day, that makes sense. But then this hairy mass on their chin getting sweaty and dirty, which takes as much or more upkeep. At least it *should* get upkeep."

"They're popular now. Athletes, like you said. Celebrities."

"That's why you want a beard? Because they're popular?" Then I turned crafty. "I read a study that said men grow beards in an effort to show off to their fellow men how manly they are."

He stroked the side of his jaw. "I read a study, too. It said men who grow beards these days want to show they're their own man. Not part of the corporate expectations to be clean-shaven. Independent."

I eyed him, feeling a shrewd guess coming on. "You're rebelling against police department regulations?"

"Or celebrating not needing to adhere to them anymore."

Celebrating?

That didn't land quite right.

Was he truly celebrating not needing to adhere to rules? Or trying to find silver linings about being kicked out of the club?

I opened my mouth. Closed it. Started again. Differently.

"Well, let me warn you if your celebration gets caught in a saw or curled around a drill or pulled when a ladder folds on it, I'm not coming to your rescue and you get no workman's comp."

He grinned. "Understood."

Sternly ignoring the grin, I said. "I thought you were done measuring. Besides, it looks like you've started constructing."

"Not construction the way you mean it. I'm building braces to support the ceiling for when I take the wall out. Probably isn't necessary, but you don't know for sure until you find out to your sorrow that it *was* necessary and then you're in a mess. Besides, remeasuring told me we're going to have to eat into one room or both. The overall depth's not enough."

"I measured when I first had the idea." I'd laid two hangers end to end and they'd fit fine.

"Did you allow for the thickness of the wall and space for the clothes to hang?"

No. I hadn't. "Make the wall between the backs of the two closets super thin."

"Super thin walls cause issues like sound transmission, not to mention a good knock from a hanger could go through it. And even if I forgot my carpenter's oath—"

"Carpenter's oath?"

"—to build sturdy and lasting, there's no way to make a wall thin enough."

"I'm sure with your skill, you can find a way."

He scowled.

I'd have to work on my flattery-to-get-what-I-wanted skills.

"You'd have to have the closets completely open to each other and the ends of the hangers from one side overlapping the ends of the hangers from the other side. *Which,*" he continued loudly when I parted my lips, "is not up to code and not something I'm willing to do. If you're going to go shoddy, get somebody else."

I scowled back at him.

He relented. "Look, I'll show you."

He took out the tape measure, started to extend it, and caused a crisis. A loud crisis.

But with him using the tape and me holding Gracie, he created taped off areas on the floor.

Definitely eating inches.

Then I looked at how far the closet needed to come into the master bedroom and compared it to an existing jog in the wall. I had an idea.

"Teague?"

"Uh-oh."

"How can you say uh-oh when I haven't said anything?"

"I remember that tone and expression from the shelves projects and it always meant more work for me."

"They turned out well, didn't they?"

"Yeah."

"Okay, then. How about if you build bookshelves framing the closet doors. Shallower—"

"Sheila?" Clara's call reached us from downstairs. "You ready to go to the yoga studio?"

"Upstairs," I called back.

Teague frowned. "Yoga studio? I thought they canceled classes until next week."

"We're going to help prepare for a remembrance gathering tomorrow for Xanthe." Then I resumed my description. "Make the shelves shallower close to the doors, deeper where the wall jogs."

He squinted.

"Might work. Could support them mostly like floating shelves, but they'll need more support at the far end or they'll tip."

"Great." I was pleased. There's no such thing as too many bookcases.

"But it'll cost time and money. Hey, Clara." She'd poked her head around the corner, looking curiously at the work zone. "And, since you're adding another wrinkle, I'll have to start over with figuring the dimensions."

"*More* measuring?"

"You've heard of measure once, cut twice?"

"Yes. But quadruple? It's your own business how much time you take, since you're not working by the hour, but couldn't you take on more jobs if you finished faster?"

"Might not finish faster if I don't do all the measuring, then mess up. Undo and redo always take longer than getting it right the first time."

"Why would it be messed up? Do you have trouble with numbers?" Clara's warmth removed any potential nosiness from the question and left caring … with maybe a little curiosity.

"I don't see well out of my left eye. In fact, I'm legally blind in that eye."

A resounding *click* sounded in my head.

The way he swung his head to look at things—and people—from one angle, then another. Checking and rechecking input from his impaired sight.

"Teague," Clara said with more warmth and caring, yet without a hint of the pity that would send most males running.

"It's not that big a deal. I have some sight in it. Enough. I can do pretty much everything I need or want. Including drive, teach, hang out with Murphy, even carpentry work, as long as I'm careful, especially with measuring." He grinned, slightly lopsided, yet genuine.

"But not be a law enforcement officer," blurted out of me without warning or my permission.

He did that head shifting thing I'd thought meant he doubted what I'd said, but now had an entirely different explanation.

After a pause, he said, "The medical retirement lists my eyesight as the cause."

Utterly even, those words created a vortex of questions. How did he feel about that? How did it happen? Was retiring his idea or forced onto him? But how could I ask those or the others piling up behind them when I didn't want him to ask questions about me and my past?

"Well, their loss is our gain. And the school system's. Your old department are idiots." Clara's outrage abruptly shifted. "Are you talking to our sheriff's department about getting a job here?"

"No. Why?"

"Oh. Just wondered." Her airiness wasn't entirely convincing. "It would make sense. They'd be lucky to have you."

"Thanks, Clara, but I'm liking the way this is working out now. All except my current boss's brainstorms."

Before I could retaliate, Clara said, "You're a big fake, Teague. You love her improvements. I see that gleam in your eyes when she comes up with something new. But right now I'm going to steal her away to talk over this murder on the way to the yoga studio."

He groaned. "I might even prefer the constant change orders to that."

CHAPTER TWENTY-ONE

WE TOOK A quick detour to the Roger—the supermarket—for Clara to pick up dog food for LuLu. Feeding that skinny canine was like shoveling enough coal to keep steelworks running.

On impulse, instead of heading directly to the studio to help with the remembrance preparations, I walked across Beguiling Way, to the front of the barbershop, then turned my back on its window to consider the studio.

Not as the Beguiling Way yoga studio per se, but as a building.

On the left was the flower shop. On the right the stubby opening and then the music store.

For the brick on the studio's mirrored wall to be a consistent surface as Tina had said, that wall had to run deeper than the stubby opening.

What was behind the end wall of that gap?

The music store looked as deep as the studio, perhaps built at the same time. Each backed up to a two-story building that occupied half, possibly a little more, of the depth from Tanner Street to Beguiling Way. The flower shop, though, had a much smaller footprint. A three-story building loomed from behind, leaving the flower shop a thin slice of real estate.

"What are you looking at?" Clara joined me, waving to someone in the barbershop before turning to mirror my view.

"The buildings. Wondering about their history."

"Now? We don't have all the time in the world to solve this thing, you know."

I pulled my gaze from the buildings to her. "Why not? It's not like they've accused the wrong person. Or even suspect a wrong person." Which was a nice change, since one of the people they'd suspected last time had been me.

"Because I've signed up for a course. And it starts soon."

"Course? What cour—Oh. How to be a virtual assistant?"

"Yes. The one your aunt's friends said was solid. It has great reviews and testimonials from people I can see have set up their own businesses. It starts the end of next week. So, I sure hope we've solved this by then so I can concentrate."

I chuckled. "Getting practice at meeting deadlines, huh?"

"Exactly. Now, if you want to know about the history, you should go to the historical society."

"I didn't know there was one."

I'd delved a bit into the area's history, but from brochures and what Amy Kackley, a librarian who lived down the street from me, had said.

Clara huffed. "We have a lot of history."

"I don't doubt that. I just didn't know about the historical society. I wonder if Amy could direct me to a good source about the buildings."

"Amy? You don't need Amy. I know the perfect person. Give me a minute."

She whipped out her phone and began thumb-tapping a text.

"There. That should—" Before she could finish or put away her phone, a ping announced a reply. "Great. You're all set for tomorrow. Urban will meet you at the historical society—it's the original courthouse building behind the New New Courthouse."

North Bend County never let go of courthouses. Even after they'd built a new one and repurposed the old, it was still call courthouse. There was the New New Courthouse—the one actually functioning as a courthouse—the Old New Courthouse, the Old Courthouse, and the Old Old Courthouse, now the historical society.

"That's great. Thank you." My gaze still wandering over the buildings, my peripheral vision caught her smile and wave at someone across Beguiling Way.

"*Now* who are you—?" It was Alan, the grandfather from the florist shop, walking past the studio, heading south, away from his shop.

"C'mon, let's go help at the studio," Clara said. "And see what we can find out."

"You go ahead. I'm going to stop by the florist."

"No way are you going without me. You think she's there?"

"Sign says open and with Alan gone, it seems likely."

Likely turned into certainty when we pushed opened the door and heard the cheerful bell.

Mamie's welcoming smile fell when she saw us. She tried to rescue it without full success. "Hello, we're closing real soon…" When that didn't turn us around, she released a breath. "May I help you with something?"

"Yes. Are you absolutely sure about what time you left Monday night, Mamie? We know you didn't reach the hospital until much later than usual."

She glanced around, as if her grandfather could have been lurking unseen in the tiny space.

"It was my usual time."

"The hospital knows it wasn't."

"What difference does it make? Some maniac off the Interstate killed her. That's what the sheriff's department said."

I looked at her steadily. "That is what they said."

"You… You don't think it was?"

"No. We don't. So, you can see, if you were here later than you said and you saw Xanthe or anything, it could be important. What you didn't see could be important, too."

"I wasn't here later." That shot out of her. She looked at Clara. "It was like you said, class was still going on, she was still alive, with all of you there when I left."

Clara appeared on the verge of patting her hand and saying, "There, there."

I spoke before she could. "Mamie, that doesn't add up. You can't have left here at eight, yet been an hour late to the hospital. Unless…"

She licked her lips. Pulled in a breath as if to speak, then let it back out, looking down.

The cheerful bell sounded behind us.

"I was telling these ladies the flowers are all set for the studio tomorrow for the remembrance," Mamie said hurriedly.

We turned to smile at her grandfather.

We each left with another bouquet, suspicious looks from Alan, and no eye contact from Mamie.

CHAPTER TWENTY-TWO

TINA ALREADY HAD a protective covering over the hardwood floor in the studio area. It usually only felt our bare or sock-covered feet, but tomorrow there would be street shoes and the folding chairs a few volunteers were wiping down. Others were cleaning the cubbies in the vestibule while a couple more cleaned, straightened, and organized the props cubbies from convenience to precise order.

Tina and Liz were on ladders, hanging a poster-sized photo of Xanthe over a section of mirrors.

We stopped near the bottom of Tina's ladder and waited.

"Hold your side in place a second," Liz instructed Tina.

Tina looked down at us. "You didn't have to bring flowers. We're getting them tomorrow from the florist next door."

"We know. We were just there. These are for home," Clara said.

"Nice. Now—"

Before Tina could set us to work, I had a question.

"Tina, when you were renovating, why couldn't you put the mechanicals where you wanted?"

"The inspector said something about the strength of the wall not being right on that side of the building and made us swap. Guess it's okay if it falls in on someone using the loo, but can't have it falling in on the furnace and stuff."

I thought of the patched arch behind the sink and guessed that was the weak area. If it gave way with someone in there, which was worse? Bricks tumbling down on you while you washed your hands or bricks tumbling down next to you while you were using the toilet. Tough call.

"But the rest of that side's okay?" Did Clara envision crumbling brick and drywall descending, perhaps turning shavasana into true corpse pose?

"It's only a patched area in the restroom. The rest is plenty strong. But that side looked messy anyway. This side—" She nodded toward the mirrored wall. "—is all one brick. The brick on the other side was from two buildings with a patch of a third color in between."

"There," Tina and Liz said together.

With the photo secured, Liz climbed down her ladder with a "Bathroom break, be right back" explanation to Tina. She nodded to us on her way.

I smiled up at Tina.

"You've got quite a crew here. All the people wiping down the chairs and—"

"Eloise has done the hardest work. She picked up the chairs from a church lending them to us. We formed a line to unload them, but she'd loaded them all into truck she borrowed by herself. And now she's gone back for a couple tables. She's pushing herself too hard."

"I wonder if Eloise is feeling bad about not being there for Xanthe."

"Why would she feel that way?" Tina sounded even more distracted than uninterested as she looked over her opposite shoulder for a view of the chair-wipers.

"Being at the ballgame with you and the others Monday night."

"She wasn't with us at the game. She joined us when we came back and had a drink at a bar in Stringer." She frowned and turned toward me. "Why would—?"

"After the game? Must have been late." I was glad Clara asked that, because she made it sound like a casual question, and Tina's frown disappeared. My follow-up would have sounded like an alibi-check.

"Game went pretty quick. Pitcher's duel—"

Clara nodded wisely. I needed to ask her later if she knew the phrase pitcher's duel and its implications for us, because the game would have been shorter than usual.

"—so we stayed for the last out, but we were getting out of the parking lot there well before ten. Called Eloise then. She was waiting at the bar with the first round for all of us. Xanthe was originally going to come, too, but she chose to sub for Liz over going with us. Just as well."

"Why?" I asked, doing quick math that added up to Eloise having an hour plus after our class ended to kill Xanthe and get to the bar.

"Hmm?" Tina responded absently, her attention now on what she could see of the vestibule area. "Could have been a little awkward. Xanthe's dating Eloise's ex and he was with us."

Refusing to look toward Clara, though my peripheral sight caught her eyes going big, I produced a casual, "Oh?"

"Yeah. As it turned out, it gave him and Eloise a chance to see each other casually, without—" She froze, her face going stiff with dismay. "I didn't mean—I wasn't thinking. It wasn't a big deal."

"Totally understand, Tina. You were back in the moment of that evening. That's all. Don't kick yourself."

"I was. For an instant I forgot. I actually forgot."

I reached up and patted her wrist. "You have to now and then. It's the way to cope. Do you know Eloise's ex from banking?"

"Banking? No. He's a fireman."

"Of course. That was Xanthe's ex who was in banking."

"Was he?" Her focus was all on me now. So was her frown.

I smiled. "You need to put us to work. What should we do?"

That snapped her back into her happy place. Organizing. "There's a spare bulletin board in the closet across from the restroom. It probably needs to be cleaned. And there's an easel over there. We want to set up the board on the easel and put photos on it. The photos are in a cubby out front."

Clara sidled up to me as we headed for the closet. "Xanthe was dating Eloise's ex. *That's* a motive."

"And her timeline just developed opportunity."

WE FOUND MORE than we expected when we went in search of the bulletin board.

First, at the back of the mini hall between the restroom and furnace area, a door stood open, revealing a deep, dark closet we'd never seen before, and didn't choose to explore.

Next, we found the wood-framed board, fortunately at the front, yet festooned with enough cobwebs to make a Halloween decorator proud.

Then, Clara went into the restroom to dampen paper towels and found Berrie Vittlow.

"I'm cleaning in here," she said, the defensiveness as much of a giveaway as her having no cleaning supplies at hand and the restroom already being clean.

"Right." Clara shot me a look through the open door. "Answer our questions and we won't tell Tina you're hiding out."

"I'm tired."

"Because of the cancer?" I asked.

"No," she snapped. "I'm cancer free, even if the doctors won't say it. I don't need your pity. Go ahead, ask your stupid questions."

She'd hide out, she'd fib about working, she'd whine about being tired—that I expected of Berrie. But not accept sympathy for cancer—that was unexpected.

But psychoanalyzing this woman was not my goal.

Refocusing, I asked, "When you told us before class Tuesday about Tina coming in and telling Liz about Xanthe being killed, you said someone was going to crumple to the floor—who?"

"What do you mean, who?"

I considered saying *who* was basic and widely understood. But that was Aunt Kit speaking and I didn't think Kit would get much out of Berrie.

"Let's go back a bit. Where were you when you heard Xanthe had been killed?"

"Getting signed in by Liz."

"Good. What happened next?"

"She signed me in."

I resisted grinding my teeth. "And then?"

"I took off my shoes and put them in a cubby. I do my shoes first so they're not on top of anything else, because sometimes the shoes get things on them from the dog park."

"You don't have separate dog park shoes? With all the—?"

I interrupted Clara—not because I didn't agree with her sentiments, but to keep this going. "You, put your shoes in—" I made a mental note to notice which cubby she favored and avoid it from now on. "—the cubby and then everything else. What happened next?"

"She came in and said she'd been shot and I thought she'd fall down right there."

"Who came in?"

She looked at me as I were dense. "Tina, of course."

"Tina said Xanthe was dead?"

"That's what I said."

"It *wasn't* what you said," Clara objected. "You threw in a bunch of *shes* until nobody could possibly know who you were talking about. Who came in? Who said Xanthe was dead? Who—"

"Tina, I told you. Weren't you listening?"

"—nearly dropped to the floor?"

"Tina, of course." She clicked her tongue at our stupidity.

"It could have been—"

I touched Clara's arm to stop her from saying Liz's name. "Tina looked like she'd fall to the floor?"

"Yes," she snapped. "Was white as all get-out and nearly hyperventilating."

"How about Liz? How did she react?"

"Liz? I didn't notice. Shocked, I guess. But I had other things on my mind."

Like getting into the studio to be the town crier with the news before Tina or Liz could.

"Did you really see Liz with a man Monday?"

"Yes."

"Do you know his name?"

"No."

"Have you seen her with him before?"

"No. Don't know more about him. But I'll give you an answer for free—she didn't look sick to me."

Clara asked, "Berrie, what did you tell the deputy when he asked if you were the last one to leave class Monday night?"

"I didn't tell him anything, because he didn't ask."

Clara and I exchanged a look. Berrie must have had Eckles. Had he missed only her or failed to ask any of the people he interviewed?

"*Were* you the last one?"

"No. That skinny, pretentious woman was still there and so was the one who's falling apart after having a baby."

"But everybody else was gone?"

"I said that, didn't I? I've answered enough of your useless questions. You're not the only ones who can figure things out. That florist girl saw something, didn't she? Hah. I thought so. Now, leave me alone."

WE DIDN'T LEAVE Berrie alone immediately. We took time to dampen paper towels to clean the bulletin board.

That would show her who was in charge.

After setting up the board on the easel in the front corner, we went into the vestibule to get the photos.

An instructor was protesting. "Fern, you don't need to do this. We've got plenty of people who can—"

"I've been scrubbing for twice as long as you've been alive, Natalie." The octogenarian's face was flushed and shiny. "No reason to stop now."

"You know, Fern," Clara said, "we could use help going through all these photographs and deciding which go on the board in the studio. Would you help? I'd put them all on."

She clicked her tongue. "Editing is key, along with placement. Come along, you two."

The younger woman gave us a grateful smile.

I hurried ahead to place a chair in front of the board for Fern.

Clara and I sat on the floor on either side of the chair, handing her photos and hopping up to place them on the board when she selected one. A photo of Xanthe and a boy in graduation cap and gown, who had to be her son, took the center spot.

We'd filled half the board with holiday shots, yoga poses, and candid pics, when Fern held up a larger photo.

"Ah, this is a lovely one of Xanthe, Eloise, and Liz here at the studio. I'm glad they're talking again."

My eyes met Clara's as she said, "Xanthe and Eloise? They weren't talking? Because of that guy?"

"I don't know about that. It was Liz who wasn't speaking to Xanthe when she began teaching here. Something about money. Such a shame she and her husband are having a difficult time."

WE GOT NO more from Fern.

I suspected she was playing vague on purpose, regretting what she'd said.

If so, she played it very, very well.

Though perhaps not quite as well as Eve and Julia, who arrived to "help" as we were wrapping up. Well before they came in, I'd seen them through the front window, both tapping away at their phones in the middle of Beguiling Way, so I strongly suspected the timing was deliberate. They volunteered to stay to clean up, but under Tina's directions we'd done that as we worked, so we all headed out together.

Clara went down the first of two steps from the studio door to the sidewalk just ahead of me and stopped.

Mamie was walking along the sidewalk from the flower shop toward us and heading for—yes, the van parked in the tiny spot between the studio and the music shop.

The girl had guts or ironclad practicality to park there, especially with Beguiling Way sinking fast into darkness while the streets at either end remained bright from the evening sun.

Clara waved.

No response.

Mamie was going to ignore us.

Clara didn't give up that easily. "If we can get her aside for a minute…" she muttered. Then she called loudly, "Hi, Mamie."

The girl nodded toward us, but with no smile. She couldn't have waved even if she'd wanted to because she carried a three-foot wide box, with flowers apparently blooming from its top. I suspected this was one of the boxes I'd seen in the shop, used to secure vases for transport and to separate bouquets to avoid mashed up flowers.

Clara stepped down the next step. "Can we talk to you, Mamie?"

She swung wide of Clara, going off the sidewalk and into the alley-way. "I don't have time. I'm running late as it is and—"

The vehicle seemed to come from nowhere, its engine loud with the strain of acceleration.

But, of course, to get here so quickly it must have already been off of Haines Avenue and onto the pedestrian-only Beguiling Way.

No headlights.

No license plates.

A small, beat-up old van that looked like it had been painted dark gray with cans of spray paint, blending in to the dimness of Beguiling Way.

I noticed all that in a snapshot.

Then an instantaneous calculation of complex intersections of speed and direction I couldn't have accomplished in a month with paper and pen—

"*Mamie!* Look out!"

She stopped. The van didn't.

I was too far. I couldn't reach her.

Clara, in front of me, leaped forward, both hands going around Mamie's left arm, spinning the girl and herself back toward the studio like an Olympic hammer-thrower in reverse.

The motion jerked Mamie's left hand from the cardboard box. She kept hold of the right side, but the rest floated in the air.

Until the van side-swiped the box, wrenching it from Mamie's hand as she and Clara collapsed backward and I tried to haul them up the steps, even though the van was past now.

"Call 911," I shouted.

"Calling," came back in a calmer voice than mine. Tina's, I

thought.

"Are you okay? Mamie? Clara?" We were untangling ourselves from each other, with me at the bottom of the pile and the edge of the top stair digging into the back of my thighs.

"Okay. I'm okay," Clara said. "Mamie?"

"I... I don't know." Her voice shook.

"Okay, slowly, slowly," Clara instructed.

Shredded flowers, the broken glass of vases marked the point of impact that would have been van and girl instead of van and box, if not for Clara. The smell of vegetation and wet cardboard surrounded us.

"Oh, my God," cried Eve. "The crazy drivers these days. Of course, she *was* walking in the middle of the street."

"Pedestrians only," someone grumbled at her from the back.

I looked around at the people behind—above us.

Belatedly, now that danger was past, Julia Trippen clutched her friend Eve's arm with both hands. Whether to pull Eve further from the path of the vehicle or to hold herself up I didn't know.

Several voices rose, but Eve screamed over them. "They came right at her. She must know something. She must know something about the murder!"

"What?" sputtered Clara. "You just said—"

"Blood." Tina's voice came from behind us. We all turned. She was on the phone, leaning over from the doorway. "There is blood on at least one of you three down on the steps."

"It's you, Sheila. You must be bleeding. Don't move," Clara ordered.

CHAPTER TWENTY-THREE

THE BLOOD WAS on me, but it wasn't mine. It was from a cut to Mamie's arm, caused by flying glass.

But that determination didn't come until EMTs and deputies had arrived, and they followed well after Mamie's grandfather, who wrapped her arm tenderly with his shirt until medical care arrived.

She kept apologizing about the destroyed flowers and deliveries they'd miss.

Mitch from the music shop, who'd been locking up at the time, volunteered to deliver what was in the van. He took only a little paint off their van when he backed out.

No one had gotten any better description than I had. They dispatched deputies to see if anyone on Haines Avenue had seen the van beforehand or if anyone on Court Avenue had seen it after.

I wasn't optimistic.

Neither was Deputy Hensen.

He said as much when he took Clara and me aside to go over our statements again.

At the end, he eyed us for a moment before saying, "O'Donnell says you two are observant."

"He did?" Clara glowed.

"But don't exercise enough caution. So, watch it." Hensen walked away.

Clara grasped my arm before I could express my opinion of those opinions, and said, "A near-death right here where Xanthe was murdered? That was no accident. That poor girl could have been killed.

She nearly was. And not by some maniac off the Interstate. Berrie…"

"I know. But she probably told a million people whatever she thinks she knows."

She breathed out. "Still, we need to figure this out before someone else *is* killed."

I agreed. Though what I most wanted to do was talk to Mamie. If someone thought she knew something, she'd be far better off if she told it to as many people as she could. Starting with Clara and me.

Okay, maybe starting with her grandfather and the sheriff's department, but then Clara and me.

But I could hear her telling a deputy I didn't recognize that it must have been an accident and she'd been in the alleyway, so they must not have seen her.

✧ ✧ ✧ ✧

THE HEADLIGHTS OF Clara's car fell on Teague sitting on the back steps of my house, flanked by my dog and his.

"Uh-oh," she said, echoing my internal response. "Will you think I'm a chicken if I drop you off? I need to get home and tell Ned about this before he hears. I could use some aspirin or something, too."

"Dropping me off is fine. Definitely take the aspirin. And get a good night's sleep. We'll talk tomorrow."

"Okay, thanks. You, too, with the aspirin."

I walked slowly to the back steps.

Three sets of eyes regarded me. Two of the sets, however, accompanied their regarding with tail-thumping.

I'd been determined not to speak first, but my eyes had adjusted to the level of illumination from the backdoor light and curiosity won.

"Why does my dog's muzzle have orange on it?"

"Mine does, too, you can't see it against the black."

"Cheetos?"

"They were upset because you were so late getting back from the yoga studio."

"It isn't any later than when we have night class."

"They might have heard something about a hit and run at your location."

"It was an almost hit and run. But how——? Do you listen to a police scanner?"

"It's an app."

"Of course it is." Silence settled again.

I couldn't reach both dogs without being right in Teague's face, so
I petted mine. Murphy, no dummy, got up, went behind his human
and wedged himself in next to Gracie, so I could pet him, too. I did.

Something about petting the dogs let me say, "We're okay, Teague.
Mamie, the girl from the flower shop took the brunt of it, but she's
okay, too."

"Sit down. Tell me."

He and then the dogs scooched over, making room for me next to
Gracie.

I sat, the dogs between us. I told.

He didn't say much. He asked good questions.

But lying in bed later, after a long hot shower in hopes of keeping
stiffness at bay, I wasn't sure it had gotten us anywhere.

With the investigation, I mean.

DAY FIVE
FRIDAY

CHAPTER TWENTY-FOUR

CLARA AND I shared soreness reports at our dog park rendezvous.

We'd both live.

Clara went home to bake a cake in preparation for Ned's birthday party the next night.

After lunch, with no sign of Teague or Murphy today, I showered and dressed several steps up from dog park attire. It took a while to find the right pieces in the various places I'd stashed them. While I was at it, I found a suit from my Manhattan wardrobe and hung it on the shower curtain to ease out a wrinkle across the back of the jacket.

Then I headed toward the Old Old Courthouse behind the New New Courthouse.

URBAN PARHEM WAS shorter than me and wiry. He had a gray brush mustache and mostly gray hair. His glasses were dark and businesslike. It was either the glasses or a resemblance to someone I'd previously known, but either way I immediately trusted him.

That sentiment might not have been reciprocated.

"You're truly interested in these buildings? It's a fascinating history," he said, as if he usually had to persuade people. "But…"

"I am interested, and I'm looking forward to it."

The skepticism fell away and his face shone with the joy of a dog tasting whipped cream for the first time.

Not that I'd know what a dog looked like tasting whipped cream for the first time. Not that my dog comes running at the sound of it coming out of the can. Not that my dog can distinguish the sound of a whipped cream can opening from any other container in the refrigerator.

But even if she could distinguish the whipped cream can, at least it wasn't Cheetos. Never Cheetos.

Urban handed me a pair of gloves and an old-fashioned magnifying glass, then went to a wide cabinet with many shallow drawers, selecting the bottom one.

He lovingly placed a large map on a table. "This was the town's original plan. A copy, actually. The original is in the archives, but this is a faithful copy from more than a century ago."

I recognized the Haines Tavern town square immediately. The handwritten street names marked its rectangle, then echoed out in ever-larger iterations. The extensions of the streets around the square created shorter blocks to the east and west and longer blocks to the north and south.

"It's elegant," I said.

He beamed. "Like the design of a formal garden or a table by a master woodworker. Interestingly, the four sides of the square—which, of course, is not actually square—initially spawned different areas. Beyond the churches—" He pointed to the east. "—a few wealthy families established an enclave. Beyond the courthouse—" His gloved finger pointed north. "—the middle class built their homes. Doctors, lawyers, and shopkeepers. Convenient for the lawyers with the courthouse right there. And for the shopkeepers, because this area became what you might call the commercial center."

Now he pointed to the streets to the west, past the hardware store, post office and library on Market Street.

"And the southern quadrant? The area beyond Haines Tavern?" That historic building took up as much space on this map as the courthouse across from it, with outbuildings scattered behind the inn.

"Ah. To the south was the area of glamor and seediness, possibility and poverty, ambition and despair."

I raised my eyebrows.

He twinkled a bit, but otherwise remained solemn.

"The tavern brought all sorts together. It was the closest thing the county had to a playhouse. Indeed, there was an effort at one point to change its name to the North Bend Opera House. The Haines of that time had fallen on rough times. But a younger brother returned from Chicago where he'd built a fortune, bought the property, settled all debts, and secured its name.

"Whatever its name, it was the entertainment center for all of the county and beyond. There is a legend Charles Dickens stayed and lectured there on one of his American tours, though no proof has been deemed strong enough to earn the tavern a *Dickens slept here* placard. Still, well-known singers of the day, traveling plays, and such were all held there. And then, in the streets beyond it came a section of bawdy houses—interestingly close to the wealthy houses. Behind the bawdy houses, poor worker cottages. It was glamor in the front and seedy in the back.

"That's how it was for a long time. In the post-World War II boom, they started building up here." He pointed past the northern-most road on this map, into the territory where my house was. "Working from close into town to farther away on the north, west, and east. Then, gradually, they built on the edge of the southern area. Down by the sheriff's department." In Gracie's map of the world, that was down by the dog park. "It's only been the past decade they've moved in closer on the south side. Infill and renovating. What was once the most notorious bawdy house is now fixed up, looking like a million dollars."

He replaced the map and selected another from a slightly higher drawer. The design was immediately recognizable, but with much more detail, showing buildings not only immediately around the square, but growing out like rings of a tree.

"What you want is over here." He pointed to the western section, moving aside to let me get closer. "This is how Beguiling Way was organized in 1891. Of course it would be a hundred years and more before it was called anything but the alley behind Tanner Street. Still, it had a certain energy all its own, even then."

In this plan, the fronts of buildings lined up neatly along Tanner Street, but the backs resembled a jack o'lantern's grin, right down to a stub of a building representing a broken tooth.

I squinted to read the handwriting. "Does that say barber? Oh, general store and these are stables on the other side of the alley."

"Yes, and next is a mason's office with storage behind. All gone, now. They were mostly frame."

"Including the mason's buildings?" I asked.

"Yes, indeed. Precisely like the cobbler's children having no shoes. Although that had become a brick building by the turn of the century."

"What's this long one in the middle?" I pointed to a building nearly reaching to Beguiling Way.

"A furniture store. Just a moment…" He went to a different cabinet, opened a drawer, seemed to fall asleep an instant, then snatched at something like a bird diving on a worm. "Here."

He came back with a photograph in the faded monochrome that made you think history was experienced in black and white.

What looked like the float trailers we decorated for homecoming in high school held a dozen young women. The trailer was towed by four horses with two bowler-hatted men driving.

"Here it is." He emphasized it with a stubby finger.

Beyond the eye-catching trailer and girls was a brick building with an awning over two large windows flanking a front door. The next floor had three double windows, with another three single windows under a slanted roof.

"Green's Furniture Emporium."

"Emporium?"

"Angus Green had aspirations of building a dynasty. Didn't work out that way, but his handsome Furniture Emporium building does still stand. Smith-Flarenge occupies the first floor."

I mentally matched the drawings on the unfamiliar map to what I knew of the block.

"That's the little flower shop on the Beguiling Way side, right."

"That it is—both the flower shop and little."

"So, this empty spot on the map must be where the yoga studio is now? What does it say on the building facing Tanner Street at the front of the lot?"

"Boots, shoes, and repairs, speaking of cobblers."

"No wonder they had trouble getting all that in. And the big empty space behind it?"

"That was the yard for the building. A number of the trades needed space for their craft. If they were tanning leather, the neighbors probably wished it was a bigger space. Here's another photo." He placed it atop the others. "This is after they'd torn down the frame building with the boot, shoes, and repair shop, and before they built the current building. You can see Green's didn't quite take up the full depth of its lot."

It was a side view of the Emporium building with two empty lots between it and the camera. A crew of men in work clothes stood in the nearer empty lot, posing for the camera.

In the alleyway to the left, a horse stood patiently at the end of the building, possibly enjoying the shade of the overhanging roof beside the loading dock. Toward the back of the building a woman's figure wearing a light-colored apron blurred in an open door in the side of the Emporium. Not posing for the camera, but blurred by motion.

I peered closer with the magnifying glass. She was emptying a bucket. A woman hard at work.

"When did all this—" I gestured to the gap-toothed look of the map on either side of the then-alleyway. "—get filled in to become Beguiling Way."

"It was filled in mostly during a building boom in the 1920s. Then there was a clean-up around the Bicentennial—" He quirked a grin at me. "That was 1976, young lady."

I grinned back. "That I knew."

"Very good. Well, the next spruce up was in 1998—our county's bicentennial. That was when interest in what became Beguiling Way took root, though it didn't become what it is now until the past seven, eight years."

"What about more recent building? Say, after the current configuration existed."

"Let's see." He hummed to himself a bit as he pulled out one higher drawer, then another. "After World War II, they had aerial photos done of the entire county. Most useful in locating early building sites amid fields and open lands. Ah. Yes, yes."

He brought back an oversized aerial photograph, this one showing only a slice of the western edge of the square, Tanner Street, the alley that became Beguiling Way, and the block beyond it.

Growing more accustomed to connecting these overhead views to what I knew from street level, I zeroed in on what would become the yoga studio. And had a surprise.

"This area, this would be between what's now the yoga studio and the music store, right?" I didn't wait for his confirmation. "But the gap between them goes full depth. The gap's only about a third as deep now."

He peered at it. "Oh, yes, that storage area was built much later. I recall it being added to serve offices accessed from Tanner Street as well as the buildings on either side—now the studio and the music shop. That was only done twenty or so years ago. I distinctly remember watching Elmer Branter and his son, Fred, laying the bricks."

CHAPTER TWENTY-FIVE

"**THAT MUST BE** her son, with the ex-husband behind him." Clara used her eyes to indicate the corner without moving her head. "And his mother."

We'd just arrived at the remembrance gathering for Xanthe Anstead.

The area by the front steps had been cleared of glass and other debris. The blood was nearly invisible on the steps.

The studio was packed, with Xanthe's son, ex-husband, and ex-mother-in-law in the back corner by the prop cubbies and near the large poster photo of her smiling face. Her son took surreptitious looks toward it between greeting those who found their way to him.

Ethan Branter, easily recognizable from the graduation snapshot as well as his resemblance to Xanthe, stood tall and straight.

His father and grandmother resembled each other, which wasn't flattering to either of them. He might have been a solid specimen as a young man. Now he was a lump.

"Let's split up to cover more ground," Clara said. "I'll see what I can find out over by the bulletin board."

"Good idea."

She went right, I made my way toward the back left to where Liz was talking with Alan and Mamie from the flower shop. I didn't see a likely candidate to be Liz's husband. Perhaps she'd come alone.

Before I arrived, Liz said something to the grandfather and granddaughter and went the other direction.

Had she seen me approaching? I thought she had.

Half-tempted to pursue her, manners won out, because Alan and Mamie had definitely seen me.

"How are you, Mamie?"

"I'm fine. Really." She cradled her bandaged arm with the other hand.

"She's cut, shaken up, bruised, scraped and it's a damned miracle she didn't get hurt worse. Idiot drivers not looking where they're going."

Ah. She'd given Alan the same story as the sheriff's department.

Mamie looked away. "Accidents happen, Gramps."

"Then responsible people stop to see if they hurt somebody, not to mention, not driving like a maniac on Beguiling Way in the first place." He held up a hand when she would have spoken. "Doesn't matter. You're not going anywhere alone. Not even the thirty feet from the shop door to the van."

"Gramps, we can't keep the store running if we close up for you to come with me on deliveries. Plus, you need to be there so early to get the deliveries and overnight orders…"

"Then we'll lose the shop. I'm with you every step of the way tonight and tomorrow night and Sunday night and—"

"Not Sunday night, Gramps. You can't miss your meeting."

I didn't know what the meeting was for, but from his expression she'd scored a point. He rallied. "I'll be late. First time, but it's worth it. I'll get you packed up and on your way to the hospital, then I'll go to my meeting."

"Okay, Gramps."

But as I said I hoped she healed quickly, then left them, I had the feeling Mamie had gotten what she wanted.

SINCE I WAS already at the back, I cut across to the other side, where Xanthe's son stood.

I moved close enough to listen, but kept three-quarters turned away, so it wouldn't be obvious.

"All these crazy-ass yoga types don't know the least thing about that no-account girl. Boo-hoo-hooing all over the place."

Joyce Branter was talking. About every fifth word her otherwise penetrating voice stretched out the syllables into a whine.

"It's what Ethan wants," said a male voice like a downshifting gravel truck.

I glanced over my shoulder. The speaker had to be the man identified as Fred Branter.

Unless he was disguising his voice now or had disguised it Monday night, he was not the *What are you doing here?*" interrupter.

I hadn't realized I'd had high hopes he was until they sank. I had no idea how Urban Parhem's news that Fred had assisted his father in constructing the storage area fit in, but it sure seemed like it would. And if his voice matched…

But it didn't.

And Ethan remained silent, so I made no headway there, either.

I mingled through the gathering, looking for men I didn't recognize from class and trying to listen to their voices with no luck until I was down to the last option.

Ethan.

Xanthe's son had moved away from his relatives and was talking with Eloise.

I edged closer, while turning away from them with a half-raised hand, as if acknowledging someone.

"Well, he's got nerve to ask you for an invitation." Eloise sounded decidedly un-Zen-like.

"He wanted to come. And Mom wouldn't have stopped anybody from coming if it would make them feel better."

Not the voice of the class interrupter. Maybe in a few years… But too young, too light.

Eloise sighed. "You're a good soul, Ethan, but I hope he's a no-show. Oh. Hi, Sheila."

Apparently, my edging closer had gone over the edge into obvious lurking.

"Eloise. Hi. I didn't see you there. This is a lovely gathering. I'm so glad you did this."

"Thank you. This is Ethan Branter, Xanthe's son, who did a great deal of the planning for this." Her gaze slashed toward the young man's father and grandmother, who—her look clearly said—had done nothing. "Ethan, this is Sheila Mackey, one of the many students your mom impacted."

That wasn't exactly true—along with using impact as a verb, which she'd have heard about from Kit.

"Excuse me. Looks like Tina needs me." Eloise squeezed his arm and left us.

I extended my hand and the boy shook it.

"I'm so sorry for your loss, Ethan. Your mom's love of yoga and of teaching it came through clearly in every minute of class with her." That was absolutely true.

He nodded. His jaw working.

"I didn't know your mother as well as a lot of people here, only from the studio."

He looked up, blinked hard, and dropped his head again. "She loved it here. It changed her. Made her happy. Sorry. I gotta—"

"Of course." I patted his upper arm and turned away. Both to let him believe I hadn't seen the tears and to block others' view of him.

Teague O'Donnell appeared by my side, also with his back to the teen.

"Lovely event," I said, to mask the sounds behind us. Then whispered, "What on earth are you doing here?"

Ignoring the question, he said in his normal voice, "It is a lovely event." After a pause, he added, "Until you made a kid cry."

"Teague—"

"Don't worry. He's gone. What did you say to him?"

"That I knew his mother from the yoga studio. He said it made her happy and it changed her. His own words did it. Nothing I said."

"Uh-huh."

I narrowed my eyes. "Silent observer," I reminded him.

"That's why I came. To observe." He took a small sip from his cup. "Is all this stuff healthy?"

"Yes. No Cheetos allowed at the Beguiling Way Yoga Studio. You can go observe somewhere else. I need to talk to people."

I'D HEARD THE whispered name Smith-Flarenge and connected it to a group of four that stuck closely together. A late-thirties overly groomed man, a woman with blonde-streaked hair in her early twenties with those eyebrows that look like they're pasted on from a photocopied sheet, and two women older than him with smiles that looked as if they hurt.

On my way to them, my path crossed with Eloise's for a third time.

That's the way with some of these events. You aim for someone else, but somehow your mingling keeps bringing you back to the same person.

Even though people were talking quietly, the number of conversations made it difficult to hear, so I took her arm and leaned close to say, "This is a great turnout, Eloise."

"It is. Maybe that will help Ethan. Even his father and grandmother are—*Unbelievable*. He *would* show up."

I turned to see who she was looking at.

A man in his early thirties, talking with—more accurately, pretending to listen to—Fern.

He was attractive in the way the heroine's wrong-for-her former boyfriend in a feel-good made-for-TV movie is attractive. Good hair, teeth, features, body, coming together in a way that wasn't quite right. Like his former co-worker he was groomed to an unrealistic gloss.

"We don't want him here. They don't want him here." A jerk of Eloise's head indicated the Smith-Flarenge knot, all facing away from the man, except the blonde-streaked young woman, who was regarding him curiously.

"Xanthe's ex?" Who had figured largely in Professor Andronski's account. "The one she dumped for yoga?"

Eloise chuffed. "That's him. Vincent Shornfell. At least he didn't bring a date."

He wore an overly confident smile, but his eyes kept flicking past Fern toward the back door. Looking for an escape.

"A date?"

"Yeah. Xanthe said after she dumped him, he'd show up places she'd be with different dates, each one younger and more bimbo than the previous. Except the most recent one a month or so ago. Xanthe said she only got a glimpse, but she seemed more normal. Definitely a grown-up. Oh, God, now he's going to try to talk to the financial people? What an idiot. They frog-marched him out the door after firing him. Xanthe'd broken up with him right before because, she'd said, she'd finally had her eyes opened to what he was. Then she quit herself. If he thinks he's going to talk to Ethan—"

She broke off as she pushed into the crowd, heading for Xanthe's son.

Shornfell was on the move, but not for Ethan. His target was the hair-streaked young woman.

Trying to catch Clara's eye, I made a beeline to intercept Shornfell, hoping to hear his voice. But Clara was in earnest conversation with the auburn-haired woman from our class, who had covered her gray roots since I last saw her.

"Sheila."

I would have ignored being hailed at a volume that could snag a cab in Manhattan, but Berrie also grabbed my arm, swinging me around, so I had to apologize to three other attendees I bumped before I was brought face to face with Berrie and Laura, the new mother.

"Tell this woman she has to get a dog."

"My baby—"

"That's my point exactly," Berrie interrupted her. "Dogs help kids' immune systems. They also teach responsibility. With a dog a kid's never alone no matter how mean other kids are. The dog actually listens." A glimpse into Berrie's childhood?

I looked over my shoulder.

Vincent Shornfell was having words with the man from Smith-Flarenge. Not audible from this distance, but obvious. A few heads turned toward them. They both smiled. The other man's not pleasant, Shornfell's aimed at the hair-streaked young woman.

"It's practically child abuse not to have a dog." Berrie continued at a volume that gave me no chance of hearing what was being said between Shornfell and the other man. "You have to get—"

Laura, her vacant gaze pinned over my shoulder, looked even worse than usual. None of her clothes were inside out or stained with dubious substances, but her face was so dead white I yanked my arm free from Berrie in the expectation that I'd have to catch Laura any second.

"—at least one. Boston terriers are best. I have a couple I'm fostering. Come over tomorrow and—"

"Excuse me." Laura pivoted and plunged away.

"No sale, Berrie." I spun around to head back the way I'd been going.

I was almost to the Smith-Flarenge group when I realized Shornfell wasn't there anymore. I scanned the room and caught his profile as he exited toward the vestibule, moving like a man who wasn't going to linger and chat.

Desperately, I looked for Clara or Teague. If one was near the door and I could make eye-contact with them...

I couldn't spot either one.

After a shoulder-slumping second of disappointment, I side-stepped close to the compact knot.

"Well, that was interesting," the young woman with blonde streaked hair said.

"Awkward as hell," came a male voice from the other side of the group.

"What was he thinking? Showing up? Talking to us?"

"Us? What about his wife. And he didn't even come with her."

Wife? Xanthe's ex, Vincent Shornfell was married? Was that recent? Or—

"I can see why he didn't come with her," said the first woman. "She looks awful."

"She just had a baby," snapped the oldest woman.

A baby? A woman who'd just had a baby? Was there another one here? Could there be two? Of course, there could, but... But ... My brain slowed, like cogs in an engine smothered in molasses.

"Probably wouldn't have come with her anyway," said the Vincent clone. "Cramps his style for fooling around. Started way, way before Xanthe. I went to his wedding, you know, and he was cheating before and after. Hell, he probably cheated on Laura *during* the wedding."

My brain exploded. Cogs spewing this way and that, molasses all over the inside of my skull.

Laura.

Laura, the new mother, was married to Vincent Shornfell.

Still reeling, I tuned back in.

But they'd moved on to a new topic.

"I swear, that breakroom is haunted or something. First, Vinnie goes nuts in there after not turning a hair about being fired, then there's a murder, then that prospective client woman ends up there yesterday, and a couple days ago, that weird sound. Remember?"

No, no, tell me more about Vincent Shornfell...

"Weird sound? You mean the pipes from this place's bathroom? We hear those all the time."

"No, it was something different. Just for a little while, then it stopped. Sort of like an alien or something from behind the refrigerator."

"It would have to be an alien to be behind the refrigerator. The inside's bad enough, I can imagine how disgusting it is behind. Remember when that one cleaner pulled it out a few inches, took one look, then slammed it back in place?"

"Besides, you can't blame the murder on the breakroom. Xanthe's murder had nothing to do with us."

In the way of such gatherings, it had suddenly gone quiet and the words of the young woman rose above all others like a rocket launch.

Everyone turned to see who had spoken. With her co-workers looking away from her and her face scarlet that was an easy guess.

Tina stepped forward from near the bulletin board.

"Thank you all for coming today for this remembrance of Xanthe's life. We're going to have a few people speak now of this remarkable woman and her life. Eloise? Will you start?"

CHAPTER TWENTY-SIX

THE REMEMBRANCE BEGAN to break up as soon as the formal remarks ended.

The first to leave, as if making an escape, was Laura, the new mother. Laura Shornfell, I now know.

Had Xanthe known Laura, the student in her morning class and again when she substituted for Liz, was the wife of her former boyfriend?

She must have. The system included last names, and Shornfell wasn't common.

Had Laura known about Xanthe?

That was trickier.

I got a hold of Clara's arm, resorting to tugging when she seemed inclined to chat and linger.

Outside, I drew her out of the path of others departing by going across to the closed-up barbershop, then spilled the headlines, starting with Laura being Vincent Shornfell's wife.

She said *no* and *you're kidding* a lot, finishing up with a *wow*.

"And about the best thing I got," she lamented, "was Tina telling me she and Mitch from the music shop agreed to go in together on someone installing security cameras and motion sensor lights. That way everything will be covered. No gaps. No dark corners."

"That's good."

She sighed. "Yeah. For preventing anything else, but not for figuring out this murder. Did you see Teague in there?"

"Yeah. Which I don't understand, since he has no interest in this investigation."

"Oh, I think he might be taking an interest in the investigation. He's the one who got the barbershop's security footage before it was recorded over. And he was back there talking to folks to see if they might have missed anybody who'd seen something."

The gears in my brain took a moment to mesh. *"That's* who you waved at yesterday in the barbershop?"

"Umm-hmmm."

Hell, he didn't even need the app.

ABOUT TO GET in her parked SUV, Clara and I stopped when the door of a car two vehicles down the street swung open and Joyce Branter shouted, "Get in this car now, Ethan."

He kept walking past the open door.

"Get in here!" she shouted again at her grandson.

He didn't stop.

His father, Fred, half-stumbled out of the vehicle, as if he might have been pushed. It gave him the momentum to catch up with his son. "Get in the car with Grandma."

"No."

"Ethan—"

"No. I'm not listening anymore to her bad-mouthing Mom. Not today, not ever again. Until she stops, I'm having nothing to do with her. Or you as long as you live there."

"I can't make her stop and—"

"Have you ever tried?"

"—I gotta have someplace to live—"

"Try getting your own place. We could be together summers and breaks—"

"—and besides, she needs me, now your grandpa's dead."

Ethan looked at his father for a long moment, then away. "I'm going with the Clarys. I'm going to stay with them until school starts. If you want to see me, we can meet somewhere, Dad, but not with her and I'm not going back."

DAY SIX

SATURDAY

CHAPTER TWENTY-SEVEN

THE SUMMER PREVIEW heat had backed off, remembering it was still spring, so Clara and I had agreed to meet at the dog park in the afternoon.

That would give her a chance to prepare for the family party tonight for Ned's birthday.

And give me a chance to call Kit without taking my life in my hands by doing so before she was awake.

"Kit, do you know of a way to open a bank account with a modest amount of money not traceable to you, me, *Abandon All*, or my main accounts? I'd rather it didn't connect to my accounts here, either."

Silence greeted this question.

A long silence.

Then Kit cleared her throat. "Probably. Let me find out. How much? How soon?"

"As soon as possible." I named a figure.

"I'll call you back after I talk to Beatrice."

She hung up.

In her younger days, Kit had ghostwritten a number of financial advice books. She'd already been adept at stretching every dime—as she said, as important a skill for a career writer as imagination, grammar, typing, and accepting delayed gratification.

One book was by a bus driver who'd saved enough money over her working life, even after putting three kids through college and saving a good retirement for herself and her husband, to fund a scholarship for kids from the local high school.

Beatrice was the bus driver's daughter, and shared her mother's common-sense approach.

Sharp-minded and sharp-tongued Beatrice did Kit's books and knew her way around banking, finances, and investments.

I suspected she'd suspected something was fishy about the financial dealings between Kit and me at the start of our *Abandon All* association, but after money started flowing into Kit's accounts at an even faster rate than mine, she stopped giving me the side-eye. Presumably, she'd decided I wasn't trying to bilk Kit.

To my knowledge, she'd never asked Kit what was going on and Kit had never told her.

My phone rang.

"Beatrice says the account will be set up tomorrow, funds available Monday. I'll call with account number and password."

"Thank you. And tell Beatrice thank you from me."

"Already did."

"You didn't even ask why."

"It's your money. It's not ransom money or get out of the country money, so it couldn't be anything too serious. Besides, I figure it has something to do with that murder at your yoga studio."

"Have I mentioned lately I love and adore you?"

"Say it with cookies, kid. I haven't received a shipment in a while."

She loved the caramel dipped cookies my family called acorns. "Right away."

"No. After you solve the murder."

I laughed. Had to love her priorities. "That's a deal,"

"Care to share what you're going to use the money for?"

I did.

At the end, she said, "I see why you don't want it connectable to your other accounts. If they knew your net worth, they'd never let you go."

✧   ✧   ✧   ✧

"**WE SHOULD HAVE** grabbed Fred when we could," I grumbled, as Clara and I sat on our favorite table at the Torrid Avenue Dog Park. "If we're considering suspects, we have to include him."

Saturday brought out weekend warrior dog owners to the park, so the tables could get crowded. But with enough patience, we'd outlasted the most recent group and had the space to ourselves, while our dogs took a break in the shade under the table.

"Are you still on about that? Last night was not the moment," Clara said again. "His son had as good as walked out of his life. Besides, would you have wanted to talk to him with Joyce there?"

"No."

"Okay, then. I have something else to talk about. I've been thinking. What if Mamie was the target all along? What if it was a hit and somebody only knew they were supposed to take out a female who parked there."

"A hit?" *Take out* coming from Clara should only refer to food. "On a high school kid? Besides, she's not the only one to park there. Liz does, too."

"So that puts Liz in the category of possible victim, not suspect," she said in triumph.

"Remember the murder weapon? Who better to know Xanthe would have a strap available as an on-hand murder weapon than someone who teaches yoga?"

"Nobody," Clara acknowledged miserably. She looked up. "But what about what Tina said. Eloise doesn't have an alibi. Though that does seem extreme over an ex?"

"Murder's pretty extreme. There's probably a five- or ten-minute window when Xanthe was killed. Between the time she locked up, left the studio, and got in her car. But that window can move. It could have been later, when Eloise was with Tina and the others at the bar or it could have been earlier when Eloise has no alibi. Eloise stays on the list."

"*Everybody* stays on the list," she said, disgusted.

"Let's look at it a different way. Who would your top suspect be, Clara?"

"That mother-in-law, Joyce Branter."

"Really? Why?"

"Because the mother-in-law- daughter-in-law relationship is fraught with dangers."

"Speaking from experience?"

"No. I had a terrific mother-in-law. But I'm the exception who proves the rule. I say my thank yous every day for Ned and his family, along with how well he gets along with my family. He and I think it's normal, then start talking to other people … holy moly. And you know what we've heard about *this* mother-in-law."

"That's a fair point. But from what Donna said, that's been a bad relationship since Ethan was a baby, maybe before. Why would Joyce kill Xanthe now? Especially with her grandson about to go off to college."

"First, you never know when those family things are going to explode. Second, she might have felt she had less to lose. Or—" She drew out that short word for all it was worth. "—she was looking ahead. Ethan marrying and having children and all this going on to future generations and she ran into Xanthe and snapped."

"Spur-of-the-moment murder?"

"That's what the sheriff's department is saying. Only some stranger off the Interstate, while I think a family member is more likely."

"But if Xanthe stayed late, Joyce would have had to wait around and that's the opposite of snapping."

"Okay, so she didn't stay late or at least not super late. But, still, Beguiling Way would be awfully deserted as soon as the last students left."

"Which brings us to those last few students as possible suspects. We can't rule them out. Each had opportunity and means, assuming Berrie is correct about Xanthe being strangled with a yoga strap. In fact, that points even more to class members, because they all saw Xanthe pull one out of her bag."

"But why? What would their motives have been? And don't say she worked us too hard in class."

"You know," I said thoughtfully, "you combine that with lack of sleep, crying baby, projectile vomiting, postpartum depression, and Xanthe's dog keeping her baby awake, and that could give Laura motive."

"I suppose." Clara brightened. "Now, if you'd said Eve Kraft, because Xanthe used the same idea for table decorations or has already booked the videographer Eve wanted, *that* I'd believe."

"Except she and her tackling buddy Julia left before the last few did."

"I know." She said it with sorrow, but shook it off. "What about the guy who interrupted class?"

"And said, *What are you doing here.*" I sat up straighter. "I've been thinking about that. Who says that? Someone who expected the place to be empty—and why would anyone expect that? The schedule's public, plus we're there every Monday at that time.

"The other reason someone says that is they didn't expect to see *that person*. Say he did know *what* she was doing, but he hadn't expected *her* to be the one doing it. And that could fit Fred."

The dogs emerged from under the table, trotting purposefully toward the opposite side of the park, then veering off to wrestle ferociously.

"You mean… I don't know what you mean."

"All those motives you had for the mother-in-law go for Fred, the ex-husband, too, only stronger, because it's his son, along with the divorce scars, and seeing her completely changing her life, while he's still living with his mom. *But—*"

"But you said his voice was all wrong."

I subsided and acknowledged, "But his voice was all wrong."

We sat in silence, watching the dogs, now sniffing the same spot with great attention.

"I think we know what we need to do next," Clara said. "See Laura Shornfell."

"And try to hear Vincent Shornfell. But not today. It's Ned's birthday."

"Yup. Today's for the party. I wish you'd change your mind and come. I have the meat he'll grill marinating and the cake's ready. It'll be great. Investigating will wait until tomorrow. What are you doing today?" She swung around on me. "You're not doing anything on the murder today, are you? That's not fair—or safe. You can't without me."

"I plan to be lazy today," I promised. "Though I have an idea for next week. In fact, I've started the ball rolling on it."

I reminded her about my conversation about Smith-Flarenge with the professor Donna had connected me to, then explained my idea, and told her I had set up an account, skipping mention of Kit or Beatrice.

"Sheila...?"

"I know, I know. But it's not connected to anything else I own, and I'll do my best not to sign anything. I don't want to lose the money. But I have to have something to show I'm serious so they'll be interested."

Her frown shifted.

"You think Xanthe's death had something to do with people un-happy about Smith-Flarenge and Vincent? Those things the professor said?"

"I don't know. We do know it's something the sheriff's department isn't investigating. Remember what Eloise told us. How Xanthe's old life was driven by money. Then suddenly she gave it up. Quit her job. Dropped the guy. Changed her life. Smith-Flarenge was the job she quit, Shornfell was her boss and the guy she dropped. All for yoga, to be an instructor."

"So he sees her unexpectedly at the studio and kills her because she left him?"

"That might be jumping too far."

She wasn't listening. "He could have been stalking her and she was hiding, then he walks in and one moment of bad luck—"

"Whoa. She couldn't have been trying too hard to hide if she lived close enough for her dog to bother his baby, worked practically behind where they used to work together, and listed her name on the studio's website for classes."

She breathed in sharply through her nose. "Right. Okay. You

know, I think this break is going to be good for us. Shake up our thinking."

A BREAK, YES. A shake-up in thinking, no.

I wrote for maybe an hour.

Then I fell asleep in the hammock I'd put up in my back yard under the shade of a maple tree, and stayed there until my dog's stomach alarm went off.

I TRIED A stakeout by myself that evening, which I knew I'd hear about when I told Clara the next day.

Even though it was only following Mamie in the florist van.

And, as it turned out, it was uneventful enough that not even Teague O'Donnell could have objected.

I followed in the twilight as Mamie and Alan went directly to the hospital in Stringer, unloaded deliveries, then she drove to their small house on the west side and they went inside.

I was just as bad. I went home, played with my dog, and went to bed.

And I didn't even live with my grandfather.

DAY SEVEN
SUNDAY

CHAPTER TWENTY-EIGHT

GREAT AUNT KIT'S call came as I tried to get in the back door.

She began reciting digits while I juggled keys, dog leash, door handle, and cell phone as Gracie and I returned from the dog park.

"Wait, wait," I pleaded.

"I can't wait. I have a lunch date with a cute widower who thinks I'm fascinating."

"You *are* fascinating and—" I bit off *rich* as Teague leaned around the corner from the dining room and handed me a pencil from the stock he kept on the table, while Gracie and Murphy bumped and nudged each other as if they hadn't parted minutes ago at the dog park.

I grimaced as orange Cheetos dust sifted down to the paper from the pencil. Complaining, though, would come under the heading of looking a gift- and much-needed writing implement in the mouth.

"Just remember—"

"I know, I know," I interrupted Kit.

"I know you do and Beatrice knows you do, too, or we'd never let this happen."

"Gee, thanks for the compliment. I think."

"Take them as you get them. Ready?"

"Ready." She delivered the numbers machine-gun style. This widower must be really cute.

"Something interesting?" Teague asked when I disconnected the call.

"Not really," I said airily.

"You and Clara planning something today?"

"She and Ned have plans until later." After which Ned would leave for a pre-Reds-game on-field special event, followed by a cookout with retired Reds in the parking lot, and then the game, all of which Clara had bought tickets to for him and his favorite cousin as a surprise birthday gift. She'd found a great last-minute deal online from someone who couldn't go. "Then we thought we might take the dogs for a nice, quiet stroll."

Teague's eyebrows rose, but he said no more before going upstairs for another pass at measurements.

I watched him go. Wondered how his one eye had become legally blind. Thought about him losing his career and taking on two more.

And decided he could measure as many times as he wanted, with no interference or smart remarks from me.

CHAPTER TWENTY-NINE

THE SHORNFELL HOUSE had the tallest grass and lowest curb appeal.

We spotted that on our first pass around the block with Gracie and LuLu in this still-naked development of small, uninspired houses in no-man's-land southwest of Haines Tavern.

Rather than walking back and forth, we went around the block to view Xanthe Anstead's house on the far side. It looked both well-cared-for and oddly forlorn.

"Donna said Xanthe's dog's already been adopted," Clara said. "Ethan wanted to take it, but with going off to college in a few months…"

Perhaps it was the lack of the dog—and the woman—who should have been there that made it forlorn.

The dogs insisted on smelling every new spot and, since every spot here was new to them, our progress was slow.

We'd passed the Shornfells' a second time with no sign of life and had reached Xanthe's side of the block again, when Clara said, "Somebody's there. At Xanthe's house."

A woman came out of the house and walked toward a car in the driveway, carrying mail. "Eloise."

Tugging on leashes in a rare role reversal, we hurried our pace to intercept her.

She looked up at my call and smiled.

"Clara, Sheila. What are you two doing here?"

"Walking our dogs." If she concluded we lived in the neighborhood, good. "How about you?"

She lifted the accumulated mail she held. "Picking this up for Ethan. The sheriff's department said we could now." She looked over her shoulder toward the house. "Guess I'll be helping him sell this place when we can do that."

"You're doing so much to help him. He must be very grateful."

She shrugged at my comment.

"The remembrance gathering was lovely, Eloise."

She thanked Clara, but her lip twitched.

Guessing at the cause of the lip-twitch, I asked, "How was Ethan afterward?"

"Good. Actually, surprisingly good. He told his father and grand-mother he's staying with friends until he leaves for college. When he told me the next day, he sounded so strong and grown up." Her expression turned wry. "More grown up than I was feeling at the end of Friday night. Those two new students said they'd help clean up and then the blonde one spent all her time in the restroom and the other one wouldn't stop talking about some wedding. Tina practically had to throw them out at the end. I went home and practiced for two hours, to work out my desire to hit them. Or maybe the Branters. Or Xanthe's ex. Or all of them."

Clara and I grimaced our complete understanding of the desire to hit those people, though not the two-hour yoga practice.

"Her ex was there at the remembrance?" I didn't do innocence nearly as well as Clara, but Eloise didn't seem to notice.

"Yeah. Vince Shornfell." More lip-twitch, this time accompanied by a glance past Xanthe's house to the one behind it. "He lives over there. Well, his wife and kids do. I don't think he's around much. Pretty ironic Xanthe moving in here right as she broke away from him."

"Really?" Clara's eyes went big. "How awkward for Xanthe. Espe-cially if he was trying to get back in her life?"

"She didn't mind. It was over, she had no trouble making that clear to him when she needed to, he wasn't around, and she said the wife didn't know. Just ranted about Xanthe's dog barking."

"Did her current boyfriend come to the remembrance?" Clara

asked with her superior innocence.

"She didn't have a boyfriend."

Clara didn't let Eloise's staccato response throw her off. "I understood she was dating someone."

"Oh. I guess. He was on duty Friday night. Fireman. Couldn't come."

"It must be so hard for him. We heard they were supposed to go to a baseball game the night she was killed. For him to know she'd be alive if she'd stuck with that plan, she—Oh. You said were with them, didn't you?" Confusion clouded Clara's face. "But Tina said…"

Eloise looked down and to the side, appearing to focus on my knees. "I met them right after. For drinks."

"Was Xanthe supposed to join you all after class?"

"I guess. I'd thought she was going to the game. I didn't know about her teaching instead." Something crossed her face. "He—the guy—didn't, either, until Tina told him. He wasn't happy, especially when Xanthe stood him up after, too. Or so we thought."

We thought.

"So, you four must have been trying to contact her, see where she was…"

With clear reluctance, she said, "Tina and her husband left before it was real clear Xanthe wasn't coming, but he tried to reach her. Sorry. I've got to go now. Didn't realize it was so late."

She wasted no time in getting in her car and pulling out.

"One thing for sure," Clara said as we waved at the departing car. "Eloise wasn't as over her ex as she pretended. I wonder how long she sat with him in that bar, drinking, while he tried to contact Xanthe, getting more irked, both of them drinking more and more … with less and less to suppress the old feelings. Want to wager whether they slept together that night? And now the guilt…"

"Might not be any guilt if that was her goal from the start. She could have skipped the ballgame because it was too hard to see her ex with Xanthe *or* she could have skipped it to end their relationship for good." I said. "Either way, there's definitely one other thing for sure—Eloise doesn't have an alibi."

✧ ✧ ✧ ✧

As we continued our circuit around the block, we talked about trying to find the bartender on duty the night of Xanthe's murder, but since we already had a plan for tonight, it would have to wait until Monday night.

The dogs were far less patient on this go-round. They'd hit the high-value sniff spots and were ready to move on.

That's when the garage door of the Shornfell house opened and out came our quarry.

✧ ✧ ✧ ✧

"No, *no*... she'll scream. She'll—She's not screaming."

The baby kicked, pumped her fists, gurgled, and cooed as Gracie snuffled at the bare feet.

Her mother—Laura Shornfell—stared on in amazement.

Clara chuckled.

Laura had emerged with the baby in a stroller. A toddler clung to her leg. A more autonomous boy headed straight to the mud in a corner of the yard.

Gracie alerted to the kids as if they were new versions of treat. She wouldn't chew them, but licking them to oblivion might have been on her agenda.

She made first contact with those bare baby feet, while the toddler watched with cautious eyes from behind Laura.

LuLu watched with a mix of boredom and astonishment that Gracie would want to spend her time this way. She tore at a dandelion with her teeth.

But baby and Gracie were an item from the start.

It was probably the tickle of breath or whiskers—or the combination—on her feet producing the baby's reaction, but it seemed as if she looked straight at Gracie's long face and bonded instantly.

"I... I can't believe it. She cries at everything. Not just cries. Banshee howls. That's amazing," Laura said.

I tried to figure out how old the baby was and add nine months. I kept coming up with Vincent Shornfell impregnating his wife during his affair with Xanthe.

"Obviously a dog lover," I said with a smile.

"Not all dogs," she muttered.

"No, I heard there was an issue with Xanthe's dog barking."

She jerked the baby's feet back, which sparked a howl to make a banshee blanch.

Laura showed good sense by releasing the baby's feet, restoring dog and child contact, and quieting the world-is-ending siren. But she continued to glare at Clara and me.

Then the glare went both darker and confused. "I know you two."

"Yes," Clara said encouragingly, "from yin yoga at the Beguiling Way studio."

"Yeah," she said slowly. "That's right. What are you doing here?"

"Walking our dogs. We like to give them some exercise." As if this were exercise compared to the hell-bent sprints, endurance circuits, and acrobatic rolls of the dog park.

Laura looked down at the clinger. "Go play with your brother."

I glanced at the oldest child. Laura might as well have added *In the mudhole* to the order.

The child gave her a doleful look, but shuffled silently toward mud and sibling.

"Do you know my husband?" Laura asked abruptly.

"Your husband?" I repeated.

"Vince Shornfell. With Smith-Flarenge."

My blank look got a big boost from her second sentence. She thought he still worked for Smith-Flarenge when he'd been fired nearly a year ago?

"No. Never met him," I said honestly.

"Me, either," Clara said, when Laura looked at her.

Laura muttered something under her breath, sounding like *You're the only ones in town, then.*

Clara's eyes flickered, but she otherwise didn't betray she'd heard it, too. Cheerfully, she said, "By the way, being around dogs is really good for babies and kids. There are all sorts of studies about how it helps prevent their getting allergies, especially to animals."

"That's what that other woman said." She sounded and looked suspicious.

"Berrie. She was right. About that."

Something sparked in her eyes at my dry tone. A flicker of kindred spirit. She looked from me to Clara and back. "You really never met my husband?"

"Never."

"You two were at the sheriff's department, too. The other day. About that murder."

Someone more curious—or less defeated—would have wondered what we were doing here, on her street. Laura Shornfell's questions about her husband appeared to have exhausted her wondering.

"Yes." I said. "Horrible thing to happen, wasn't it?"

"Yeah," she said without emotion.

"And then all the questioning," Clara added shrewdly.

That drew more reaction. "It went on and on and on, after I *told* that deputy I had to get home to my baby." She looked at the child and her mouth softened.

"I know. And he kept asking where I was at the time of the murder, even though he couldn't even say what time." Clara's hearty agreement with Laura's complaint made such headway with the younger woman that I resolved to stay quiet and let my dog's feet-tickling be my contribution.

"Exactly," Laura said. "Where was I? Where am I ever? Here."

"Well, you're at yoga sometimes."

"I swap with my neighbor. I take care of her kids for her three classes a week and she takes care of my kids for my three classes a week."

"Your husband doesn't help?"

Laura looked at her blankly for a long moment.

Clara said, "You said something about your husband. Doesn't he care for the kids? Give you time off?"

"No." The word carried a full measure of hopelessness.

Clara gently touched her fingertips to the woman's forearm, as if anything but the lightest contact might break her.

"You recognized his voice when he interrupted class Monday night, didn't you, Laura?"

As if in a trance, she said, "He was surprised to see her. I'd wondered, but he was surprised. And she sent him away. They were really done." Her voice went wooden. "But there's another. There's always another."

"You can leave him. Take your kids and go. You don't have to stay with him. There are ways."

"I was going to leave. I was all set to last year…" Her gaze slid to the baby. "Maybe later. When… When I can…"

"There are places you can go. You and your kids. They'll help you. If you need a name—"

"He doesn't *hit* us, if that's what you think. That would take too much energy and he doesn't have any left from all his other *activities*. Except … now and then." She looked at the baby again. "Plenty of time to lie on the couch and have me fetch and carry for him while he brags and brags about this idea and that brilliant scheme and how much better he is at everything than anyone else. And he spins his dreams. All the things that are going to happen—someday. He'll be swimming in money. Someday. Have a big house and a boat and vacations all over the world. Someday."

Bitterness pinched her young face. "Him. It's always him that will do it. Never us. He doesn't even think I notice the kids and I aren't in any of his dreams. As for me? I can barely drag myself to those classes. Three hours in the whole week. Only time I have for me. And then it turns out that bouncy, skinny, energetic teacher was one of his—"

She swallowed it with a gulp.

But we already knew.

WE SAT IN Clara's SUV, waiting for the swirl of tails and fur to slow behind us, weighed down by what we'd heard and seen.

"Poor kid," Clara said.

"Laura or her baby?"

"Both. All of them. The whole family. Except him. I was think-ing... What Eloise said about Xanthe having no trouble making it clear to him it was over. That could mean he kept trying."

"It could."

She expelled a breath through her nose. "I got our families talking about some of the people in this last night at Ned's party. Nothing to really report or I'd've told you already. But there was a fair amount about Shornfell being a blowhard, full of talk, real pleased with himself for no good reason when he's just a hound without the brains to stay on his own porch."

Staring straight ahead, I removed a dog hair from my mouth where Gracie's tail had hit me on her most recent pass.

"No disagreement from me. But where does it leave us?"

She sighed. "Laura seemed to believe they were over, her husband and Xanthe."

"Seemed to. But it could have been an act or she could know it now, but didn't until ... after. Motive, means, and opportunity," I said heavily. "She could have run a little late last Monday night, just long enough to murder Xanthe Anstead before relieving her co-op babysitter."

"Everybody has means—the yoga strap—and opportunity." Clara's vigorous defense collapsed with her next words. "God knows she has motive."

"But why kill Xanthe now? Almost a year after they broke up?"

Clara glanced at me. "Now you're going to argue the other side and make me say, maybe Laura just found out. Or it was spur of the moment because Xanthe was the one she had the opportunity to strike out at."

"Pushed over the edge by her skinny bounciness," I muttered.

Clara sighed. "Okay. We can't eliminate her. But, if it was her—and this is a harsh, wicked thing to feel—she should have killed *him*."

CHAPTER THIRTY

"I KNOW WE'RE supposed to have snacks for a stakeout, but I'm stuffed after dinner at the café," Clara said. "I might not even have the strawberry pie they boxed up for me until tomorrow."

We were parked on Haines Avenue with a good view up Beguiling Way.

Mamie had parked the flower shop van in the stubby gap between the yoga studio and music store. She wasted no time loading it up. And she was alone. No sign of Alan, so maybe he had gone to his meeting.

"This might be another waste of time," I warned Clara. I'd told her about last night's effort.

"Or not. Because—*Ahh!*"

A rap on the passenger window by her head made us both jump.

Clara twisted around. "Berrie?"

I scooched down to get a look at the window-rapper as Clara lowered the window.

"What are you doing?" she demanded as soon as it was cracked.

How many times had I been asked that question this week? Too many.

"Talking," Clara said.

"About the murder? You two still going around poking into that?"

"You could help, Berrie."

"I've helped plenty. I told you I saw Liz with a guy that day—Monday."

Clara jerked upright. "When we tried to ask details, you said you didn't remember anything about it."

"Of course I remember. It was at the doctor's office. OB-GYN. And—"

"*OB-GYN?* Why didn't you say so?" Clara demanded.

"—she was with a guy, like I said. So I *did* say so."

"A guy? Or a doctor?"

She clicked her tongue, indicating our stupidity. "The doctor is a guy."

"Was Liz seeing him as a doctor or a guy?"

"I can't tell you—"

A vehicle passed us. The flower shop van.

"We have to go." I started the engine and pulled away before Berrie finished.

"She might know more," Clara objected. Then immediately added, "Or she might be confused or she might be stringing us along. You're right. Let's see where Mamie goes."

"THAT'S NOT THE way to the hospital," Clara said when the van turned right off the highway to Stringer.

"No, it's not."

It was the way to a park with ballfields, tennis courts, and creekside picnic areas. The flower shop van came to a stop in one of those, beside an aged pickup truck with the tailgate down and a young man sitting on it.

Clara voiced the breaking dawn for both of us. "A *boy*. That explains her missing hour."

I drove past, skipped the next pull-in, then used the third to turn around.

"Maybe. We need to confirm it."

I pulled into their picnic area, parking the car at right angles behind them to make it hard for either to leave until we did, unless they went over railroad tie curbs.

The boy had flopping brown hair and the giraffe gangliness of a recent growth spurt. If they weren't the same age, he wasn't much older than Mamie.

He watched us with easy surprise, but Mamie pressed her hands down at either side of her hips on the tailgate, poised to jump down and flee.

"Stay where you are," I ordered her.

Clara smiled at the boy, who now looked from us to Mamie with concern. "Hi. Don't worry. We have a few questions to ask you. You aren't in any trouble, but we need the truth. Were you with Mamie for about an hour Monday night, starting around eight o'clock?"

"Yeah, but—"

"Don't. Don't. Gramps will kill—"

"He won't." I interrupted, "But this *is* about a killing."

"Mamie?"

Clara didn't give the girl time to answer all the questions the boy packed into her name, saying to him, "Tell us about Monday night and if we can avoid letting her grandfather know we will."

"I called Mamie and told her I'd be here. Hoping she could get away. She can't always, but that night she got here about quarter past eight. We were talking and, uh... talking until she saw the time and bolted to get the flowers to the hospital."

Mamie groaned, tears coming to her eyes.

"Mamie?" Clara asked.

After a heavy breath, she jerked her head down, then up in a reluctant nod.

"Good," I said briskly. "Now tell us what you know about Liz Whyte that you kept to yourself the first time we talked."

"I don't know—"

"If you don't tell us the truth, we won't be able to avoid telling your grandfather everything." Her attempted denial had come after her eyes widened when I said Liz's name. She wasn't getting off this hook.

She looked at the boy. He nodded.

"A week before that other teacher was killed, I saw Liz in her car. I was going to ask her to let me park there because I had a gazillion orders for the hospital and that deputy was hanging around. But when I got close, I saw she was sitting there crying and crying. I thought I'd go away, but then she spotted me in the mirror and rolled down her window and said she'd move and I said no, no, don't do that. But she was going to anyhow and then I said, what's wrong. And she started crying hard again and I reached into the window to pat her shoulder or something I guess and she grabbed my hand and held on so tight and she said I shouldn't worry and everything would be sorted out one way or the other soon and then it would all be over. She kept repeating that, about it being over soon—decided, she said. And then she said again about moving her car and I said no, because how could she drive sobbing like that. But then she stopped and she was almost like herself, just like that."

"Okay. Good. That's—"

"Tell them the other thing, Mamie," Robbie said.

"Robbie," she protested.

"Go ahead. It's safer if more people know. Not just us."

Smart kid.

"Tell us," Clara said.

"I was arriving at the shop after school—the week before the last week—and I heard shouting in the studio. The blind was up on the door and I saw them. It was her, the one who was killed, and a man I don't know. They were yelling at each other. I couldn't hear words," she said hurriedly. "Not enough to make sense of it. Just angry, you know? Then I heard someone coming from behind me, so I just went to the shop. I forgot all about it until... Then I told Robbie."

"What did the man look like?"

"I didn't see him real well. The blinds and stuff. But he had a real low voice. Gruff." She looked from me to Clara and back. "That's all I know. Honest. Please don't tell Gramps about Robbie. Please."

I stepped closer, put a hand on her knee and shook it a little. "Don't be silly. Tell your grandfather everything you've told us and all about Robbie. Quit sneaking around. Both of you."

Color rose up in both their faces.

"You don't understand," Mamie said. "Ever since my mom got into a mess with drugs, Gramps won't let me out of his sight. He's especially worried about boys. He'd never approve of Robbie."

"Don't be so sure. Robbie is your alibi for murder. That will warm your grandfather's heart."

DAY EIGHT

MONDAY

CHAPTER THIRTY-ONE

WE HAD OUR plan for Monday.

It started, naturally, with a trip to the dog park.

While there, we wrote a list of all the things we wanted to know. It was long. Discouragingly long.

But, as Clara said, we could only do one thing at a time and we'd already decided what to do today.

With the dogs tired out temporarily, Clara and I picked up lunch and ate at her house, away from the ears of Teague O'Donnell.

I double-checked that the money was in the account. Of course it was. Beatrice was on the job.

Then I showered and dressed in Clara's guest room. I wore the narrow-skirted suit and heels from my *Abandon All* days, drawing a *Wow* from Clara.

"That is *gorgeous*. I had no idea you had clothes like that."

"Not dog park attire. Or yoga. Or library, post office, grocery store."

"Good point. You'll make them sit up and take notice."

I removed any Sheila Mackey identification from my purse and gave it all to Clara.

We drove to my house, but with Teague's vehicle there, Clara took Gracie in while I stayed in the car. No sense risking this outfit stirring his detective instincts.

She would wait for me across the street from Smith-Flarenge in the pocket park behind the post office. She said she'd see if she could arrange a time to talk to Fred Branter about his involvement in building the structure that helped form the little parking spot where his ex-wife was murdered.

The one thing I kept connected to Sheila Mackey was my phone. I was to call Clara if I ran into trouble.

Though what kind of trouble I might run into neither of us could have said. Maybe Professor Andronski's take on Smith-Flarenge had us on edge.

THE BUILDING THAT originated as Angus Green's Furniture Emporium and now housed Smith-Flarenge, was close to the bakery's drool-worthy display window, not to mention smells wafting from inside. Taking no chances, I approached Smith-Flarenge from the non-bakery side.

They had either restored or preserved the original look I'd spotted in the photo of the horse-drawn trailer of girls, with a central door between two large, flanking windows in the narrow façade.

For a second, coming out of the bright daylight, I wondered if I had stepped into the old Furniture Emporium. Not that the furniture was old, but it seemed to extend as far as I could see.

A blink to refocus and I realized it was sitting areas, striving to look like friendly family rooms. Among the love seats, cushy chairs, and side tables sat a shining wooden desk with bookshelves behind it and the young woman from the remembrance seated at it.

I headed for her.

"Hello, I have an appointment to see an advisor."

She held up a finger to indicate I needed to wait.

"Yes, that's right." For a moment I thought she was talking to me. But she wasn't making eye contact. As she continued, I decided her full hair hid earbuds.

At the back of the seating areas, a doorway on the right side revealed a hallway extending into the building.

"Bring all your statements, tax returns from the past three years,

your most recent mortgage statement and credit card statements....
Oh, that's the minimum. Full and complete access to your finances is
the only way we can give you the best possible advice. ... Yes, we'll see
you then."

She turned to me, with no sign of recognizing me. "May I help
you?"

"I have an appointment to see an advisor. I requested someone
experienced."

She made a show of checking a sheet in front of her. Even upside
down I spotted my name on a line next to "Jordy."

"Hmm. Everyone's so busy. But I think Jordy will be best. He's
been dynamite since he joined our team."

She led me to the door, then down the hallway. We passed glassed-
in offices, their far walls whitewashed brick. One held the Vincent
clone staring intently at a computer screen. I'd bet anything he was
playing solitaire. My spirits dipped. I'd hoped for him.

"I did say someone experienced," I said to the woman's back.

"Jordy is perfect." She kept going toward a closed door at the end
of the hallway that had to be nearly to the flower shop by my guessti-
mate.

I was oddly disappointed when she stopped short of that door and
gestured me in to an office like all the other offices we'd passed. The
occupant was younger than those at the remembrance except for Ms.
Streaked-Hair. He nearly flinched when the receptionist said, "You'll
love Jordy."

With that order, she pivoted and headed toward the front.

Talking my seat, the light caught an irregular pattern on the brick
side wall where it met the office's back. From the pattern and position,
it had to be part of the archway where the woman in the photo had
stood, with her white apron and her motion-blurring gesture of tossing
out something.

"How long have you been with the company, Jordy?"

"Uh, two weeks." Not a whole lot of dynamite. That also meant he
wouldn't have known Xanthe or Vincent Shornfell.

I waited for his pitch, but none came. He almost seemed wary of me.

Not able to take the awkward silence any longer, I asked, "What can you do for me, Jordy?"

It was like squeezing a talking doll in the right place.

"I help people plan for their retirement or to put their kids through college or—" Here a pause for a rehearsed chuckle. "Both. If you're not comfortable meeting here, I can come to your house. We can consult by phone, if that's better for you. You'll get monthly statements. And the plan will be tailored exactly to you because every situation is different and every person is different and sometimes things happen to them in life that are unexpected."

He went on in that vein while I looked around the office, my gaze returning to the brick.

The rest of the doorway had to be in the room behind this, the one the closed door led to. The breakroom, probably.

I swear, that breakroom is haunted or something. First, Vinnie goes nuts in there after not turning a hair about being fired, then there's a murder, then that prospective client woman ends up there yesterday, and a few days ago, that weird sound.

"How much are you looking to invest, ma'am?"

I told him.

He didn't hide the disappointment. "But you'll be adding more?"

"Oh, yes, I plan to. I've got a little set aside for renovations. But if I could make it work harder for me, maybe I could do more with the house."

"That's what we're here for. Now, if you'd give me your social security number…"

"Oh." I opened my eyes wide, innocent, and not too bright. "I totally forgot to bring it. I brought my account number, but I had no idea you'd need that. Perhaps if I talk to someone experienced, who could figure out a way…"

His young face turned crafty and cool. I suspected the people with experience had swooped in on him enough already that he wasn't welcoming more.

"No, no. That's quite all right. I… I, uh, think we can transfer the money over today with an account number, then we can deal with the rest later."

"Really? You can do that? Right now? I have account information." I pulled out a copy of the information Kit had given me and handed it over.

"I think so. Let me check."

He left the room.

My phone vibrated. Forget it. I had minutes at best, the phone would wait.

I was out of my chair and practically on his heels out the door. But while he turned right toward the front of the building, I turned left.

A few short feet and I was inside, closing the door softly behind me.

CHAPTER THIRTY-TWO

IT WAS A breakroom.

Not the worst I'd ever seen. But not a whole lot better.

Cabinets held supplies on this side of the room. A worn counter-top supported a coffee pot, microwave, sink on the other side of the room. Four stools and a table the size of a placemat.

In the corner closest to Jordy's office, its back to the brick wall, was a full-sized fridge.

Sort of like an alien or something from behind the refrigerator.

For a wild moment, I considered pulling it out, checking if the wall was solid behind it.

Like, what? Someone broke through it to get into the Beguiling Way Yoga Studio?

Why?

There was nothing to steal there. It wasn't like it was a bank vault.

No… But what about from the studio into here? There wasn't cash here, either, but Smith-Flarenge did deal in valuables of a kind—investments, account numbers.

What was it the professor said Vincent Shornfell did? He created more accounts to get bonuses from the company. So he had access to accounts…

Before my mind caught up, I found myself with my face smooshed against the brick wall over the sink and beside the refrigerator, peering along it to see if the patch brick within that archway was gone, leaving an open passageway…

Nope. A solid wall.

And it wasn't as if we wouldn't have noticed on the studio side if the archway suddenly was gone, revealing the back of a dirty fridge.

I sighed.

My phone vibrated again.

I ignored it again, because I heard footsteps coming down the hall.

No way I could get back to Jordy's office without his seeing me. I grabbed a Styrofoam cup and splashed in some coffee. Drew a low breath and eased it out to slow my heart and my breathing, then opened the door.

He looked startled and stopped.

"I was looking for coffee." I smiled at him.

Slowly, he approached.

He looked past me into the breakroom, skittish. "Coffee? Is that all?"

I was about to assure him it was all when inspiration hit.

"Well, I did hear it's haunted, and I was fascinated. I couldn't help myself."

"Haunted? Is that why…? Another woman came in here last week and she was real weird about it. Creeped me out, to tell the truth. It was right after another woman came in yelling we were all crooks and she wanted her money back. And I'll tell you, it shook me up. Shook me up, bad. I debated all weekend whether I should come back today at all." Belatedly, he realized what he'd said. "Not that she was right. We aren't crooks. Not at all. And I'm going to make a career of this, work here for Smith-Flarenge as long as I can, because it's a great place."

The darned phone buzzed again. Exasperated, I took it out to turn it off.

"I know you're not crooks," I lied earnestly. "What did the woman look like? The one who was upset."

"Older. Like your age."

Jordy was never going to make it with Smith-Flarenge.

As I went to turn off the phone, I caught a glimpse of the latest message.

NOW!

It was Clara.

Hurriedly, I scrolled back through earlier versions of the same message until I came to one that said: *Ethan and Fred here any minute. Come now.*

"Jordy, I have to go. It's an emergency."

"But—"

"I'll return in a day or so." To ask more questions, if nothing else.

I started off, then turned back to him.

"But, Jordy, I have a flair for these things and I have to tell you, this place is definitely haunted."

"I knew it. Damn, damn, damn, I *knew* it. I'm getting the hell out of this place."

My good deed done for the day.

AS I CROSSED Tanner Street as fast I could in the restrictive heels and skirt, I saw Clara, Fred, and Ethan standing in a tense triangle in front of the solitary bench in the pocket park.

"…better if we all sit down," she was saying in a soothing voice.

"You think he had something to do with my mother's death?" Ethan demanded of her.

"I never said—" Clara tried.

Fred talked through her. "I would never do that to you, Eth."

"To me, but what about to *her*? That would be okay?"

"I didn't—"

"Don't—"

"Stop. All of you," I demanded in my best taming-the-media voice. The surprise allowed me to continue in command. "Fred, we know you were involved with the construction of the storage area at the back of the little parking area where Xanthe was killed."

"What?" the uncomprehending blankness made father and son look more alike than I'd previously seen.

"What does that have to do with—?"

I held up that ever-useful stop-sign hand to Ethan and demanded of his father, "You and your dad did the brick work, didn't you?"

"Who *are* you?" he muttered.

"Didn't you?" I snapped.

"Yeah, but—"

"Is there a door hidden in that brick work?"

"A what?"

"A door. Some sort of secret door. Or passageway."

Now Clara looked as if I were nuts, too. But the connection of the brick work covering up the old doorway between Smith-Flarenge and the studio, plus Fred and his father doing the brickwork at the end of that nub of a parking spot had fired up my synapses.

"Are you nuts?" But he didn't stop with asking that question, perhaps the habit of obeying his mother's demands too strong. "No secret doors or passageways or anything. It's storage space. Mostly for the units facing Tanner. Then some divided between where Mitch's music shop and Tina's yoga studio are now."

…or maybe my synapses misfired.

"We'll have to get inside there to see for ourselves."

"Well, I sure as hell don't have a key. Haven't even been in there since we built it, Daddy and me, when I was a kid."

"Who does have a key?"

He started shaking his head with my first word. "I don't know. I…" He stopped shaking his head. "Maybe Fern. Probably Fern."

"Why would she have a key?"

"She owns all those buildings. They've been in her family since they were built."

"I know where Fern lives," Clara said. "We can go ask her."

"Okay. We'll—"

"What does any of that have to do with my father and my mother's death?" Ethan demanded.

That jerked my synapses back to our original purpose in wanting to talk to Xanthe's ex.

"Fred, we know you were arguing with Xanthe at the yoga studio a few days before she was killed."

His son rounded on him. "You *what?* You said you hadn't talked to her in years. Ever since the restraining order. You swore to me—"

"I didn't hurt her, Eth. I didn't. I was asking her why you had to go away, why you couldn't take classes here. Stay around so I could see you, like. I even said it would be okay with me if you lived with her. And she said something sharp about how living with my mother had turned out so well and she wasn't going to do that to you. And then Fern came in."

"And?" Ethan demanded.

Having him ask the questions worked fine for me.

"And that was it."

"That was it?"

"I left right after. It was clear your mother wasn't going to change her mind about you going away forever at the end of the summer."

"Do you swear you didn't hurt Mom?"

Fred lifted his large head and met his son's eyes. "I swear it. When I left her there, I thought it was the worst that could happen, you going off to school in a couple of months. Only then Xanthe got killed and I saw how that hurt you in a way I never wanted to see my boy hurt. Broke your heart. And then you got so mad at your grandma and me and went off to the Clarys and now we don't even have until the end of the summer."

Ethan put a hand on his father's shoulder.

They stood still for a long moment before the boy spoke.

"Dad, I'm not coming back to Grandma's house, maybe never. But you and I can have time together away from there this summer."

"We can?"

"Yes. And after the summer, too."

The man shuddered with a sob.

Clara and I left them.

"**IF WE GET** the key fast and get a move on, we can look at the storage area before anybody arrives for yoga and wonders what on earth we're doing," Clara said.

I'd filled in the minuscule amount I'd learned at Smith-Flarenge, including spotting that side of the patched doorway, and how that had led to some of my questions for Fred.

"Good plan." I said that despite still wearing this narrow skirt and heels. If I were in my right mind I'd say we'd put off exploring the storage area until I could change.

But she was right about the time being tight. If I changed, there'd be no time before yoga. We'd have to wait until everyone cleared out after class ... which would have us exploring in the dead of night.

I've seen horror movies. I'm not stupid. No way.

But wait until tomorrow? Dodging daytime yoga classes and curious observers who'd wonder what we were doing in the studio and be sure to report it to Tina and half the county? Also, no way.

Okay, yes, and I didn't want to wait the extra hours, either.

I'd forged through Manhattan rain, snow, and slush in this suit. It—and I—could withstand a storage area in Haines Tavern, Kentucky.

Fern lived south of the Historic Haines Tavern in a tattered gingerbread house on a block where more than half of the houses had been restored or were new.

"You think this used to be one of the houses of ill-repute Urban told you about?" Clara asked as we got out.

"Oh, I hope so."

She grinned.

When Fern opened the door to us with an expression of delight, Clara probed discreetly. "This is lovely, Fern. Has this home been in your family for a long time?"

"It has, indeed. Passed down from one generation to the next. We'll have to see who's the best steward to inherit the next generation. One of my sisters' grandchildren it'll likely be, since I have none. Won't you come in, sit down."

She led us past a well-preserved but faded formal parlor and dining room that would have been fashionable when the house was built, then into a kitchen with a sitting area that had ushered in the 1970s.

"What can I help you girls with?"

"Fern, we understand your grandfather owned the buildings the yoga studio and music store are in now—"

"Grandmother. She had them built and owned them, not our grandfather." She twinkled slightly. "She was an excellent business-woman."

Was she saying…?

I clamped down on my curiosity. "We were wondering if you have a key that might let us get in to the storage area between the yoga studio and music store."

Her eyebrows lifted, making her bright eyes look as they must have in her younger years. She must have been formidable then. She still was, despite the twinkle. "Your murder investigation? You think there's a clue there?"

"We don't know," Clara said. "That's why we want to check."

"My, oh, my. How exciting." She stood. "I don't suppose if I assured you there's nothing of interest in there that it would satisfy you girls. No, no, I know it won't. Of course, you may have a key and see for yourselves."

She went to a rack of keys near the back door, detached a small ring with two keys and brought it to us.

"One will get you in the studio and the other into the storage room. Door's at the back, by the restroom and furnace room. The light switch is inside the door, on your right."

The door to the closet where the bulletin board has stood, that we didn't go any deeper into. Also the door Vincent Shornfell kept looking at…

"…a dear man, but not much of a businessman," Fern was saying. "Still, the town needs a music store. And the café does well enough to subsidize Mitch."

"You own the café, too?" Clara asked.

"The building. Not the business. Those folks've worked real hard. I thought they'd succeed and I was right. Have to admit, the one I'm surprised about is the yoga studio. I was happy enough to do it to help family—"

"Tina's related to you?"

"—twice over. Tina's my sister's granddaughter. And Liz is the granddaughter of another sister. Like I said, the studio helped family twice over."

She smiled at us, clearly noting our reactions and enjoying them.

Clara looked at me, leaving the decision to me.

Any other time I would have voted to stay and ask questions. But we had no time to spare.

"Thank you, Fern. We'll return the keys as soon as possible."

"No hurry. No hurry, girls."

CHAPTER THIRTY-THREE

"Nothing," Clara declared.

Starting from the door in the yoga studio, we'd moved the bulletin board once more stored there to continue to a storage area not much wider than the hall and lit by hanging bulbs.

It hadn't taken long to work our way across it to where we now stood, by the music store door.

"Nothing except cobwebs and dust." I brushed some of each from my jacket lapel. "Unless Mitch is hiding drugs in that drum set he's stored back here."

"Very dusty and cobwebby drugs if he is."

We'd opened what looked like a freestanding double locker and discovered dust and cobwebs inside, along with a drum set.

No door led to the outside or to the part of the storage area that served the Tanner Street units.

I sighed. "Sorry, Clara. I saw that brickwork on the Smith-Flarenge side like the patch in the studio's restroom and mixed it up with Urban's history and went completely off the rails about secret doorways and hidden passages. You're a good sport to explore this with me."

"With this area so close to where Xanthe was killed, I was curious, too."

"Should have stayed at Smith-Flarenge. Maybe I can go back and if Jordy's gone, I can get that guy who knew a lot about Shornfell." I sighed at lost opportunities. "I should have known better. Especially with this area being built so recently. Now, if it had been built a hundred or two-hundred years ago ... We should have asked Fern more about Liz, since they're related. Did you know about the family connections?"

"No. Although almost everybody who's from here a couple generations or more is connected some way. But with all the married names in can be hard to sort—Oh, God. Look at the time. We've got to get out of here." Clara pushed me back toward the yoga studio.

"You know, if this were a movie, someone would have locked us in while we were searching."

"Shut up, Sheila Mackey."

"Just saying."

She pushed me from behind again. "And I'm just saying we better move our bustles if we hope to get home, changed, and back for yoga before our friends grab our spots."

I said a nasty word and moved as fast as I could. Heels and skirt. Now I remembered why I hated them.

✧   ✧   ✧   ✧

I RACED INTO my bedroom, heels off, skirt hiked to get up the stairs faster, jacket off, the top two buttons of my blouse undone.

And screamed.

Beyond the open closet door was a construction—or destruction—scene, with the wall dividing it from the other closet nearly gone. But that wasn't why I screamed.

Teague O'Donnell stood in front of the open closet door, his gaze focused where I'd been about to unbutton the third button.

"Don't let me stop you." Despite the amusement in it, his husky drawl did things to nerve endings of mine that had no business coming to attention.

"What are you *doing*?" My hand went from unbuttoning to clasping the top of the blouse closed.

"Thought that was obvious. Though what *you're* doing is not."

"No time."

"Hey, I want to talk to you about these new bookshelves."

"No time. I have to change for yoga."

"I think they'll work better in the other bedroom. The way the stairs come up, you'll lose less storage over there."

"I can't discuss this. I have to change and leave. I'm already late."

"I need a decision. Can't wait around for you and Clara to finish playing detective and—"

"*Playing*—" I swallowed down the screech and told him with slightly flinty dignity and absolute reasonableness, "Since you have to break through the sidewall no matter what, finish that first, then we'll look at it."

"That's not going to change the measurements."

"It might change your perspective."

He scowled harder. Then he ducked into the closet.

"What are you doing?" I asked. But I didn't wait for an answer. Since he wasn't leaving my room—at least not the closet—I ducked into the bathroom, resumed stripping and hoping to heavens I had something that would work for yoga in here.

"I'll finish knocking out the dividing side wall while you're at yoga, you look at it tonight all you want, and by tomorrow morning have a decision on which room you want to take the extra space from."

CHAPTER THIRTY-FOUR

I HAD NEVER needed yin yoga more.

My shoulders didn't release as I stretched my arms and legs out from flat on my back, but at least I was aware of how tight they were, which I hadn't been until now.

"It's our turn to be in the corner. You were there last time."

I opened one eye to see Eve looming over us from the bottom of our mats.

I'd changed in record time, broken a few speed limits, barely let Clara in the car before backing out of her drive, broken more speed limits, and we still were much later for yoga than usual.

Yet we were here before Eve and Julia and secured the corner. Things were looking up.

"Let them have it, Eve. It doesn't matter."

"But—"

"Forget it." That was sharp enough to penetrate Eve's self-absorption. Even her wedding absorption.

"Okay. You don't have to—"

"Sorry. Just—I'll be right back." Julia went in the restroom.

When she returned in a moment, she'd regained her calm, judging by her voice, since I had my eyes closed.

"What were you saying about the peach sashes?" she asked Eve.

And there went my calm.

"Oh, yes. Yes. It's a heavenly color. I know I should have waited, had them put on hold, and let my daughter look at them. But it's like you said to your friend on the phone, sometimes you have to stop being cautious and strike, before all opportunity is gone."

Julia swore. Which seemed an extreme reaction to being quoted.

Then I heard Berrie's voice. "You left this."

I did the one-eye open trick. To my relief, she was not talking to me or Clara, but was holding out Julia's bag to her.

Julia stared at her.

"Here. You left it in the restroom," Berrie said.

Julia took the bag, gave a mechanical smile, and said, "Thank you."

"Took you long enough to say thank you," Berrie grumbled and walked away.

That interruption past, I went back to thinking about my trip to Smith-Flarenge. Especially one piece.

"C'mon," I said to Clara as I stood.

Fern was turning away from the cubes with a supply of props and I wanted to intersect her before she returned to her mat.

"But—" Clara rolled her eyes toward Eve and Julia.

"We'll keep an eye on them." I didn't bother to whisper, since Eve was back to droning about the wedding.

Clara hopped up and joined me. Fulfilling my promise, I half-turned Fern as I said hello so I had a view of our mats and neighbors.

"Fern, here." I placed the keys in her hand. "Thank you so much."

"You were absolutely right," Clara added with a wry smile. "Nothing."

She smiled. "Ah, well. You have to hit a lot of nothings before you find something."

As she started to turn away, I said, "Fern, what can you tell us about the difficulty Liz and her husband are having over money?"

She looked at us blankly.

"You said something earlier about difficulty over money?"

She blinked. "Not *them* over money. Liz and Xanthe over money. Mad as fire, Liz was. But then she got calm and determined, the way she does. Has it all worked out. Went to that place a couple days ago, asking for her money back, recording the whole thing. It's one of the steps in her plan."

Ah. The "older" woman demanding her money back that Jordy

mentioned?

"But at the remembrance you said Liz and Gregson were having trouble."

Surprisingly, she smiled. "Yes, they were. That's all over now. People my age sometimes grumble about modern ways, but then something like this happens and it makes all the fiddling with space-age buttons and such worthwhile."

"Over now?" I repeated, at a loss.

"Something like what, Fern?" Clara asked.

"They're pregnant—I *do* like saying *they*, rather than *her*, because it takes two. In fact, it took more, what with the in vitro fertilization, the doctors, and I don't know what all else. That's why Liz was so unhappy with Xanthe about losing that money."

That's why Liz's emotions were all over the place. *In vitro fertilization... Hoping... Fearing...*

"Liz had invested it, hoping to make it grow faster, because they'd tried once, it hadn't worked, and they needed to save up to try again. Wouldn't take a penny from me. Stubborn as her grandmother, that girl." Her smile echoed happy wrinkles across her cheeks. "But this time it worked. Liz gave her grandma a copy of the ultrasound. Just touched their phones together and there it was. Then I got to see it soon as Liz left her grandma ... So, she wouldn't know I knew yet. I'll have to act all surprised. But I'm good at that."

She reached out a hand to each of us. "Oh, but don't tell anyone, please. It's still a secret for a while. You know how superstitious young people can be. But I wormed it out of her grandmother. My younger sister, you know." She winked. "Told her I might not be here when they get around to going public with the news."

"Fern, you will be dancing at their baby's wedding."

The smile wrinkles deepened. "That's my plan."

The lights dimmed.

Julia stood. Clara and I hurried to our mats, but the blonde tackler headed for the restroom again, not for our spots. Fern made her way majestically across the space. Liz, who'd come in, closing the doors behind her, gave the older woman the right of way. Julia returned and class began.

So did my thinking.

But no matter how I tried to direct my mind, I didn't get far. It circled, circled, circled. Snagged on Fern's grandmother, Eloise's ex, and Tina's skylights. Then turned around and circled the other direction. Getting nowhere.

And then it was time for shavasana.

Directed thinking hadn't done much, so with my eyes closed, I tried to let my mind float.

If this was my mind floating, it was going to drown any second.

It was more inclined to click from image to image like an old slide projector my grandparents had. The one that was my window into my mother's childhood, teen years, then my parents' courtship.

Baby Mom being held by Grandma and Grandpa. Click.

Her and her siblings roasting marshmallows in a cabin. Click.

Dad with his arm tight around her waist. Click.

The man coming into class. *What are you doing here?* Click.

Wait, where did that come from?

Be quiet, Sheila. Just watch the show.

Urban's old photo of the woman standing in the doorway. Click.

Xanthe substituting for Liz. Click.

Vincent Shornfell, fired from Smith-Flarenge, looking for an escape, walking in to the studio. His voice saying *Everything's okay.* Click.

Eloise on Xanthe's past. *She got caught up in it. Her job, her life, her image, the guy she was involved with, it all revolved around money.* Click.

Then more…

A woman talking about her bragging, unfaithful husband. The studio being closed until today. The women who'd shown up at Smith-Flarenge. Preparations for the remembrance.

Click. Click. Click. Click.

They followed one after the other until I had why, the outlines of how, and one who.

But there was still so much more. Small on their own, but adding up to doubts. Huge doubts for anyone I'd have to try to persuade.

Especially without being absolutely sure of the second who.

"Begin to bring movement back into your hands and feet," Liz's voice instructed.

No, no, no. Let me stay here. Let me think. Keep everybody quiet and still.

A few more clicks. That might be all I needed.

C'mon, slide projector. C'mon, brain. A few more clicks…

"Now return to your easy seat as we conclude our practice tonight."

Eyes still closed, I tried to reach out, to grab a few more clicks, a few…

They wouldn't come.

Routine carried me through the fog that encompassed me. I found myself in the vestibule, shoes on, wallet and keys in hand, about to push out the exterior door. Some of the class already gone, others still milling.

Clara grabbed my arm, stopping me. "Oh, look at this workshop on yin that Liz's doing." Clara's gesture rustled the paper on the bulletin board. Her grip turned me toward the board, then toward Liz. "It looks amazing, Liz. To do yin yoga at the park in the evening? That's inspired."

"I think you'd both enjoy it."

Without thinking, I stepped backward. Away from the instantaneous image of mosquitos feasting on my body as I yinned in the itchy grass of a park.

The arm Clara didn't hold swung behind me—some instinct to protect it from mosquitos, probably—and connected with the key protruding from the deadbolt lock on the door.

Click.

That wasn't the sound of the lock closing. It was the sound in my head.

A big, resounding, reverberating *click.*

The second who.

CHAPTER THIRTY-FIVE

"C'MON, CLARA, LET'S go."

Too late, I'd realized I'd accompanied the *who* click in my head with a turn to look at one particular person.

Had it been noticed?

I wasn't sure.

"I think I'll get the key lime tart tonight instead of strawberry pie," Clara said as I hurried her out.

"We're not stopping at the café."

"You want to go straight to the bar?" That was our plan, to see what we could find out about Eloise and her ex from a week ago. "I thought we'd do better a little later. Like after key lime tart."

"We're not going there, either. Not tonight. We're going home."

"Are you feeling okay?"

I was aware of being watched.

Or I was being paranoid.

Either way, I wanted to get to where I could check if the pieces I thought fit really fit and work this all through in my head, nice and neat. Then talk it over with Clara. Run it past Kit.

Only then would I consider presenting it to Teague. Or a deputy.

I hurried her to the car. "Get in. I'm fine. I'm driving you home."

"But my car's at your house."

"You can get it tomorrow. I'm dropping you off at your house."

I wasn't taking a chance with Clara getting hurt, if I was right. From a practical point of view, I could operate better without looking out for her, too.

Besides, Ned would never forgive me.

I would never forgive me.

"What's going on, Sheila?"

"Nothing. Nothing's going on—"

But if there *was* something going on, if my mind had been read, if that car that seemed to be following us really was following...

"—I need time to think."

"I won't interrupt your thinking. What are you going to think about, though? Because—"

Rather than try to answer—or not answer—I asked, "Clara, remember when Mamie was nearly hit by that van?"

"Of course. It was terrifying. I was so scared it would hit her."

"It didn't because you grabbed her and spun her around."

"Only because I was in front. If you hadn't held the door open for me, you would have been the one to grab her. I wish people would listen to me about that and stop—"

"No, no. They're right. You were there and you saved her. And because you were doing that, maybe you didn't notice the people behind you afterward."

"I ... I did, though. It all slowed down. Like slow motion. And I saw you reaching toward her, too. Laura standing on the steps with her mouth and eyes wide open. Eloise staring, frozen. The spot-stealers a little closer, with Julia holding onto Eve like it kept her standing. And—"

"Wait. Stop there. That's what I thought at first, too. That Julia was holding on, either to keep Eve back or to support herself. But think about that again. Close your eyes. Clear your mind of expectations. Just think about their body positions. If you saw that without knowing the circumstances, no van, no Mamie for them to react to, instead, you saw a photo of them in that position, what would you say was happening?"

Beneath her lowered eyelids, movement showed as she seemed to survey the scene brought up from her memory.

"I think... I think I'd say Julia was issuing orders to Eve." Her lids popped open. "Giving orders. Like a coach right before she pushed the player onto the field."

"Or a director giving an actor her lines?"

"I guess. But… Oh. That's why Eve changed from saying accident to saying Mamie had to be a target because she knew about the murder? But why would Julia tell her to say that?"

"Misdirection."

"Misdirection? But—No. Wait." She held up both hands. "That's not why you got all weird at the studio just now. Was it something about the door?"

"Did you ever wonder how Vincent Shornfell got in to interrupt class that night?"

"Xanthe forgot to lock it."

"Maybe."

I pulled as far into her driveway as I could get, so she had the least amount of territory to cover to get to her door.

"Will you please tell me—?"

"I'll call you in the morning." She paused, staring at me. I looked back, letting impatience creep in. "I have to go."

Finally, she opened the car door and got out. "First thing in the morning," she ordered.

I waved good-bye cheerily. And waited until she was inside before starting to back out.

As soon as I was clear of Ned's vehicle and on track to back into the street smoothly, I tried Teague's phone number.

Forget thinking everything through, carefully placing the pieces. If I was right…

Three rings, then a pause.

My stomach sank.

Voicemail.

His recorded voice invited me to leave a message.

I was *not* going to leave a voicemail. I'd sound like a crazy woman.

"…so leave a message after the tone," his voice said.

Then came the tone.

I left a voicemail.

"Teague, it's Sheila. Listen, I, uh, I need to talk to you tonight. In fact, if you could, uh, come by the house, that would be great. Right away. Immediately. And if you wouldn't mind calling when you get here, so I know it's you at the door." I tried a laugh. It wasn't good.

"Hope to see you soon. As soon as possible. Bye."

I hung up.

Worse than a crazy woman.

He'd probably think I was calling about finding a new design of vents. Or a different configuration of clothes rods. Which, I had been thinking about—

Not the time for that, Sheila.

Not. The. Time.

I had a choice.

I could drive to the sheriff's department. A bump up the curb and onto the wide sidewalk and I'd be right next to the door.

The car definitely following me now wouldn't follow me there, surely.

And even if it did, its occupants would not possibly risk shooting at me at the front door of the sheriff's department.

So that was a good choice.

Except, it wouldn't prove a thing.

Deputy Eckles would roll his eyes—even if he didn't do it physically, he'd do it in his head—and dismiss everything I said as insufficient or unsubstantial.

My other choice was to try to draw them out.

It would take good timing. Really good timing.

But I'd have homefield advantage and my secret weapon with four paws and a tail.

I drove home.

QUELLING THE INSTINCT to run, I walked at a normal pace through the kitchen, past the opening to the dining room, which could be seen from the street through the front window.

Then I sprinted toward the living room, pulling the basement door open behind me, because it would prevent most of the light from the kitchen from bleeding into the living room.

Staying in the shadows of the living room, I was in time to see a car go past slowly. Very slowly. It was probably two houses down when, through the living room's side window, I caught the glow of its brake lights.

Parking? Or coming around for a second pass?

The downside of not waiting to know which for sure was blowing this whole effort.

The downside of waiting to know for sure and having them on top of me too fast was a whole lot worse.

I called the North Bend County Sheriff's Department. I reported an attempted break-in in progress at my address. My dog and I were going to take shelter upstairs.

As the dispatcher instructed me to stay on the line, I muted the phone, left the line open, and slipped it in my pocket.

Only then did I greet Gracie.

She had her nose out of joint by that delay, and she has a considerable nose.

I walked back through the kitchen, dining room, then up the stairs, as I would any other night coming home from yoga.

Gracie trotted along behind me, her tail happily disturbing the atmosphere around us.

They might already know the layout of my house. In case they didn't, I turned on my bedroom light. I needed them to know which room was mine.

Then I opened the closet door, letting light show, but blocking the view into the room for anyone outside.

The view of Vincent Shornfell and his confederate, Julia Trippen, outside my house.

CHAPTER THIRTY-SIX

I CALLED GRACIE, who'd been sniffing around in the hallway, to come into the room with me. She came in with an air of skepticism, but a willingness to let me prove I'd be entertaining.

I closed the door to the hall and took ahold of her collar. From the baggie in the pocket of the lightweight robe hanging from a closet doorknob, I gave her a treat.

Two chews into her three-chew routine, she stopped.

Her ears went up.

She swallowed the rest of treat whole. Swiveled her ears to pick up more sound.

They were faster than I expected.

I reached down and held her nose to keep her from barking. She swiveled her eyes at me, not happy.

With the other hand, I unmuted the phone, said, "They're in my house. Definitely in my house." I gave the address again. For good measure, I added, "I caught sight of them trying to get into my back door. I think they're armed. I'm in the upstairs hallway bathroom, locked in. With my dog. Don't shoot us."

I suppose lying to the police isn't the best idea, but I intended to be in the hallway bathroom. Soon. And the door would be locked. Soon.

I hoped.

"Hurry." My urgency was totally convincing because it was real.

"Stay on the line with me, ma'am. We have someone on the way. Just stay on the line and—"

I muted the phone again and slid it back into the pocket. I needed both hands.

Especially since Gracie had heard more noises and was now trying in earnest to bark, her eyes swiveling as far as they could toward the door. My hand wrapped firmly but not hard around her narrow muzzle let only muffled *whompfs* escape.

I used my other hand to guide her toward the open closet door.

A pair of two-by-fours stood upright in the otherwise empty closet.

I had to release Gracie's collar. One-handed, I moved the first out of the way.

As I reached for the second, Gracie abruptly tried to back up to free herself from my hand on her nose. My hand slid.

I propped the two-by-four against my hip and grabbed at her as the second half of a partially muffled bark erupted.

The stealthy sounds from downstairs stopped.

The two-by-four started to slip down from my hip, heading for a resounding crash against the hardwood floors.

I raised my knee, catching the two-by-four in its crook, but needing to keep my foot raised so it didn't slip the rest of the way.

One hand wrapped around Gracie's collar, I pulled her toward me again, when all she wanted to do was get to the hallway door—as close as she could get to those stealthy noises—and bark her head off. I barely got my other hand back around her nose before she would have deafened me, the intruders, and half of the county.

Making eye contact, I said, "No!" Giving it barely any volume, but plenty of vehemence.

She *whompfed* again.

"No barking. Quiet." Still in that vehement no-sound delivery. I had a portion of her attention anyway. "It's okay."

She rolled her eyes from the direction of the door to me with a clear *Hell, no, it's not okay* message in them.

"No. Barking," I repeated in a tone I'd never used with her before.

I had her attention.

Good thing, because my leg was cramping from the awkward half-raised position needed to keep the two-by-four from crashing down.

I hop-slid back an inch at a time, bringing Gracie with me—far more by her willingness than by my hold on her.

I released her collar again. She didn't pull away.

I reached back. No two-by-four.

Another couple inches and a yoga-worthy twist, and I made contact with the two-by-four, lifting it away from my leg. Carefully, quietly, easing backward so I could lower it silently to the floor and out of the way.

Now we could back up to a galloping two or three inches at a time.

We had to angle from the door on my bedroom side toward the guest room closet door. Deconstruction had left little obstacles eager to trip me up.

And now we had an added difficulty. I needed to close the closet doors behind us, so the intruders wouldn't peer in here the second they got in the room.

I pulled the door partly closed. And cut our light in half.

Gracie jerked and I recognized what she'd reacted to.

Footsteps at the bottom of the stairs.

That close already?

Coming too fast?

Would I have time?

Reaching behind me, I found the knob and opened the door on the other side of the closet out into the guest bedroom.

I stretched over Gracie to poke the hinge side of my bedroom's closet door. One poke gained about two inches. The second only half an inch. I was up to six pokes before I could reach the knob and pull it closed, then secure her collar again.

Barely any light reached us now, but I could feel the opening behind me that would take us into the guest room.

I backed up. Gracie balked.

With nods, and smiles—none of which I would have been able to see, but I hoped she could with her better low-light vision—I coaxed her through the closet and into the guest bedroom, still holding her nose.

The footsteps reached the top of the stairs.

My heart *ka-thudded* hard in my chest.

Too close.

Holding my breath, I closed the closet door on the guest room side as quietly as I possibly could, ending with the faintest click.

If they opened the closet door from my bedroom and looked straight ahead, they would see the wall still intact. If they looked to the side, I prayed it would look like blank walls there, too, with not enough light reached that back corner to see a door leading out this opposite side.

As their stealthy footsteps reached my bedroom door, I crept toward the hall door of the guest bedroom, one hand holding Gracie's collar to keep her beside me so I wouldn't accidentally step on her in the dark, the other on her nose.

I heard a whisper from next door, but couldn't make out the words. I was pretty sure the response was, "Shut up."

Releasing Gracie's collar, I slowly, slowly eased open the guest room door.

I didn't remember it having a creak, but I hadn't paid much attention, either. What if I was wrong, what if it gave me away?

I'd have to make a dash for it. Though whether we could get down the stairs before they reached the top of them... Worse, whether Gracie would—for the first time—obey all the lessons about waiting for humans to clear the stairs before starting down them.

If they didn't have a weapon, maybe we could make it.

If they did...

But I had a backup plan. One that added the element of surprise.

I hoped.

The guest room door eased open under my shaking hand.

The hallway was dimly lit from what came up the stairway. I appreciated the light now, but it would make Gracie and me more visible if we tried to go down the stairs.

My bedroom door was slightly open.

I'd feared that might happen. Because they'd need light to try to find me in the room.

"She's not in here," came what I thought was a male whisper.

"Shut up. Check the closet."

With the door already open, thus cutting a couple precious seconds in the head start Gracie and I would have, the stairs shaped up as a worse and worse option.

But I couldn't worry about any of that until this next—and potentially most vital—step.

Once again holding Gracie's collar, we crossed the guest room threshold and into the hallway. I pointed her nose toward the door to my bedroom.

Tightening my grip on her collar, I removed my other hand from her nose.

CHAPTER THIRTY-SEVEN

NOTHING.

I'd expected lunging, frothing, ferocious barking.

She remained perfectly still and totally silent.

I leaned down and said softly by her ear, "*Speak.*"

She didn't.

She didn't even look at me, having suddenly switched from a herding dog to a pointer with all her focus on my bedroom door.

"Gracie, *speak.*"

A floorboard squeaked under an intruder's foot and her head cocked.

But did she bark?

No.

Still whispering, still with my mouth close to her ear, I repeated, "Gracie, *speak!*"

Along with the command, there was urgency in my voice. I know there was. Probably fear, too.

Our escape all depended on the intruders feeling pinned in that room.

Just for a moment. Just long enough for us to get away.

And that depended on Gracie barking like a demented being, the way she would if a squirrel or chipmunk or dangerously skidding leaf were in that room.

But here, now, she wasn't having any of it.

During the nose-holding trek from my bedroom, through the closets, then through the guest room to here, I'd made my point so thoroughly about being quiet, she wasn't barking no matter what.

Her look clearly said she wasn't falling for that just to be yelled at. Uh-huh, not Gracie Louise. She was too smart for that.

I could shout, but that was unlikely to scare the intruders into staying in the room. Even saying I had a weapon—

And then I heard steps nearing the door.

Whether they'd heard my desperate whispers to Gracie in the hall or they'd finished their search of the room and closet, they were approaching the door.

They'd see us any second.

I looked around, aided by the faint light from the hallway sliding into a slice of the guest room, hoping, praying—

My prayers were answered.

I grabbed it from where Teague had spread out the tools of his carpentry trade atop the dresser, thumbed the control to open it, and shook it out.

The metal tape measure extended, snapped, bent, and twanged like a miniature thunder machine.

Gracie went ballistic.

Bouncing off the plaster walls and echoing up from the uncarpeted floor compounded her barks until I thought I'd go gloriously deaf.

Gloriously, because deaf wasn't dead.

A scream came from inside my room. The steps stopped.

Then they rushed back to the door, slamming it closed.

"Don't let it in, don't let it in." The man's words stumbled over each other.

Clinging to the dog collar, I extended the tape measure toward the door, waving it. The movement and the faint noise upped Gracie's barking.

Another scream. This time I could identify the screamer.

Him, not her.

"We're trapped. We're trapped. We can't get out past that vicious dog and she's not even here. I told you this was stupid. I told you—"

"Shut up. Be quiet." Though why she was urging quiet after the siren of that scream, I had no idea. "We *saw* her in here. And don't be a wuss about the dog. Just shoot it."

They had a gun.

No way were we taking the stairs.

I heard a police siren in the distance. Then another siren.

Coming this way.

But not here yet.

How fast could they get here?

Footsteps approached my bedroom door again from the inside.

Those sirens weren't going to get here fast enough.

All those people in my room had to do was pull the door open and cover a few feet.

And they had a gun.

Which could cover a lot more feet a lot faster.

I stirred Gracie into another frenzy of barking with the tape measure, but this time the footsteps didn't retreat. I dropped the tape measure and urged her back with me into what I hoped to heaven was a strategic retreat.

I HEARD STEPS pounding up the stairs, then a single male voice shout, "North Bend County Sheriff's Department! Halt! Put your hands up!"

They'd sent one guy? *One?* And from the sounds reaching me, the bad guys weren't halting or putting their hands up.

"They went in there. That other room."

The guest room? Had to be.

Then a squawk and a heavy thud.

Before I heard a shout of pain. "You *bit* me."

Who thudded?

Who bit?

Who was out there and who was winning?

I could wait to see who won the scuffle outside or I could act.

I acted.

First, I got Gracie into the bathtub.

Not as easy as it sounds.

We had never worked on the command "Get in the tub." And even with no water in it, she was not viewing this as an invitation to heaven.

Finally, with me standing in the tub, she acquiesced. Grudgingly. Lifting one foot after the other like she was on hot coals, and making it seem like there were a lot more than six feet in this bathtub.

Bathtubs were good for tornadoes—though preferably not on the second floor—but I had no idea what protection they offered from bullets.

I heaved the window open, not caring about noise. There was enough noise in the hallway to mask whatever I did. Including pushing out the screen and letting it skid down the sloped roof to the ground.

I got one leg up and out of the opening, then turned so I did partial splits over the window frame—I knew that Sleeping Swan position would prove useful someday—then reached back down for Gracie.

I couldn't reach her.

"Come, Gracie." I patted the top of my thigh, indicating she should put her front feet up on it.

She stared at me like I was nuts.

"C'mon, Gracie. Come."

She jumped up enough that I could get my hands under the equivalent of her armpits, but her back legs had little purchase on the porcelain finish.

I heard a shout from the hallway. But all that registered was its closeness.

I had to get this sixty-five-pound dog up, then her and me out of the window to slide down the porch roof. I had to do it *now*.

"*Sheila!*"

This time the voice registered.

Just before the door crashed in.

We all froze.

Me. Gracie. The door crasher.

Someone came up behind Teague O'Donnell as he stood in the doorway, but Teague held his arm out sideways, blocking the listing doorframe and stopping the motion behind him.

Softly, like he might be talking someone off a ledge, he said, "What the hell are you doing, Sheila?"

CHAPTER THIRTY-EIGHT

"YOU SHOULD HAVE seen Sheila's face when Eve Kraft—that's the mother of the bride—returned to class *with* her daughter," Clara told Ned and Teague.

The four of us were on their back patio on a Saturday night, having eaten a lavish spread thanks to Ned's grilling and Clara's everything else. I brought cookies and Teague brought beer and wine.

The dogs, having had a glorious day at the dog park, followed by a couple hours of chasing each other around Clara and Ned's back yard, and a few special treats, were now contentedly sprawled under the table, making it impossible for the humans to stretch their legs.

The best news was that Clara had told Ned all about her involvement in solving two murders.

He appeared to be simultaneously concerned and proud. A reasonable reaction.

Clara and I had started to share yet another round of explanations before she detoured to this news from our most recent class.

"The bridezilla was at your yoga class and you didn't tell me?" Ned asked.

"That's the thing. She's not a bridezilla at all. She's really nice," Clara said.

I had to agree.

Nice *and* a loving daughter.

"Poor Mom," she'd said. "That Julia woman turning out to be involved in a murder on top of how she's been stressing over my wedding." The daughter was talking to me, because I'd moved to the far side of the vestibule while the rest of the class members rushed Eve Kraft to ask her questions.

The young woman shook her head fondly, watching her mother swell at being the center of attention. "Justin and I would have been happy to elope. Or just have the families. But she wouldn't hear of it. I think she's been planning my wedding since I was born."

It was the only way she could have thought of all those details she'd tortured us with at yoga.

I smiled back at the bride to be.

A soft smile and slight shrug indulged her mother's fantasy.

I also mentally apologized for jumping to the conclusion she was a bridezilla. She was a nice young woman with an admirable tolerance for her overzealous mother.

I resolved to cultivate a similar tolerance for Eve.

I had to admit, that goal seemed a lot more attainable when she'd been mortified over being Julia Trippen's fool.

"Okay, but go back to the actual murder and what those two were up to," Ned said.

"Vincent used to work at Smith-Flarenge. That's how he and Xanthe met. Eventually he got himself fired—not for overcharging customers, but for trying to bilk the company. But before he went, he noticed a flaw in the security. At first, it was probably something to brag about at bars and such. But as time went on and he wasn't making a fortune any other way, the idea might have taken hold of him."

"Or Julia took a hold of him," Clara said.

"Or that," I agreed. "She sure seems like the stronger personality."

"I bet she did the killing. He was probably only an accomplice."

Ned nudged a dish of carrots, celery, and olives toward his wife. "That's because you haven't liked her since she and that mother of the bride stole your favorite spot at yoga."

"It's an indication of character." Clara roughed up the edges of that dignified response by quickly adding, "And she really was a stinker."

"Getting back to what happened," I reminded her, "Vincent Shornfell had recognized that those old renovations put the side of the yoga studio up against that door from the original building. Brick stops electronic transmissions, but it was porous enough that someone with the right equipment could suck up the information through it."

"Suck up information? Is that the technical term?" Teague grinned.

"Close enough."

"They had it all planned, including Julia Trippen using Eve Kraft's mother of the brideness as a distraction from what she was doing. With her loud oversharing, Eve drew attention, leaving Julia free to operate."

"The idea was to get some sort of receiver into that corner of the yoga studio?" Ned asked.

"Simpler than that," Teague said. "It was a phone to phone transfer. Shornfell loaded up a spare phone with data the day he was fired, then left it plugged in behind the refrigerator in the breakroom because that's where the old door was. Everywhere else, there was a double layer of solid brick—one from each building."

He had definitely been talking to the sheriff's department. That detail had not been reported in the media.

"Why not sneak it out?" Ned asked.

"Smith-Flarenge examines everything belonging to departing employees, including their personal phones."

"He left it there nearly a year?"

"That's what Sheila meant about Julia being the stronger personality. He's not exactly a self-starter. It took Julia Trippen to get things going." Clara reached for a baby carrot. "That's why they moved our stuff and tackled Sheila. To get to that corner."

"That first night Julia tried having her bag in the back corner of the main studio, thinking that would get a phone close enough to gather the data. It wasn't. The next day, when Clara and I staked out our corner first, Julia nearly lost it. She must've tried to pick up the signal from several feet over. When she couldn't, she improvised by taking her bag into the restroom and leaving it there during the class. She tried to get back in first, but Rowena ran her over. I wondered about Julia constantly fiddling with her bag the first class, then leaving it in the restroom the next class, but it seemed weird, not nefarious.

"The one thing they didn't count on was Liz needing a substitute that night—because she felt strange and was terrified something had gone wrong with her pregnancy—and the substitute being a woman Shornfell had dated. In fact, was dating at the time he got fired and had told of his plan."

"As we know now and you only guessed then," Teague said.

Vincent had started blabbing that night in my house and apparently hadn't stopped since.

If Julia could have gotten her hands on him, he would have been the next victim.

"Where did Xanthe come into this? Was she part of it?" Ned asked.

"If she had been, they wouldn't have needed to kill her. From what Eloise said of their relationship, I can imagine him bragging to Xanthe when he came up with the plan, showing off how clever he was. And maybe she thought he was clever initially. But when she had a change of heart and a change of life, she was no longer impressed by money. Or him."

"But why kill her?"

"She was a loose end. First, she knew about the plan—"

"That was a leap until Shornfell said it," Teague interjected.

"You know what they say about leaping. Take a leap and the net will appear under you. And it wasn't much of a leap. He told Julia, his current girlfriend. Why not the previous one? In fact, it's more likely he'd tell Xanthe because she worked there with him. I bet he asked her to do something with his setup after he was fired and that's why they broke up. That was right when she changed her life."

"Plus," Clara added, "she had seen him at the yoga studio. She knew who he was. She knew the plan. She could put it all together."

"But Julia had no idea who Xanthe was during class, so she went ahead with the plan and unlocked the door for him."

Clara explained about how the door was locked during class.

Her husband asked, "But once they killed Xanthe, why not take her key and finish up what they needed to finish?"

Clara beamed at him. "You're good at this, Ned. That's a great question. The answer is the security system. Xanthe set it before she left at night. And Julia knew about the security system, because she could see it from her mat that night. Plus, there's confirmation."

She turned and joined me in eyeing Teague.

"Hey, why look at me?"

"Because you either saw whatever security video the sheriff's department had or you heard about it in detail. You know what happened after Xanthe was killed."

"Nothing definitive."

We kept staring, now joined by Ned.

"Okay, okay. It's not good enough for court anyway. There's one set of footage that shows an unidentifiable figure—more a blob of shadow—approaching the studio. It hesitates, then a light flickers from the direction of Court Avenue, and the blob of shadow, with an even less defined blob joining it, takes off toward Haines Avenue."

"The light?" Ned asked.

"Part of Shornfell's monologue at Sheila's house was about whether they should have used Xanthe's key—he said yes, she said no—then getting spooked by a car and running like hell."

Ned had another question. "But why did Shornfell come to the yoga studio at all?"

"*Everything's okay.*" Clara quoted. "We're supposed to leave our phones out in the cubbies. If he'd called Julia Trippen to let her know the Smith-Flarenge employees had cleared out—because they were concerned someone there might hear something—everybody in class would have been aware of what she was doing."

"And they did hear something the next day," I said. "A Smith-Flarenge employee was talking at the remembrance about an alien sound from behind the refrigerator. Until it stopped abruptly. Julia must have successfully transmitted some from the phone behind the fridge to her phone in the restroom during that Tuesday class." I turned to Teague. "Until the battery ran out?"

"It did." He grinned. "It came unplugged because someone started to clean behind the fridge. The connection to Julia's phone during that daytime class was its last gasp. They didn't know that, though. With

Tina closing the studio, Julia tried a couple times to be there alone by volunteering for cleanup duty. She also tried going to Smith-Flarenge. And, of course, at the next class on Monday night."

"When you put it all together," Clara said.

"Only when you showed me the flyer for the workshop. It was the rustle of the paper, like Fern described. Remember, Clara? The day at the sheriff's department when they interviewed all of us. We were asking about what she remembered about the guy—Vincent—interrupting the class, but she thought we were talking about earlier, before class started, when Julia jumped up and went into the vestibule, supposedly because she forgot she had her sunglasses on.

"To put her sunglasses away, she'd have stayed on the end of the vestibule where she was visible through the glass doors. But she didn't. She went out of sight. And Fern heard her rustle against paper—the paper on the bulletin board, like I did when you turned me to look. It put my back to the door and my hands right by the lock, with my body blocking anyone else from seeing if I unlocked the door.

"That's all Julia had to do. Stand with her back to the door, pretend she was looking at something on the board, say something to Xanthe to distract her, while she unlocked the door for Vincent."

"But you couldn't have known for sure that night," Ned objected.

"We didn't know all the ins and outs, but we'd found enough of the pieces to be pretty sure. When we looked at motive—" I slanted a look toward Teague, and Clara chuckled. "—it made sense. In class they started coming together. Unfortunately, I'm afraid I let Julia see the one about the door."

"I knew Sheila had a breakthrough, but she insisted on dumping me off here and going home alone." The second I'd dropped Clara off at her house, she'd called Teague, leaving me to get his voicemail. "She didn't fill in the gaps for me until the next day."

"But you were the one who talked to the media." Ned sounded bemused by his wife's second brush with the spotlight.

"Oh, Clara does a much better job of making it all clear and tidy," I said.

"Does she?" Teague muttered under his breath.

Apparently only I heard him, because Ned and Clara were occupied smiling at each other.

To distract Teague, I said, "It was when I got home that night that the fun started."

"Security system." This time Teague's mutter was for the whole table.

"Us, too," Ned said. "Never thought I'd see the day in Haines Tavern, but…"

"We have a security system—LuLu," protested Clara.

"And I have Gracie."

"Right."

"Stop, you two. Let Sheila finish the story," Clara ordered.

CHAPTER THIRTY-NINE

"**...AND TEAGUE BREAKS** down the door—ruins the doorframe—"

"Which I'll fix as soon as the closets are done."

"—and shouts *What are you doing*? I don't know why he needed to ask. It should have been obvious. I was saving myself and Gracie."

"I never would have thought on my feet the way you did, Sheila," Clara said. "It was so clever to go through the closets and get Gracie to bark outside the bedroom door."

Teague said, "Oh, yeah. Brilliant."

"Sarcasm is the lowest form of wit," I primly quoted Oscar Wilde.

"But the highest form of intelligence," Teague and Oscar shot back.

Darn. I hadn't expected him to know the second half of that quote.

Satisfied he'd won the round—and he had, darn him—he drank from his wineglass.

Ignoring the exchange, Clara continued, "But I'm not so sure about going out the bathroom window that way. Maybe you should have put Gracie out first."

"I thought about that, but I was afraid she would skid down the roof and get hurt. But if I was there—"

"You could *both* fall and break your necks," Teague said.

"That wasn't the plan."

"That was a plan? You actually *planned* it?"

"Well, the backup plan."

"Backup plan?"

"Quit repeating what I say."

"I wish I'd taken a picture so you could see what I saw." Teague turned to Ned. "Imagine one of those smaller windows in older houses. She's straddling the window sill—I can't even see her outside leg—and the she's bent the other leg—"

"Sleeping Swan," I said to Clara.

She nodded wisely.

"—trying to haul that considerable amount of furry dog up out of the bathtub. And the dog turns her head around and gives me this pleading look like she's saying save me from this crazy woman."

The dog in question was lying at my feet, in fact, with her chin resting on one of my feet, and surely never had such a disloyal thought in her head or heart, much less an expression someone who barely knew her, like Teague, could accurately interpret.

I satisfied myself with a short humph.

Gracie stirred.

"You stop picking on Sheila—and Gracie. I think Sheila was *brilliant*. If she hadn't done something, they would have had plenty of time to hurt or kill her before you and the deputies got there." Both men stopped laughing. "And Gracie did what she needed to do to scare those two killers. *Murderers*."

Clara had tears in her eyes. Ned put an arm around her shoulders.

"Sheila was smart and used what she had and bought the time she needed to keep herself and Gracie from getting shot. She and Gracie were incredibly brave."

Teague put his glass down. "You're right, Clara."

He turned to me, stretching out his hand to cover mine. "She did what she had to do to keep those murderers from getting her."

"And Gracie," Clara prompted.

"And Gracie," he agreed, looking into my eyes.

After a moment, I broke the look. "You guys should have seen Gracie with the new closets. She sniffed from one corner to the other of the closet in my room. Then she ran around to the other room and explored that just as thoroughly—"

"Is that why there was dog hair in the wet paint?" Teague asked.

"—and came back and stared at me, like she was requesting the wall be removed for sneaky exits. I told her it did what we needed it to do then, but this works much better for everyday life."

"How about sticking with everyday life from now on?" Teague requested.

"You don't have to be involved, Teague. You can stay far away from anything we do that doesn't resemble everyday life."

"No, he can't." We all looked at Clara. She looked back, smug. "He has to fix that bathroom door."

The End

Thank you for reading Sheila's latest adventure!

As their bonds (human and canine) deepen, Sheila and friends look forward to some peace and quiet in North Bend County. And you might think a simple task such as grocery shopping would make that list. Instead, the executive who's responsible for widely hated changes at the biggest supermarket in Haines Tavern arrives for a tour … and doesn't leave alive. Sheila and Clara are on the scene—buying dog treats, of course—and on the case.

Death on Covert Circle

Sheila, Clara, Teague and friends ask if you'll help spread the word about them and the Secret Sleuth series. You have the power to do that in two quick ways:

Recommend the book and the series to your friends and/or the whole wide world on social media. Shouting from rooftops is particularly appreciated.

Review the book. Take a few minutes to write an honest review and it can make a huge difference. As you likely know, it's the single best way for your fellow readers to find books they'll enjoy, too.

To me—as an author and a reader—the goal is always to find a good author-reader match. By sharing your reading experience through recommendations and reviews, you become a vital matchmaker. ☺

For news about upcoming Secret Sleuth books, as well as other titles and news, join Patricia McLinn's Readers List and receive her twice-monthly free newsletter.

www.patriciamclinn.com/readers-list

Other Secret Sleuth cozy mysteries

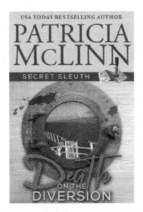

DEATH ON THE DIVERSION

Final resting place? Deck chair.

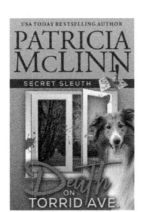

DEATH ON TORRID AVENUE

A new love (canine), an ex-cop and a dog park discovery.

DEATH ON COVERT CIRCLE

A reviled supermarket CEO meets his expiration date.

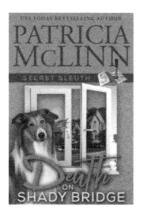

DEATH ON SHADY BRIDGE

A cold case heats up.

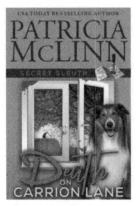

DEATH ON CARRION LANE

Murder crashes Clara's high school reunion.

"Move over Agatha Christie, there's a new sleuth in town. Patricia McLinn has created a fabulous new murder mystery series with … wonderful characters, both human and canine, [and] an interesting backdrop. I highly recommend."

—5-star review

Death on Torrid Avenue "is told with a lot of humor and the characters are good company. I thoroughly enjoyed myself and am looking forward to the next story."

—5-star review

Death on the Diversion "is such an enjoyable story, reminiscent of Agatha Christie's style, with a good study of human nature and plenty of humor. Great start to a new series!"

—5-star review

Caught Dead in Wyoming mysteries

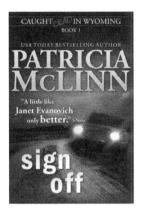

SIGN OFF

Divorce a husband, lose a career … grapple with a murder.

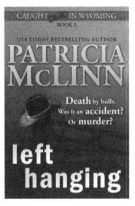

LEFT HANGING

Trampled by bulls—an accident? Elizabeth, Mike and friends must dig into the world of rodeo.

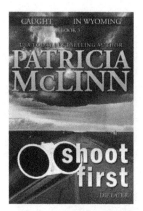

SHOOT FIRST

For Elizabeth, death hits close to home. She and friends delve into old Wyoming treasures and secrets to save lives.

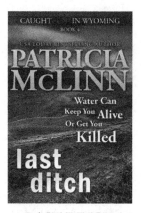

LAST DITCH

Elizabeth and Mike search after a man in a wheelchair goes missing in dangerous, desolate country.

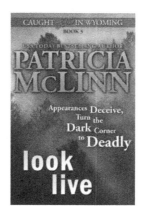

LOOK LIVE

Elizabeth and friends take on misleading murder with help—and hindrance—from intriguing out-of-towners.

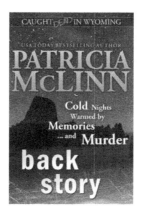

BACK STORY

Murder never dies, but comes back to threaten Elizabeth, her friends and KWMT colleagues.

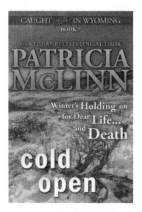

COLD OPEN

Elizabeth's looking for a place of her own becomes an open house for murder.

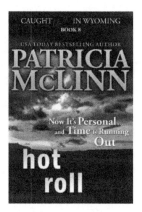

HOT ROLL

One of their own becomes a target—and time is running out.

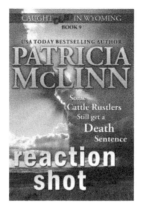

REACTION SHOT

Some cattle rustlers still get a death sentence.

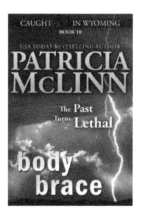

BODY BRACE

Everything can change … except murder.

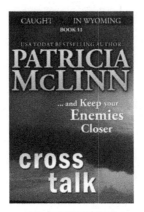

CROSS TALK

Storm clouds darken the KWMT-TV station.

"While the mystery itself is twisty-turny and thoroughly engaging, it's the smart and witty writing that I loved the best."

—*Diane Chamberlain, New York Times bestselling author*

"Colorful characters, intriguing, intelligent mystery, plus the state of Wyoming leaping off every page."

—*Emilie Richards, USA Today bestselling author*

Mystery With Romance

The Innocence Series

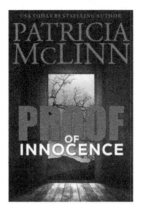

PROOF OF INNOCENCE

She's a prosecutor chasing demons. He's wrestling them. Will they find proof of innocence?

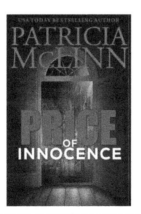

PRICE OF INNOCENCE

She runs a foundation dedicated to forgiveness. He runs down criminals. If they don't work together, people will die.

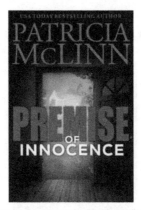

PREMISE OF INNOCENCE

The last woman Detective Landis is prepared to see is the one he must save.

"Evocative description, vivid characterization, and lots of twists and turns."

—*5-star review*

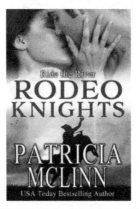

RIDE THE RIVER: RODEO KNIGHTS

Her rodeo cowboy ex is back … as her prime suspect.

Explore a complete list of all Patricia's books

www.patriciamclinn.com/patricias-books

Or get a printable booklist

patriciamclinn.com/patricias-books/printable-booklist

New! Patricia's eBookstore (buy digital books online directly from Patricia)

patriciamclinn.com/patricias-books/ebookstore

About the Author

Patricia McLinn is the USA Today bestselling author of nearly 60 published novels cited by readers and reviewers for wit and vivid characterization. Her books include mysteries, romantic suspense, contemporary romance, historical romance and women's fiction. They have topped bestseller lists and won numerous awards.

She has spoken about writing from London to Melbourne, Australia, to Washington, D.C., including being a guest speaker at the Smithsonian.

McLinn spent more than 20 years as an editor at The Washington Post after stints as a sports writer (Rockford, Ill.) and assistant sports editor (Charlotte, N.C.). She received BA and MSJ degrees from Northwestern University.

Now living in Northern Kentucky, McLinn loves to hear from readers through her website and social media.

Visit with Patricia:

Website: patriciamclinn.com

Facebook: facebook.com/PatriciaMcLinn

Twitter: @PatriciaMcLinn

Pinterest: pinterest.com/patriciamclinn

Instagram: instagram.com/patriciamclinnauthor

ISBN: 978-1-944126-48-3

Made in the USA
Las Vegas, NV
25 September 2021

31109101R00152